The Cure

The Cure

Zane Gates

Writer's Showcase
San Jose New York Lincoln Shanghai

The Cure

Writer's Showcase
an imprint of iUniverse.com, Inc.

For information address:
iUniverse.com, Inc.
5220 S 16th, Ste. 200
Lincoln, NE 68512
www.iuniverse.com

ISBN: 0-595-17484-1

Printed in the United States of America

This book is dedicated to my mother, Gloria Gates, Zane Gates Jr. and the Children of Evergreen Manor Housing Project.

Acknowledgement

I'd like to thank Francesca Kowalski for her wonderful editing and moral support. Without her, this book would not have been possible. And to Roger Lepage, the best writer I've ever met.

Chapter 1

Minot, North Dakota

The thick darkness of the ventilation shaft was as cold and empty as the fear in Nicole Johnson's heart. She fought hard to stop the trembling that shook the warm metal floor of the ventilation shaft, but the decision overtook her. Which one would die and which one would live? It was a sick nightmare that she was sure the devil himself thought up. Unfortunately, the sun wasn't going to rise and wake her from the horror. She had to decide soon, or they would both die.

The heat inside the shaft was heavy and thick, almost choking her every breath. One year ago, Dr. Loventhol came into her life with promises of a new beginning. He gave her one hundred thousand dollars and a five-bedroom house with a maid and full time cook. Jacob and Sean had more toys than the entire neighborhood back in Brooklyn. She no longer had to walk the streets in the middle of winter, hoping someone needed a warm body to lie on. But, as the months went on, she had become a cow that the doctors milked blood from each day. They extracted bag after bag from her veins despite her growing weakness during the day and cold sweats at night. They promised her they were going to stop soon, but the days became longer and the nights shorter. And when she became too weak, they started using Jacob's blood.

Tears leaked from her eyes as she remembered the look on his face as the needle went into his arms. He would fight at first, until they threatened to kill mommy. His eyes became sedate, almost ghost-like, and stared into the distance. The images forced her to fight the suffering and accept the needle, despite the overwhelming feeling of death. The question that plagued her mind every waking moment was what would happen to her children if she died? The doctors didn't care about them. They would drain her babies dry if they had too, she thought, biting her fingernails. And not a soul in the world would ever know the truth. That's when she decided they had to escape.

Nicole knew that her firm, supple breasts, long legs and silky brown skin could weaken any man's resolve. She was the highest paid prostitute on the block and the night shift guard that stood in front of her door was not immune to her power. The thought of his thick, greasy skin rubbing against her body still made her nauseated, but the suffering was worth it. Each night he came into her room, panting with testosterone, was another day he became less attentive to his duties. He started bringing food, bottles of liquor, and soft music to pretend that his violent pelvic thrusts actually meant something. Little did he know that Nicole had saved enough sleeping pills to spike his drink. The image of his large bloated body lying nude on the floor like a killer whale on a shore still brought a smile to her face. That's when she climbed up into the ventilation shaft and made her way above her boys' room.

The ten minutes of freedom felt liberating until she peered through the vent. Jacob slept in his bed as Sean snored in his crib. The peace that glowed from their faces was pure and safe. It was as if the world had placed a protective blanket over them, shielding them from the evils of their every moment. She reached inside her pocket, pulled out a screwdriver, and unfastened the first screw. The eight-month plan to escape was etched in her brain like the names of both her sons in the gold locket around her neck. It was the only thing that got her through the transfusions when her body felt like Jell-O. She never once thought she couldn't take them both—that wasn't part of the plan. But the transfusions had caused her cancer to come back. She was sure of it. It was getting harder every day just to wake up, but she had to fight or they would all die.

Nicole finished unscrewing the last bolt and unloosened the vent, all the while checking for any unfamiliar sounds. She scanned the room and saw the table she placed under the vent two days ago. She dangled her body above it, then carefully let go, falling softly on the table. She estimated it would take the guards ten minutes to fix the glitch she placed in the security camera. Her body felt like an over-stretched rubber band about to snap, as each step drew her closer to her children. She carefully planted each step, despite the shaking of her legs, and approached their beds. Thousands of scrambled thoughts ripped through her brain like the knife that lacerated her soul. Which would live and which one would die?

She first stared at Sean and knew that there was a God. Nothing mortal could create something so beautiful. His eyes were as blue and clear as the ocean. Each of his breaths was as precious as the one before it. How could she live without ever holding him in her arms again, feeling his tiny heart beat against her chest? And what about Jacob? He was her strength. His love kept her from trying to kill herself after a tough night on the streets. His deep brown eyes were strong, yet innocent. His heart was honest and pure. The thought of his tiny little eyes closing forever almost made her pass out. She regained her composure, glanced at the clock and realized they would be coming soon. Which one? Which one? she kept asking herself.

She walked over to Sean's crib and was about to pick him up, when Jacob awoke. "Mommy," Jacob said, rubbing his eyes.

"Shh," Nicole said, putting her hand over his mouth.

God had made the decision for her, she thought. How could she tell Jacob to go back to sleep? "You have to be very quiet or the bad men will get us," Nicole whispered. She picked him up in her arms all the while staring at Sean's face. How could she leave him? She walked over to his crib and was about to reach inside when a weakness overtook her. Her skin started to burn as if someone had thrown acid on it. Her legs struggled to hold up her thin frame. She leaned against the crib and looked at the clock on the wall. Two minutes to decide. She prayed for a moment and then reached inside the crib. She was about to grab her son when she heard footsteps in the hall. They were soft at first and became louder by the second. She withdrew her hands, then reached back in. She caressed her son's face and cried.

"Why are you crying, Mommy?" Jacob asked, trembling.

"We have to go," Nicole said, hoisting Jacob against her hip.

"What about Sean?"

"We have to come back for him later." She looked back at the crib and imprinted the image of Sean sleeping in her mind. His life was now in the hands of God. The sound of keys jiggling outside the door made her realize she had to move quickly. She jumped up on the table, shoved Jacob into the ventilation shaft, and followed behind. She grabbed the metal vent and wedged it in the walls to slow the guards if they followed. Nicole cried violent tears as she pushed Jacob forward, struggling to move her weakened arms and legs as fast as she could. A loud thud shook the entire shaft and she could hear heavy breathing. "Stop right there, you fucking bitch," the guard yelled.

Nicole quickened her pace, the guard followed. The shaft made a turn to the right. Hopefully, he would be too large to fit his body through, she thought. The exit to the outside was right around the corner. Jacob passed through easily. She scrunched her body into a ball and negotiated the tight corner. The guard, however, was stuck. But he wiggled his body, like a fish trying to break free from a fisherman's line, and slowly forced himself through. She accelerated her crawl, pushing Jacob ahead, trying feverishly to get to the vent that led to the back of the building. In the distance, she saw rays of light penetrate the holes at the end of the shaft. It had to lead to the outside. She unloosened three of the screws. One left, she thought. The guard finally broke free and lunged his body forward. She dropped the screwdriver and searched frantically on the floor. She could see the shadow of a person fifteen feet away. Jacob reached down, quickly found it and handed it to her. Her hands trembled as she unloosened the final screw and pulled the vent from the wall. The face of the guard appeared. He grabbed her foot. She jiggled her leg quickly, breaking his grip. She pushed Jacob outside, and picked up the metal vent. With all of her strength, she slammed it against the man's head and blood trickled from his skull as he lay motionless. She dropped the vent and climbed outside.

There was a full moon that illuminated the stars in the pristine black sky. Mountains, with tall jagged peaks, surrounded the entire area. The air was hot. The ground was dry. The facility was in the middle of nowhere; the nearest town was forty miles away. Nicole picked up Jacob and scanned the parking lot. The guard she had seduced always boasted about his supposed bumpin' ride, she thought. It was a brand new green Ford Explorer. It was at the far end of the parking lot. Despite her weakness and exhaustion, she sprinted with her child to the truck and opened the door. She started the engine and floored the gas pedal.

Nicole had escaped before, only to find the local police were on the payroll. They immediately brought her back to the lab and collected a briefcase full of money. She knew Frank Roberts was the only person she could trust and unfortunately, he was in New York. He was the closest thing to love she'd ever experienced. He treated her like a woman, not some warm body to masturbate into. But he couldn't handle the shame of being in love with a prostitute and never believed that Sean was his son. It destroyed her soul. And despite her numerous phone calls, he refused to come visit his newborn son. Now he may never get the chance to look in his boy's beautiful eyes.

The ride to Bismarck, North Dakota had been mesmerizing. The fever that boiled her brain made it almost impossible to stay awake. She looked over at Jacob and realized she had to fight the pain. He was sleeping peacefully in the passenger side. She stared at his face and began to weep. He had long eyelashes, like a woman's, that accentuated his big brown eyes. His skin was creamy brown, his body thin and long. Every morning he would bring her a bowl of cereal and juice to her in bed after a hard night on the streets. He was such a strong child for his age. Hopefully, he would be strong enough to survive if she died.

Nicole parked her car at the airport terminal and ran inside. She scanned the parking lot and found no suspicious faces. She knew that would be the first place they would look. She went to the gate and obtained a ticket with the guard's credit card. Luckily, the flight was leaving in ten minutes. She boarded the plane and plopped into the seat. For a moment, a feeling of comfort entered her mind. But it was short lived because her baby boy was still in the lab.

LaGuardia airport was filled with immigrants from all over the world. At least five different languages blared overhead, instructing the travelers where to pick up their luggage. A lot of them were on vacation, but not Nicole. She was struggling to keep her eyes open because the room seemed to be spinning. She was lightheaded and burning up, like a match, with fever. Nicole could tell by the empty look in Jacob's eyes that he knew she was sick. But nothing could stop her now; she was in New York City.

Nicole arrived outside and flagged down a cab. She reached in her pocket and smiled; she had enough money to get her to Frank's police station in Brooklyn. She glanced over at Jacob and fought back the tears. He looked like a zombie. His steps were trance-like, as if his legs were moving on their own without any guidance from his brain. His body was as rigid as a corpse. Nicole reached inside her soul and grabbed enough strength to hold him in her arms, trying to comfort his fears. She jumped into the cab and collapsed into the seat. The Middle Eastern cab driver looked at her with concerned eyes. "You all right lady?" he asked with a thick accent.

"Take us to the 42nd precinct, in Brooklyn."

"You look like you need a doctor."

"Just do it," Nicole said, now struggling to breathe.

Nicole felt her body drifting away. She started seeing things, such as creatures with long purple heads with horns and bugs that seemed to crawl under her skin. "Mommy, please don't die. Take us to the doctors…Mommy's sick," Jacob cried, grabbing Nicole's hand.

"Sean, save Sean. Bismarck, North Dakota. Loventhol clinic, Loventhol clinic. Please Frank, save your son. Save your son," Nicole screamed, tears running down her cheek. The hallucinations were starting to control her mind. "Can't breathe…help…God…please don't let me die. My babies. Make the bugs get off my skin."

"Lady, I'm taking you to the hospital," the cab driver said, his face expanding with fear.

Nicole's mind slowly disconnected from her body and an overwhelming peace overtook her. At first she fought it and worried about her two sons; the only thing that gave her the will to fight. But, a powerful comfort consumed her and she knew it was now all up to God.

Chapter 2

Brooklyn, New York

Dr. Robin Vastbinder sat at her desk trying feverishly to finish the stack of post-mortem charts, wondering why she became an oncologist in the first place. It was a struggle to relive the memories of the people she once gave hope. They all had terminal cancer and came to her for a promise of a new beginning. Unfortunately, the disease was much smarter than she was. They all had died and left nothing more than a stack of papers that recanted tales of their suffering. They were husbands and wives, sons and daughters that left behind nothing but regret. The regret of not seeing another day. And they were all much too young to die; most of them were no older than forty. But that was her life, one tragedy after another.

When she was in her training, she thought she could shield her heart from the pain. She had been at it for five years and had visited death more often than she would've liked. The University's Oncology unit was the last hope for most of these people. Sadly, most of her patients died. But, Robin took pride in the fact that once in while, she had all the answers. It was the other seventy percent that drove her nuts. But, it was the hope of the cure that kept her getting out of bed every day.

Unfortunately, things were moving too slowly for her to handle. Her patients were short on time and too young to let go of life.

It was nine o'clock in the morning and Robin had already been at work for three hours. She combed her hands through her short, curly red hair and rubbed the little makeup she had left on her face into her hands. The long days were making her age beyond her years. Her once creamy white skin had become pale, her brown eyes now had satellites of bags eclipsing the glow of her smile. Her long, healthy frame had slimmed, making her once firm curves disappear. The days at the gym had been long gone since the accident. She stared at the three bookshelves in her office and realized that work was all she had left.

Robin continued examining the pile of medical records on her desk when her pager went off. The annoying beep interrupted everything she did. It was difficult to get anything done, especially her research. She depressed the key and picked up the phone. It was an Emergency Medicine doctor asking her to come down and see a leukemia patient who was critically ill. She grabbed her jacket and stethoscope and went to the elevator at the end of the hall.

Another train wreck in the E.R., she thought as she rode the elevator to the second floor. The only time they called her was when it was too late to do anything. She exited the elevator and walked towards the nurse's station. The E.R. was crowded, as usual, with patients in every room, ranging from critically ill to a common cold. Nurses scurried from exam bay to exam bay, with frantic tired eyes. Residents and Interns fumbled around the halls, reading their pocket handbooks, trying to figure out what the hell they were doing. It was July; the worse time to be in a teaching hospital. The interns were brand new and everything seemed quite overwhelming. She laughed to herself thinking about her first day. She didn't even know where the bathroom was located, let alone know how to treat a sick patient.

Brooklyn University hospital was as old as the Liberty Bell, or so it seemed, Robin thought. The dusty, green tiled walls were chipped, and the floor had more cracks than an old sidewalk in Brooklyn withering in the wind. The equipment was ancient. The blood pressure cuffs and ophthalmoscopes were at least twenty years old, but that was typical of an inner city university hospital. The research facilities were plush and elaborate, but the hospital was barely one step above a third world country.

Robin looked at the board and found her name beside the patient in room twelve named Nicole Johnson. She walked around the corner and spotted a black woman, in her late twenties, struggling to breathe inside the room. Three nurses stood around her administering I.V. fluids and adrenaline, trying to get her blood pressure up. A young resident barked out commands with a look of terror on his face. Robin entered the room and assessed the woman. Her hair was long and silky black, her breasts were large, probably fake, Robin thought. Her skin was pale brown with multiple bruises, her breathing labored. She looked like a fashion model that overdosed on drugs, but her labs showed she probably had end stage lymphoma, which had infiltrated her bone marrow.

"I'm Dr. Vastbinder, from oncology," she said, calmly shaking the nervous resident's hand.

"Tim Jackson," he replied, hyperventilating while looking at the monitor. "I've given her five liters of fluid and I still can't get her pressure above sixty."

"Where is the attending?" Robin asked, calmly glancing through the chart.

"Over in the trauma bays with the bus accident victims."

"So, I guess I'm all you got," Robin said, putting on a pair of rubber gloves. "What pressor's do you have her on?"

"Dopamine and neosynephrine," the brown haired, blue-eyed resident replied. "Her white count is fifty thousand. All blast."

"She needs chemotherapy," Robin said, glancing at the monitor. "But, we have to stabilize her first."

Robin pulled out her stethoscope and was about to listen to Nicole's heart when her eyes suddenly opened. Her arms and legs flailed back and forth, almost knocking herself off the gurney. "Save my babies…Jacob, Sean," Nicole screamed. "My babies, where are my babies?"

"You better get her intubated, her oxygen saturation just dropped to eighty," Robin said, holding down Nicole's arms and legs. "How many intubations have you done?"

"About fifteen," the resident said confidently.

"Then get to it."

The resident stuffed the tube down her throat and listened to her chest, the nurse connected the ambubag to the tube and began to ventilate the woman. "Her pressure is dropping," Robin yelled. "Double the dopamine and neo."

Robin could feel her heart race and skin tingle. But, she fought to remain calm. She looked into Nicole's eyes and the reality set in. This young beautiful woman was going to die unless she figured out a way to increase her blood pressure. She ordered the nurse to increase the pressors, but Nicole's vitals continued to spiral down like a plane falling from the sky. Then it happened. The woman went into ventricular fibrillation, the heart rhythm that was a precursor to death. "O.K., let's shock her. 200 joules," Robin barked. The woman's body jumped and the smell of burning flesh stained the air. Robin looked at the monitor; she was asystolic, no heartbeat.

"Give her 300 joules and an amp of epinephrine."

The woman's body trembled on the table then relaxed. She still had no pulse. Robin felt a nausea stream through her stomach and perspiration run down her face. Nicole's eyes fixed and dilated. "An amp of epinephrine," Nicole yelled.

The monitor beeped with only a straight line on the screen. She was drifting away. Robin grabbed a large bore needle from the tray beside and rammed it into the woman's chest. Thick, bloody fluid filled the syringe. The woman had a pericardial effusion, which disabled her heart. She wiped the sweat from her forehead, which dripped into her eyes, and glanced at the monitor – nothing but a straight line. It was over. The tightened muscles in Robin's arms and legs relaxed as a pool of stomach acid crept up her throat. She let out a deep sigh and said, "Time," ripping the blood stained latex gloves from her hands and dropping them into the wastebasket.

"10:06 a.m., July tenth," a white-haired nurse said feebly.

Robin glanced at the Intern slumped against the wall with a look of despair that eclipsed his blue eyes. He rubbed his face, trying to cover up the tears that trickled down his cheeks. He had obviously lost his first young patient, Robin thought. She walked over to his side and gently placed her hand on his shoulder. "You did everything you could," she said softly.

The intern's eyes were distant, his movements somber. "She was no older than my sister," he said, dropping his head to his chest.

"It doesn't get any easier," Robin said, pulling a tissue from her coat. "You have to remember that you really don't have any control over life or death. The decision had already been made long before they came to the ER. You just do your best and that's all anyone can ask. Why don't you go and get yourself some coffee. I'll talk with the family."

"Thanks," the intern replied, slowly leaving the room.

"Does anyone know where the social worker is?" Robin asked.

"At the nurse's station," a young Asian nurse replied while cleaning the blood off the woman's chest.

Robin went to the sink, washed her hands, and walked out into the hallway. A heavyset black woman with wide brown eyes and dread locks approached her. It was Careen Jones, the social worker. "She's gone, isn't she Dr. Vastbinder?" Careen said, shaking her head while staring at the floor.

"I'm afraid so," Robin replied. "Where's the family?"

"The only people out in the waiting room are her son and a cab driver. I've searched our old records and found that she has a brother who lives in Jersey. Called him twice, but there was no answer."

"No husband? Mother or father?"

"Not to my knowledge."

"How old is the little boy?"

"I guess he's about four or five, tough to tell. He won't speak. Poor child just stares at the wall. Definitely post traumatic stress syndrome."

"God," Robin said, rubbing her temples. "Five years old and alone. I hate this place."

"I know. If I didn't have three children and a mortgage, I'd take him myself."

"We'll need psych to get involved," Robin said

"One step ahead of you. They're already in the room."

Robin took a deep breath and followed Careen through the double doors into the conference room. A little African-American boy sat at the head of the table. His round little brown face stared somberly at the table as if the wood had all the answers. His long arms were folded against his chest. His eyes were expressionless as if the soul had been removed. A thin Asian woman was on one knee with an arm around his shoulder, speaking softly into his ear. It was Dr. Chau Dang, a staff psychiatrist. Unfortunately, nothing she said changed the expression on the little boy's face.

As Robin sat down in one of the creaky wooden chairs, she focused on the boy's eyes and the pain returned. He was the same age as her son. She remembered how soft her son's skin felt against her chest, how he would run to the door of the daycare center, jump up and hug her. She tried to swallow, but the golf ball in her throat made the saliva stick to the roof of her mouth. How was she going to tell the little boy that he would never see his mother alive again?

"May I speak with you for a moment, Dr. Dang?"

"Sure," Dr. Dang replied, following her out of the room.

"I...I was just wondering if you broke the news to the kid," Robin said, as a tear trickled down her face.

"We've been through this a hundred times, Robin. You need more time off. You're not ready."

"I just can't sit at home," Robin replied, thinking about her empty house.

"Travel. I'm sure your family would love to see you."

"Work is all I have right now," Robin replied, wiping the tears from her face.

"Listen," Dr. Dang said with a sigh. "I can't let you continue to treat patients in your condition. I want you to come by the office tomorrow and we can talk. In the meantime, I think you should go home."

"Maybe you're right," Robin said, combing her fingers through her hair and dropping her head.

"I know I'm right," Dr. Dang said, caressing her back.

"Thanks, Chau."

Dr. Dang went back into the conference room as Robin took a deep breath and walked down the hall. Maybe Chau was right. Her parents had a home in Florida and had been begging her to come down and stay since the funeral. But, work kept her mind off things. Sitting on a beach, watching the waves crash against the shore would do nothing but make her think. And thinking was something she couldn't handle right now.

Robin hopped on the elevator and rode it to the fifth floor. She walked inside her office and plopped in her chair. Three more charts, then she would go home, she thought. As she picked up the five-inch thick chart and began leafing through the pages, her pager beeped. She depressed the key, picked up the phone and dialed the number. "Dr. Vastbinder."

"Dr. Vastbinder, it's Careen."

"What did you find out?" Robin asked, leaning back in her chair.

"Well, I got in touch with her brother and he agreed to come and get the child. Both of her parents are dead and her brother is all the family she has."

"Did you get authorization for her autopsy?"

"Yeah. And I got her old records coming in from the warehouse. There's something really strange about all of this."

"What?"

"Well, the old charts are from the delivery of her son, but there are two diagnostic codes on the sheet. The first one is for labor and delivery and the other is for treatment of a cancer. Large cell immunoblastic lymphoma."

"Are you sure that's not a mistake? That's quite rare, which means the prognosis is poor. Most people die within 2 years, even with chemotherapy. Her son is five years old. It would be a miracle for someone to live five years with that disease."

"I double checked it myself. It's not a mistake."

"When will those charts be over from the warehouse?"

"You know how this place is...probably sometime tomorrow."

"Could you give me a page when they arrive?"

"As soon as they're in my hand."

Chapter 3

Robin turned on her radio and sunk in the seat of her gray Volvo, wondering if she'd ever get home. The traffic on the Brooklyn Queens expressway looked like thousands of ants crowded together, fighting for the same piece of bread. She glanced out the window, and then closed her eyes, all the while envisioning the face of the scared little boy. Of all the people to show up in the E.R., why did it have to be him?

Robin finally arrived at her three bedroom, Victorian style home in Queens and pulled into the driveway. She opened the door, walked upstairs and slipped out of her gray, wrap around skirt and put on a pair of sweat pants and a tee shirt. She walked downstairs and poured herself a glass of white Zinfandel and kicked her feet up on the couch. She picked up the remote to her stereo and the soft sounds of Marvin Gaye hummed through the speakers. The song, "Let's Get It On," reminded her of the first time she met the love of her life, her husband, Davis. It was during a party at John Hopkins medical school. She may have been drunk out of her mind, but she never forgot the look in his eyes. She knew that the first kiss meant forever and it did, until a year ago. A teenager rammed a stolen car into her husband's BMW, killing him and her five-year-old son. The look on the police officer's face when he came to her door never left her mind. It still kept her awake at night, even after a bottle of wine and a few sleeping pills.

Robin finished the last gulp of her second bottle of wine and wiped the tears from her face. She thought about trying to sleep in her bed, but it still hurt knowing he was no longer by her side. She still couldn't go into Davis Jr.'s room. The bed was made and the toys still lay on the floor, just as he left them the day before he died. She asked God every day why she deserved this. What had she done? Unfortunately, he wasn't listening. Robin reached over in her purse and pulled out a bottle of Restoril, a sleeping pill. She plopped one of the blue capsules into her mouth and tried to relax on the couch. Every day seemed a little better than the day before it, until this morning. Once she saw the look in the boy's eyes she knew she would be up all night.

A thick pool of phlegm clogged Robin's mouth, making her cough and wake up. Her head pounded and muscles ached. She pulled herself to a sitting position and looked at the clock above the entertainment center and immediately became awake. It was eight thirty. She had overslept again. Rubbing her eyes, she glanced at her living room. Clothes were piled on her love seat and papers cluttered the coffee table. She hadn't done laundry in days. Her once immaculate living room looked like a garbage dump. It took too much energy to clean. The only thing she cared about was the picture of Davis and Davis Jr. sitting on her end table. It was a shrine that she cleaned everyday. She thought about having a housekeeper come in once a week, but that was too much to think about. It was tough enough to go to work, she thought. She picked up the phone on her end table and called her office to inform them she'd be late again. She rushed into the shower and quickly got dressed. She had an office full of patients and ten to see in the hospital. She became depressed for a moment thinking about how behind she would be, but realized it was a lot better than staring at the four walls of her empty house. She grabbed a stale bagel from her fridge and rushed out of the door.

Robin trotted through the glass doors of her office with a cup of coffee in her hand and stopped at her secretary's desk. The woman shook her head and handed her a stack of charts. "You have three patients in the rooms and four in the waiting room," the plump secretary said, anxiously.

"Thanks," Robin said, applying red lipstick. "Sorry I'm late. Traffic was hell." Robin walked into her office and dropped the charts on her desk. She reached inside her drawer and took a swig of Maalox trying to subdue the stomach acid that crept up her throat. Walking out of her office she approached the first exam room and grabbed the chart from the rack on the door. Leafing through the pages, she realized her day was off to a bad start. It was Mrs. Karen Pitney, a thirty-five year old mother of three who had acute leukemia. Karen had suffered through high doses of Cytoxin, a very toxic chemotherapy agent, and a bone marrow transplant and still the cancer remained in her bone marrow. Robin remembered the look in Karen's eyes as she sat in her the hospital bed, trembling from head to toe with infection, fighting to stay alive for her children. And how she would smile each morning, despite the inside of her mouth peeling from her palate and cheeks, causing a drink of water to be a painful experience. She fought harder than any patient Robin had ever treated. Sadly, she was going to lose the battle. Robin took a deep breath and walked into the room.

Karen Pitney's frail frame hid behind a flowered exam gown that dangled over her nude body. The blonde curly wig may have covered her baldhead, but didn't cover up the circles under her eyes and the cheekbones that almost protruded through her skin. She looked like a skeleton covered with flesh. Robin pulled her stethoscope from her coat, grabbed the blood pressure cuff, trying to avoid informing her of the results of her bone marrow biopsy. Two months ago, being the grim reaper was a routine. She never once thought about it. It was just a normal part of the job. Some people were lucky and others weren't. Now, each minute in the exam rooms was worse than the one before it.

"So, how've you been?" Robin asked, pumping up the blood pressure cuff.

"You don't need to tell me the results of the bone marrow," Karen said, tears soaking her cheeks. "I know they're bad, I could tell the minute you walked in here."

Robin swallowed back the tears, trying to remain professional. "I'm so sorry Karen, but the bone marrow transplant didn't take. We can try another round of chemotherapy, maybe you'll get a…"

"No more," Karen said, breaking into a violent cry. "I couldn't take throwing up my brains and feeling like shit all the time. I want to die at home with my kids and husband."

Robin wrapped her arms tightly around Karen. "I will make sure you're comfortable."

"How…long?" Karen asked, between the tears.

"I'm not God, but most people in your condition live between six months to a year without treatment."

"Good," Karen said, relieved. "I will get to see my twelve year old graduate from grade school. The girls are so young, they don't quite understand, but he does, and I know it's killing him."

Robin didn't know what to say. How in the hell was she going to tell her children? Her husband? The thought never entered her mind in the past. It couldn't or she would've gone crazy thinking about all the people she had seen die. "Why don't you come and see me in a couple of days, think about things before you make the decision not to get chemotherapy. You may be one of the lucky ones and get a response."

"My mind's pretty much made up," Karen said somberly.

"Just talk it over with your husband and give me a call."

"Thanks."

Robin was exhausted after she walked out of her last patient's room. It was only noon, but it seemed as if she had been up two days straight. Maybe Dr. Dang was right. A few weeks at her parents place would make her deal with the pain and stop denying it ever happened. Robin went to the break room and grabbed her fourth cup of coffee, which made the pain in her stomach worse. "Probably have an ulcer the size of the Grand Canyon," she said to herself, holding her upper abdomen. As she reached in her pocket for another swig of Maalox, her pager beeped. It was Careen Jones, the social worker from the hospital. She went to her office, picked up the phone and dialed her office. "What's up Careen?"

"I got the charts you wanted," Careen exclaimed.

"What charts?"

"Nicole Johnson, you know, the black lady that died in the E.R. yesterday."

"Oh yes, I remember. Sorry, it's been one of those days."

"It's O.K. I can completely understand considering what you've been through."

"Thanks."

"I almost passed out when medical records called. It only took eighteen hours. I think that's a record."

"I'm sure they were burning the midnight oil just to get them over here," Robin said with a chuckle. "So, what did you find?"

"Well, the diagnostic codes were correct. She had large cell immunoblastic leukemia."

"What did she get treated with?"

"She left the hospital against medical advice right after her son was born."

"No outpatient records?"

"No. I even had them double and triple check the records."

"Are you sure that was five years ago?" Robin asked, still baffled how all of this could be possible.

"Positive. Come see them for yourself."

The twelve story high brownstone Brooklyn University hospital sent a long shadow across the parking lot that reminded Robin of the darkness of her thoughts. The sun was bright, the sky clear, but the warmth of the summer wind didn't comfort her soul as she walked through the glass doors. It was impossible to get a break from the pain. Every place she turned, it stood there looking at her in the face, ripping at her soul.

Robin stepped on the elevator and rode it to the fifth floor. She stepped off and walked down a hallway lined with five glass doors and covered with brown, worn down carpet and beige flowered wallpaper. Careen's office was the second door on the right. She knocked and entered to find Careen biting into a sandwich and sipping a Diet Coke while sitting at her desk. "Thanks for getting the chart," Robin said, sitting on the rickety wooden chair in front of her desk.

"Have you eaten?" Careen asked, offering her half of a tuna fish sandwich.

"No thanks. I'll get something later. So where's the chart."

"Here you go," Careen said handing her the chart. "That poor girl had a rough life."

"I'm sure she did," Robin said, leafing through the pages.

"She was a hooker, strung out on cocaine. Her brother said the last time he saw her was at her mother's funeral five years ago, a few months before her son was born. He also said something about another child but wasn't sure whether she gave it up for adoption or had an abortion."

"That poor little boy," Robin said with a sigh, thinking about his terrified little round eyes. "Hopefully, her brother will take him to get help because he's going to need years of therapy."

Robin flipped to the progress notes of the charts, which was a daily log of what the physician was thinking. On a routine history and physical she had an enlarged liver and spleen. And an abdominal CT scan showed a 5cm by 5cm mass in her liver and stomach. Her LDH and liver enzymes were elevated. And a CT guided biopsy showed lymphoma, which had disseminated throughout her abdomen and into her brain. There hasn't been any case report she could recall documenting the survival of a patient with this disease more than two years, even with aggressive chemotherapy, she thought. And this woman was alive five years later without treatment. How?

"Are you sure this is the right chart? Nicole Johnson is a pretty common name, there could be thousands in Brooklyn alone," Robin said, shaking her head.

"You check for yourself," Careen said, handing it to her, a bit annoyed. "I double checked the medical record numbers and they are the same."

"I didn't mean to offend you," Robin said, paging through the thin E.R. chart. "I just can't see how any of this is possible."

Robin checked the blood types and they were the same, O negative. She looked at the descriptions on the physical exam, again exactly the same. How could this be? And why hadn't anyone looked into this five years ago? She quickly turned the pages until she found the name of the oncologist who saw her at the time. Dr. Roderick Taylor. Who the hell was he? He wasn't one of the ten heme /onc physicians on staff at the hospital since she had been there.

"Careen," Robin said, twirling her pen. "How many years have you worked here?"

"Sixteen years in January. Why do you ask? Do I look that old and worn down?" Careen asked with a smile.

"No, I was just wondering if you ever heard of an oncologist named Roderick Taylor?"

"Yeah, I knew him. Left about eight years ago. Real nice guy."

"Do you have any idea where he went?"

"Yeah, he's the chairman of something at some hospital in Boston."

"Listen, I've got to run," Robin said, looking at her watch. "I want to catch the pathologist before he begins the autopsy. Thanks for everything."

CHAPTER 4

Detective Frank Roberts sat at his desk, struggling to type up the three-page report that was due yesterday. He picked and poked with two fingers at the keyboard of his computer, wishing the entire time he would've stayed awake in typing class during high school. The 42nd Precinct police station in Brooklyn was crowded with the usual Friday night vagrants: a drunk throwing up in the corner, a penny thief being dragged into his cell, and a voluptuous blonde prostitute trying to scam her way out of being arrested. It was the same thing every Friday and Saturday night, only the faces and names changed. The white paint that chipped from the walls and were interrupted by windows with bars, reminded Frank of his life. It seemed his self-respect was sloughing from his soul like the paint from the walls. He was trapped in his shitty job, just like the convicts in their cells.

Frank brushed his thick black hair from his face, exposing his deeply set blue eyes and long nose that had a bump in the middle. He reached in his desk and pulled out a box of Oreos and sighed as he inhaled a couple. His once trim stomach now had a soft bulge that protruded over his belt. Eating seemed to calm his frustrations. And unfortunately, he ate anything and everything. Frank finished the last of his reports, pulled his six foot four frame from his desk and walked to the coffee machine. He frowned. The pot was empty. As he walked down the hallway to the cafeteria, he saw a bald white man with a mustache and thick, muscular arms that bulged from his short sleeve shirt. It was Detective Mike Scalice. "How are the reports coming?" Mike asked, taking a huge bite from the cheese danish in his hand.

"Getting there."

"Are you ever going to clean that desk?"

"Is it your desk?"

"No, but I can't see how you find shit in that mess. Last week I came down and the most crucial piece of evidence in that Bankson case—you know, the bank statement—was sitting in the corner of some pile of shit that could've been easily thrown away."

"I guess I need to put directions in the front drawer so everyone who decides to go through the things on my desk will know where they are," Frank said, dropping his last report into the outgoing basket. "This paperwork is a bunch of bullshit anyway."

"By the way, you know that hooker you've been looking for?"

"Yeah, what about her?"

"She's dead."

Frank felt a pressure in his chest, the air seemed to be escaping the room. He took a deep breath, trying to hide his anguish. "How?"

"Well, I just picked up one of her friends for questioning in the Derube murders and she told me that she had cancer. Died at Brooklyn University two days ago. See, I told you she wasn't murdered, I know everything on these streets. You owe me ten bucks."

"Yeah…" Frank said, staring through Mike at the walls. "Ten bucks."

"Why the sad face?" Mike asked, surprised. "You weren't hitting it, were you?"

"No, she was just a nice girl who got strung out on that shit, then that fucking bastard, Smitty, pimped her out like a piece of meat."

"So, shit happens everyday. You had to be hitting it," Mike said, with mischievous eyes. "Or you wouldn't give a shit."

Frank felt a weal of rage climb his throat. "Listen, I do give a shit. That's why I do this job," Frank said, stabbing his finger in Mike's chest with each word. "She was only twenty fucking eight. Had a little boy. The shit still gets to me everyday. Once it stops getting to you, that's when you should get out."

"Take it easy, man. I was just messing with ya."

"What else did she tell you?"

"Why don't you ask her yourself," Mike said, straightening his tie. "She's in holding cell six."

"What's her name?"

"Gina Franks. And hey, I was just kidding. You need to lighten up," Mike said, patting Frank on the back. "And you shouldn't be ashamed for hitting it. I would've hit it too if I could've got away with it."

Frank strolled up the hallway, until he reached the elevator. He rode it to the seventh floor and showed his I.D. badge to the officer behind the glass doors. The door buzzed, then opened. The twenty cells, with only a toilet and two cots, lined the hallway. The jeers of the drunks echoed through the hallways as they screamed obscenities as Frank walked by. In the last cell were two women. One was a tall woman, with kinky black hair dressed in a tight leather skirt with black fish net panty hose and spiked pumps, the other a short Asian woman in skin tight leather pants and a pile of makeup on her face that barely covered the bruises. "Which one of you is Gina Franks?"

"I am," the tall woman replied, abrasively. "And I've told you all I know, understand? So, I better be out of here as soon as my man brings my bail."

"Listen, I'm not here to ask you about the Derube murders."

"Then what are you here for?"

"About Nicole Johnson."

"What about her?"

"I heard…she died," Frank said, somberly.

The angry contoured lines in Gina's heavy red rouge relaxed. She stared intently at Frank as if they had met before. "You're Blue Eyes, aren't you?"

Frank turned away for a second and faked a cough to fight back the tears. He thought about her bright brown eyes, her silky black skin and beautiful smile, and realized he would never make love to her again. She would always call him Blue Eyes every time she met him after work.

"I don't know what you're talking about," Frank said, coughing again.

"That's what Nicole called this cop she liked…Blue Eyes."

"So, what happened to her?"

"Died two days ago. Had some type of cancer. Hadn't seen or heard from her down at the spot for six months. She said she was going away for a while. Got a job somewhere out west."

"Doing what?"

"Didn't say. But, she did say that she was glad her children were getting away from the 'hood.'"

"Children? I thought she only had a little boy."

"You seem to know a lot about her, Blue Eyes."

"She was a friend."

"Wish I had a friend like you," Gina said, her eyes sultry and voice soft.

"So, what about this other child?"

"He was three months old. Honey, he was the most beautiful thing I ever saw. And he had these big old round blue eyes. Kept her off the streets for six weeks, the longest I could remember. She even quit doing the shit. She was so glad she didn't get that abortion and I can't blame her."

"Where are her children now?"

"No idea. Just heard the news from the street."

"What hospital did she die at?"

"Brooklyn University."

"Thanks."

A numbness slowly overtook Frank as he lumbered away from the cell. Everything in the hallway; the bars, the walls and floor, all seemed to disappear. All he could see was a tiny baby boy, with a plump round face and big blue blues. And the thought of the child without a father made him crazy. There was a good chance that this wasn't his child, he thought. She had been with many men of different races and creeds. It definitely wasn't his. Or was it?

Frank went back upstairs with thoughts of Nicole infiltrating his every notion. He looked at his watch and realized that there was no need to stay at the office. It was eight o'clock. His shift was over. It was time to go home, and forget about things for a while. Why did he ever let her go? he kept asking himself as he approached his blue Ford Tempo in the parking lot. She was the one woman who truly understood him.

Frank jumped in his car and drove onto Smith Street. He drove for ten minutes then finally arrived at his two-bedroom apartment on Bond Street in Brooklyn. He opened his door, went to his liquor cabinet, poured himself a shot of scotch and looked around his studio apartment. His couch was red, with splotches of coffee on the seat cushions. The lazy boy in the corner barely reclined. The once plush rug was worn to the ground. But, it didn't matter to him. He had a thirty-inch screen TV and a brand new Sony stereo. What else did he need? He could watch the Knicks and the Giants games then listen to Miles Davis. He was a divorced bachelor and had only himself to impress. He took a swig of his drink and looked out of the window. The streets were filled with blinking lights and people staggering on the sidewalks. A typical Friday night. The moon was half full. Half of the crazies would be out, he was sure of it. Thank God his shift was over.

Frank's back cramped as he walked over to the end table beside his couch. He opened the drawer in front and dug through the junk. He fumbled through piles of unpaid bills and trinkets, until he found what he was looking for. He picked up the small photo album, hidden at the bottom, and plopped it on the couch. He opened the first page and a tear filled his eye. It was Nicole and Jacob at the beach. The two-piece string bikini barely covered her large round, fake breasts and firm ass. She would always say, "Don't worry Blue Eyes, no one will ever know. I promise." And she kept her promise. Even when she got busted, she never asked him for help, even though he secretly pulled some strings to get her off. No one at work ever suspected he was in love with a prostitute. It was a lie he wished he had never lived, because she deserved so much more.

Frank tucked the photo back in the drawer, vowing never to look at it again. It hurt too much to think what could've been. He turned on his TV set and tried to watch the news. The entire time he flicked through the fifty channels of nothing, he couldn't stop thinking about sleeping with her in his arms. She had the softest skin and gentlest touch. If only it was a different time and place, he thought. But, he was a cop and she was a prostitute. And in the real world, that could never be.

When Nicole told him she was carrying his child, he didn't believe her. She had been with so many different men, the chances were slim it was his. She was just looking for a way out of the dark world that she had to suffer through every day, he was sure of it. He stopped returning her phone calls and then he never heard from her again. But, what if the child was really his? He sipped his scotch and wondered the entire night.

Chapter 5

Dr. Robin Vastbinder rode the elevator to the basement of the hospital, leafing through Nicole Johnson's chart. A soft ding sounded above and the elevator doors opened. Robin stepped off the elevator and a sharp odor stung her nostrils. It was formalin, which was used to preserve specimens and bodies for dissection. In medical school, the smell always reminded Robin of ammonia mixed with oven cleaner. She had to wear a mask during gross anatomy so she wouldn't suffocate while dissecting the cadavers. The row of lights that hung from the ceiling were dimmed from the black dust that collected on the brick walls. The coat of wax on the cement floors was embedded with thousands of black and gray particulate matter that sloughed off the wall. It almost looked like a dungeon. How could someone spend all day down here?

Robin walked down the hallway until she reached the metal door labeled AUTOPSY. She opened the door to find a tall, thin, black man, with a large Afro and scraggly beard that hung off his thin face. He had more hair than body, Robin thought. It was Dr. Orpheus Martin, chief of Pathology. He was sitting on his lab chair, with headphones on, bopping his head to music while eating an apple and examining a liver. It was the same position Robin found him every time she ventured to the "PIT", as Dr. Martin called it.

"Dr. Martin," Robin said, raising her voice while tapping him on the shoulder.

Dr. Martin jumped from his chair, knocking the apple and the liver to the ground. His thick eyebrows scrunched and forehead furrowed. "You almost gave me a heart attack," he said grabbing his chest. "What are you doing sneaking around down here?" You get lost or something. None of you white coats from upstairs ever come down here this time of day."

"Orpheus, when are you going to give up the seventies?" Robin said, smiling, while picking up the Parliament CD case.

"Why should I? Everything worth a shit came from the seventies: music, literature and even medicine. Think about it. The wide use of CT scans, the perfection of heart bypass surgery, better antibiotics, all from the seventies. I won't even mention music, because the stuff my kids listen to is a bunch of thugs talking about slapping their 'bitch' while driving in their car drinking malt liquor on the way to a drive by. What kind of music is that? I don't allow that crap in my house," Dr. Martin said, reaching to the floor, picking up the fleshy, domed shaped, maroon liver.

"That Afro gets bigger every time I see you," Robin said, laughing. "It needs a trim."

"You're lucky I'm almost finished with this thing. Been working the entire day on this. Most interesting case I've ever seen."

"That wouldn't happen to be Nicole Johnson's liver," Robin said, plopping the charts on the workbench.

"How'd you know?"

"She came to the E.R. in what appeared to be blast crisis, but her records from five years ago state that she had immunoblastic lymphoma."

"Are you sure that's not a mistake?" Dr. Martin asked, astonished.

"What are the chances of the same patient having the same name and O negative blood?"

"It's possible, especially in this place. Three weeks ago they sent me a live one. I was pulling her off the gurney when I noticed she was a little too warm to be dead. You would think after four years of college and four years of medical school that someone would be able to tell if someone was dead or alive."

"That's why I'm here," Robin said, handing him the charts. "For you to sort all of this out."

Dr. Martin pulled a pair of reading glasses from his lab jacket and opened the chart. As he turned each page, his eyes widened. "This is the same woman. Take a look at this liver," Dr. Martin said, grabbing a scalpel from the table.

Robin put on a pair of rubber gloves and rubbed her hand against the smooth capsule that covered the surface of the liver. At the top of the dome was a well-circumscribed, white lesion, the size of a quarter. It was nothing unusual for a patient with stage 4 non-Hodgkins disease. "So what's the big deal?"

"I don't want you to look at the lesion, but the area around it," Dr. Martin said, cutting out five inches around the lesion. "Notice how it scarred, as if the lesion had regressed."

"But, doesn't the liver regenerate?"

"Some, but not this much. Look at the rest of the GI tract."

Robin followed Dr. Martin past the five metal gurneys that contained bodies covered with body bags, to another room that was a library for body parts. The smell of formalin was twice as strong in the cold room, causing Robin's eyes to water and drip mucous from her nose.

"How do you put up with this everyday?" Robin asked, covering her mouth and nose."Nothing like the smell of some fresh formalin," Dr. Martin said, taking a deep cleansing breath. "It'll wake you up a lot faster than a cup of coffee."

Dr. Martin searched through five rows of white buckets, each labeled with a date and specimen number. He pulled one from the top and walked over to a workbench in the corner of the room. He lifted the lid. The kidneys, small intestine, and spleen were floating in a pool of formalin. "Take a look at the large bowel," Dr. Martin said, reaching in the bucket and pulling the long, sausage shaped organ and placing it on the table. "These are the same lesions, and look at the areas around them. All scarred as if they had been much larger."

Robin picked up the colon and examined the area. "So, you're saying that she had some regression of tumor?"

"I couldn't believe it myself until I took a look at the slides," Dr. Martin said, cutting the colon in half. "If you look at the areas where the tumor apparently regressed, the cells have all these inclusion bodies. Weirdest thing I've ever seen. Follow me, I'll show you."

Robin followed Dr. Martin to another lab that contained a double-headed microscope with five eyepieces attached, lined around a table. A tinge of excitement tickled Robin's stomach as she sat down. It had been a long time since she felt the exhilaration of discovery. What had caused this woman to overcome such a deadly cancer? She was a freak that could possibly save lives. It reminded Robin of the story she read in the newspaper about the women in Haiti that had been infected with HIV but hadn't converted to AIDS without treatment. Unfortunately, the team studying them had no clue, but maybe this time, they were on to something.

Dr. Martin placed the slide under the microscope and adjusted the focus. "You know what I've been noticing lately? Men becoming women and women becoming men. I had three bodies come in yesterday. Took me an hour to figure out what the hell they were. And this fake boob thing, what is that? I just don't get what is so exciting about plastic filled with saline or silicon. That shit would never have happened in the seventies. Everything was natural."

"Is that what you call that fifteen feet of hair? Natural?" Robin said, with a smile.

"I call it natural. Look at the kids today, starting to wear the Afro and bell-bottoms again. My own son has an Afro. You see, great style never goes away."

Robin concentrated on the cells, stained purple and pink, on the slide. "What are we looking at here, colon or stomach?"

"Colon. This section was taken from the area in-between the regenerated area and the tumor."

"What are all those long black rods inside the cells?"

"Inclusion bodies. Usually found with certain kinds of viruses. The most interesting thing about this case is the location of the inclusion bodies. All the cells with tumor are free of inclusion bodies, but the regenerated areas are filled with them. It's the weirdest thing I've ever seen."

"Are you sure it's a virus?"

"Judging from the characteristics of the inclusion bodies, it looks like a virus to me. But, it's a virus I've never seen. "

Robin pulled away from the microscope and stared at the ceiling. She remembered reading an article in the latest issue of *Cancer* that talked about the use of virus vectors carrying DNA that would shut off the genes that caused tumor growth. But, it was in the very primitive stages. "So you think that it's a virus that protected her from the tumor?"

"It would seem like that to me because if you look at all of the areas around the tumors, you find the same thing. But, I couldn't tell you what the virus is or how it works. I heard vaguely about viruses genetically manipulated to treat neoplasms, but I'm almost positive that it's never been tried on humans."

"So where did this virus come from?"

Chapter 6

The tips of Dr. Noah Jenkins' fingers tingled as he sat in the vestibule of Senator Thomas Watson's mansion contemplating his next move. He had twenty million dollars worth of promises and no product to deliver since Nicole Johnson and her son escaped from the lab. The only thing that remained was an infant without enough virus in his blood to cure a mouse, he thought. And what bothered him most was Dr. Loventhol's demeanor. He was always so calm and emotionless. If word got out about the transfusions, they would be in jail for a long time. But, Dr. Loventhol seemed to think that destiny was on his side. His ego had made him stupid, Dr. Jenkins thought.

A tall thin man with gray hair dressed in a tuxedo approached the door. Each of his steps was pompous as if he owned the world and everyone else was just renting space. He opened the door to the vestibule and said, "Senator Watson will see you now."

Dr. Jenkins followed him through the living room, which looked like a page from *Gone with the Wind*. The wallpaper was white with rich scarlet velvet in the print. A rococo styled couch and love seat were surrounded by expensive antique vases on adjacent coffee tables. The furniture was as beautiful as it was valuable. Dr. Jenkins could picture slaves serving drinks to southern generals at a dinner party during the Civil War. Senator Watson walked down the long spiral staircase with a cigar in his mouth.

He was a large man with rugged features and a potbelly that protruded from his conservative blue suit. He could've easily been mistaken for a ranch hand if he didn't have such prestige and power.

"Dr. Jenkins, where's Dr. Loventhol?" Senator Watson asked.

"He was unable to attend," Dr. Jenkins replied. "You know those genius types, very eccentric. I do all of this kind of stuff."

"That's a shame, because I wanted to thank the fella for saving my daughter," Senator Watson said, shaking Dr. Jenkins' hand. "How do you like Houston?"

"Pretty hot, but a nice city."

"You northern boys don't know anything about heat. It's actually pretty comfortable today. Sorry to make you come all the way down here, but I like to do business face to face. A very important business associate of mine is dying."

"Who is your friend?" Dr. Jenkins asked, apprehensively.

"Why don't we discuss that over dinner. Hope you like southern food."

Dr. Jenkins followed Senator Watson to the large dining room, with a huge crystal chandelier above the long mahogany table with twelve seats on each side. Dr. Jenkins sat down, the smell of barbecue filled his nostrils as he placed his napkin on his lap and took a sip of water. "How is your daughter?" Dr. Jenkins asked.

"She's gained all the weight back," Senator Watson replied, smiling. "Almost ready to go back to college. I still can't believe what you guys did. Hell, the people at John Hopkins gave her six months to live. I thought your clinic was some hocus pocus bullshit until one of my friends told me about his wife and how you helped her. It was quite amazing. What in the hell is that plant extract anyway? I would be willing to back the stuff if you wanted to mass produce it. I'm sure I could get those boys over at the FDA to approve it pretty fast. We'd make billions."

"That's why I'm here," Dr. Jenkins said, coughing anxiously, watching a heavyset black woman carry a large plate of ribs to the table. "We are out of the product."

"Now that's a problem," Senator Watson said, taking half of a rack of ribs. "These are beef ribs. I know you are Jewish."

"Thanks," Dr. Jenkins replied, placing a few on his plate. "May we have some privacy?"

"Sure," Senator Watson said, motioning his butler and cook away. "So, why can't you obtain more of the plant? Problems with customs? Is it protected by the rainforest people or something?"

"I wish it was that easy. You see, it's not from a plant. It's human serum."

"From somebody's blood?"

"What I'm about to tell you can go no further."

"Son, this won't be the first secret I've heard," Senator Watson said, moving his chair closer.

"A hooker from New York and her two children has blood that can cure cancer. They have a virus in their blood that attacks cancer cells and leaves the healthy ones alone. We've been trying for the past year to make the virus grow in our patients' serum, but we haven't been able to replicate the protein that keeps the virus alive."

"So, how did you save my daughter?"

"We transfused her with the blood from the woman and her son."

"I see," Senator Watson replied, with his eyes staring intently at the table. "So, what's your problem?"

"The woman and her six-year-old son have escaped from the lab."

"Do you have any idea where they went?"

"Somewhere in New York City," Dr. Jenkins said, taking a bite of his rib. "And we don't have the manpower to search the city. She's probably in one of the hospitals because she had been quite sick over the past two months."

"Well, this is quite a development," Senator Watson replied, leaning back in his chair. "We've got to find them. I'm sure my friend could help."

"Who is your friend?"

"Let's just say he's the head of the most powerful business in this country and that's all you need to know considering the problems you have. And I can assure you he can move mountains."

"So, what's next?"

"Let me make a few phone calls. Don't worry. We'll find them."

Chapter 7

Judd Isla scanned the airport looking for his partner, Nevin Cuff. His deep brown eyes were bloodshot and his nose filled with mucous. His allergies were acting up again. He sneezed violently, wrinkling his long face. Pulling a tissue from his pocket, he wiped his long nose. He picked up his duffel bag and brief case from the luggage rack and walked over to a small restaurant. Inside, he spotted Nevin Cuff sitting at one of the booths drinking coffee. His long gangly arms and legs could barely fit in the small booth. He was pale white with a long head and hard eyes. He was young and stupid. Judd objected to bringing him, but unfortunately his boss insisted.

Judd Isla walked over and slid his six-foot muscular frame into the other side. "I hate New York. It's the butt crack of this country. It smells like shit, looks like hell, and everyone needs to carry a piece just to walk their dogs around the block," Nevin grunted, intensely sipping his coffee while scanning the airport.

"You hate everything," Judd replied, looking at the menu. "You complained about the food on the flight, the way the pilot flew the plane, the rental car. You better get used to this or you're going to be unhappy the rest of your life."

"But this is bullshit," Nevin said, leaning closer to Judd lowering his voice. "If I wanted to be Magnum PI, I would've gone to Hawaii and chased chicks on the beach."

Judd sneezed and pulled a handkerchief from his pocket. "Fucking allergies," he said, popping a pill into his mouth. "I've been at this for twenty years and the one thing that separates a schmuck from a hero is following the objective by the book. I don't care if they want us to get this chick and her son just so they can have them for dinner. I do it, no questions. You are not paid to be a genius. Now, listen up. I've got a guy in Queens who's checking all the hospitals in the area for her."

"That doesn't sound like much help."

"If she went to a hospital anywhere in New York City over the past week, we'll know. Believe me, this guy is good."

A thin, brown-haired waitress walked over to the table. "You boys ready to order?" she asked with a pen and pad in hand.

"Eggs over easy, bacon and hash browns," Judd said, handing her a menu.

"Hot cakes," Nevin said.

"So, I'm going to call this guy once we get back to the car, then we'll go from there."

"I still don't get why the boss is so interested in this one. What has this hooker done?"

"Don't know, but one thing I can tell you. It's big."

Judd Isla reclined in the passenger seat of the Nissan Altima rental car and inhaled a deep breath as Nevin drove down the road. The antihistamine had worked. His nose was dry and throat no longer burned. He opened his cellular phone and dialed. His man in Queens had done a lot of work for the mob. He was a computer guru. He could break into any system. He set up a program that searched all the hospitals in the area with Nicole Johnson's social security number. Judd cringed as he heard the man's squeaky voice. This guy probably couldn't walk across the street and chew gum at the same time, he thought. After some small talk, Judd finally received what he was looking for. She went to Brooklyn University Hospital three days ago. But, to Judd's surprise, she had died. So where was the kid? Nicole Johnson's parents were dead. The only family member alive was her brother. Judd hung up the phone.

"She's dead," Judd said, popping a mint into his mouth. "Died at Brooklyn University three days ago."

"What about the kid?"

"Don't know, but I bet he's at her brother's. Only family she's got."

"So, what do we do now?"

"I'll give the boss a call." Judd picked up the phone again and dialed. He shook his head twice and sighed. This was going to be difficult, but he wasn't paid to think.

"Where are we going?" Nevin asked.

"To make a pick up."

Chapter 8

Robin Vastbinder sat in her office studying Nicole Johnson's chart. Her head thumped and stomach felt queasy. She slowly lifted her third cup of coffee to her mouth and took a long sip. The wine and sleeping pills were taking years off her life with each swallow. When she went home last night, a tingle of excitement raced through her bones. It was the first time, in a long time, that she felt like a scientist again and not just some overworked clinician who sees patients day after day like a soldier of precise monotony. Her work finally meant something to her again.

She had been at the library all day looking up articles on viruses used in cancer research. She even took a trip to NYU to check their library. It was almost two o'clock when she put down the books and tried to sleep. But, the lightning that thundered outside of her window brought back the pain. She pictured her scared little boy having a nightmare, jumping into her bed, and cuddling his warm little body against her chest. Mommy always made everything all right, she thought. She tossed and turned, then cried and cried. She promised herself earlier that day, no pills or wine. She drank every night for the past three weeks. It had to stop. But, the past was too much to take and the wine could cure anything.

The inside of Robin's mouth was dry and irritated. She walked over to the small refrigerator in her office and pulled out a bottle of water, all the while thinking about Nicole Johnson's case. Despite staying up most of the night, shifting through page after page, she never found any human trials using genetically engineered viruses to treat cancer. So where did the virus in Nicole Johnson's body come from? The environment? Or was it introduced? The possibilities were endless. She could be on the brink of the greatest advance in the treatment of cancer. What if the virus could be grown and transfused? It could be the magic bullet every cancer patient dreamed about. All those hopeless faces that walked into her office would disappear. A surge of adrenaline raced through her arms and fingers hoping the thought could be a reality.

Robin turned another page and Dr. Roderick Taylor's signature was at the bottom. His name was all over the chart. She was about to take another sip of her water when her pager went off. She picked up the phone and the operator informed her that a detective Frank Roberts was in the lobby wanting to ask her a few questions. Who the hell was he?

"I'll be right down," she said, pulling her coat from the back of her chair and draping it over her shoulders.

Robin stepped off the elevator and searched the lobby. Standing in front of the glass doors was a tall man, with uncombed black hair and stubble all over his face. His tie hung halfway down his shirt and his pants were baggy. She saw the man's eyes look at her nametag, then walk in her direction. Despite his gruffly appearance, he was quite good looking. His blue eyes illuminated his entire face. He had a child-like smile.

"Dr. Vastbinder," he said extending his hand. "Detective Frank Roberts."

"What's this about?" Robin asked, feeling a bit nervous.

"Is there somewhere we can talk?"

"We can go to my office. Follow me."

Robin entered her office with a twinge of anxiety tightening her stomach. What did he want? She thought of every possible scenario, but nothing made sense. Detective Roberts' eyes scanned her office. His face lightened as he glanced at the diplomas from John Hopkins and Harvard that were displayed above her bookcase.

"My cousin went to Harvard," Detective Roberts said, sitting in the chair in front of her desk.

"What years?" Robin asked, putting the piles of charts that cluttered her desk on the floor.

"About five years ago. He's a big shot lawyer on Wall Street."

"I see," Robin replied, disinterested. "Can I offer you something to drink? Coffee? Soda?"

"No thanks. Soda gives me a lot of gas and I gave up caffeine years ago. Makes my heart beat funny."

"So, what's this about?" Robin asked, thinking about all the work she had to do. He was a typical cop: intrusive, without a sense of social grace. He reminded her of one of those obnoxious athletes she'd met in college.

"Well, I wanted to ask you a few questions about a patient that died in your emergency room four days ago. Her name was Nicole Johnson, do you remember her?"

"What about her?" Robin asked, carefully choosing her words.

"What did she die of?"

"Cancer of the lymph nodes. The disease is called non-Hodgkins lymphoma."

Detective Roberts dropped his head and stared reflectively at the floor. Robin could sense he knew her personally and her death troubled him deeply. "What does her cause of death have to do with the police?"

"Well," Detective Roberts said with a sigh, "I wanted to know about her two children. Do you know where they went?"

"Two children?"

"Yeah, two boys."

"Only one came to the E.R.," Robin said, inching up on her chair, concerned. "I think his name was Jacob."

"She didn't have an infant with her?"

"No."

"Where did Jacob go?"

"With her brother."

"Nicole had a brother?"

"I guess there's a lot you don't know about Nicole, is there?"

"I guess so," Detective Roberts said, dumbfounded. "I tried so hard to keep that kid off the streets. But, she got hooked on the blow and her fucking pimp took over. Sorry…" Detective Roberts said, covering his mouth, "I get carried away sometimes with my mouth."

Detective Roberts' gruff demeanor bothered her, but the concern in his eyes made the stereotype not so typical. He truly cared for this woman. It was nice for Robin to see a man of the law really care about those whom all deem as scum. "It's quite all right, I've heard those words on television before," Robin said with a smile. "So, how can you be so sure she had another son?"

"I saw her pregnant and a friend of hers told me that she saw the child."

"Maybe she gave it up for adoption."

"I checked into that. Most hookers that put their kids up for adoption go to five agencies in the city. I checked them all. No one ever heard of her. I still have to check several others."

"That does sound odd," Robin said, getting up from her chair and walking over to her purse. She pulled out a bottle of Advil and plopped one in her mouth. "My head is killing me," she said chugging her water. "Do you have any ideas where she delivered the child?"

"That's my next step. She had Jacob here, so I assume she had the other child at Brooklyn University as well."

"I doubt it. I checked all of her medical records and I haven't found any documentation on a second labor and delivery."

"Well, I guess I have a lot of work ahead me. Do you think I could get the telephone number of her brother?"

"I think the social worker still has the number."

"That would be great," detective Roberts said, rising from his chair. "Well, I've taken up enough of your time. I really appreciate your help."

"No problem. I'd be interested myself in finding out what happened."

Detective Roberts was about to leave, when he stopped and shut the door. His once bright blue eyes seemed two shades darker. His movements were methodically grim. He inhaled a deep breath and then exhaled. "I just…want to know if she died comfortably. You know…if she suffered much."

Robin examined his face. His eyes glazed with tears that his manhood kept from dripping down his face. His eyebrows scrunched as if all that he once knew to be true was a lie.

"She was unconscious," Robin said, softly. "Probably never knew what happened."

Detective Roberts faked a smile, and then opened the door. "Thanks, Doc. I'll be in touch the moment I find out something."

Robin combed her hands through her hair and sighed. Another child? How cruel can the world be? She picked up Nicole's chart again and began examining her lab information again. Just as she turned the page, her beeper went off. Damn thing, she thought. She looked at the number; it was the pathology lab. Maybe Dr. Martin had some answers. She picked up the phone and dialed. "Robin?" Dr. Martin said with a crack in his voice.

"Orpheus, what have you found out?"

"Either this hospital is really stupid and misplaced a body or someone stole Nicole Johnson's corpse," Orpheus said, excited. "They also took her organs and blood samples. Luckily I had brought a bunch of slides in my office or we'd have nothing."

"Are you sure?"

"Positive. I've had my people tear this place apart."

"I'll be right down."

Chapter 9

The numerous cracks in the cement walls of the basement made Robin think of how easy it would be to smuggle a body from the morgue. The turnover of employees in the pathology department occurred almost weekly. Most of the lab technicians were college students working part-time to pay the bills. Five men and one woman in lab coats scampered around the dingy hallways, searching the rooms, making phone calls, with frantic eyes and nervous expression. Orpheus must've exploded, she thought. He was the most lighthearted man she'd ever met, but when he lost his temper, it was as if Jekyl had become Hyde.

Robin knocked on the glass door of his office and walked in to find Orpheus scolding a young woman without raising his voice. His short forehead, that his Afro eclipsed, was furrowed. His face was tight and stern. "So, someone on the night crew signed out the body to this mysterious mortuary without a requisition?" Orpheus barked.

The blond-haired, blue-eyed woman's face glanced at the floor, afraid to look in his eyes. She coughed and then said, "The forms all checked out. The guy even had a letter head," she said, handing him a piece of paper.

Orpheus studied the paper. "Did anyone ever think to check this out, considering that there was no prior confirmation earlier in the day?"

"We were really busy last night and…."

"That's not an excuse," Orpheus said, now pacing. "You are the night supervisor and if you want to keep your job, I suggest you find that body."

The woman's eyes welled with tears. She got up from her chair and left the office.

Robin sat down, afraid to say anything. Orpheus walked over to a Mr. Coffee machine on a table beside his bookcase and poured himself a cup. "Want a cup?"

"No thanks."

"I'm surrounded by idiots."

"Getting mad isn't going to help," Robin uttered.

"Yes it is," Orpheus said, sitting down. "It makes me feel better."

"Have you notified the police?"

"They're on the way."

"I still can't fathom why someone would want her body."

"I can. I've been down here in the PIT for almost twenty years and never saw a case like this one. This woman's blood was special and someone figured it out long before we did."

"Do you know Dr. Roderick Taylor?"

"I met him once, a long time ago. He was chief of the Oncology department before you came."

"His name is all over the chart. I was about to give him a call before you paged me. He's at Mass General. And guess what happened just before you called?"

"You won the lottery," Orpheus said, sarcastically.

"No. A detective Frank Roberts came to my office. He was asking about Nicole Johnson."

"This chick must've been popular."

"He said she had another child, an infant. It's missing."

"Maybe she gave him up for adoption."

"That's what I thought, but he already checked into things."

"This thing is getting weirder by the minute."

"I know. And take a look at this," Robin said, opening up Nicole's chart and plopping it on his desk. Robin pointed to a section of the chart that had the results of the protein electrophoresis. The test measured the amount and distribution of the different kinds of proteins that were in Nicole's blood. The results were displayed on a bar graph. The first five spikes were normal, but the sixth was five times higher than the others and unidentifiable. Orpheus's eyes widened. He moved his face closer to the chart, trying to decipher the graph. "What in the hell is this?"

"You got me," Robin said.

Orpheus powered up his computer and typed in his password. On the screen appeared the result of the protein electrophoresis he ran on the corpse's blood. It was normal. "This is amazing," Orpheus said, dumbfounded. "That protein must have something to do with sustaining this virus."

"What do you mean?" Robin asked, leaning over his shoulder looking at the screen.

"Look, she was able to fight the cancer when this protein was high, but when she got sick it was gone. The virus must need this protein to live. I sent a sample of this virus to the CDC to see if they could come up with anything."

Orpheus pounded the keys and entered on the Internet. He scrolled through his E-mail until he found what he was looking for. He clicked on the icon and a page of information appeared on screen. "It's a frigging shark virus."

"A shark virus? How in the hell would she come in contact with a shark virus? Are you sure that's not a mistake?"

"I'll give them a call," Orpheus said, picking up the phone.

"Listen, give me a page and let me know what you find out," Robin said, looking at her watch. "I've got a clinic full of patients waiting and I need to track down this Dr. Taylor."

"Why don't we have lunch?"

"Sounds like a plan."

Robin placed the last chart on the secretary's desk and pulled out her tape recorder to dictate a progress note. She hesitated at first, thinking about the seventeen-year-old girl's smile, her bright teeth that lightened up the room, and dropped her head. The girl wouldn't make it past next year. She had glioblastoma, a lethal brain cancer that killed quickly. Robin wished she could promise her she'd make it to graduation, but that would be impossible. Robin's secretary slowly picked up the chart and opened the folder. Her eyes were somber and distant. "How long do you think she has?" the secretary asked shaking her head.

"I don't know," Robin replied, despondent.

The secretary's face relaxed. She then reached out and held Robin's hand. "Honey, I don't know how much more of this you can take. I've seen you go through this almost every day since the accident. The staff is worried about you. If you keep letting it get to you like this, you're going to drive yourself crazy."

"I know Melinda," Robin said. "Thanks, but don't worry, I'll come out of this."

Robin walked into her office and started dictating a progress note. She thought about the look on the teenage girl's face if she had a cure; a magic arrow that would rip through her cancer and make her life normal again. If there was such a thing as a normal life, she thought. What if someone had found a cure and Nicole Johnson was the first patient to receive the protocol? That's why her body disappeared. Maybe they wanted to do an autopsy of their own, she thought. Maybe they were performing experiments without the approval of the FDA? If that was true, she had to know. Nicole Johnson had outlived a lethal cancer without treatment by five years.

Robin turned to the computer on her desk and connected with Physician Online. The service posted article abstracts way before they were on the computer at the library. She wanted to look up all the latest case reports on viral vectors used in the treatment of cancer she could find before calling Dr. Roderick Taylor. She typed in virus and cancer and forty abstract articles appeared. She scrolled through them and almost jumped from her chair when she saw the article at the bottom of the page. It was an abstract from the latest issue of *Cancer*, not yet in print, published by Dr. Roderick Taylor. The title was, "Shark Cartilage: The Truth Behind the Myth About it's Uses in the Treatment of Cancer."

She read the brief paragraph that gave a description about the article. It talked about the possibility of a virus that had a symbiotic relationship with a specific species of tiger shark off the coast of South Africa. The virus had an affinity for mutated cells and relied on a protein that the shark produced. It was a protein that was found in no other organism on the planet. Robin leaned back in her chair and stared pensively at the screen. Quickly, she picked up the phone and her mouth immediately became dry. Dr. Taylor had found the virus five years ago and kept it to himself. She was positive. But, why? This could possibly be one of the biggest breakthroughs in cancer treatment since the bone marrow transplant.

The operator at Mass General hospital patched her into his office. A deep voiced secretary connected her back to his phone. "Hello," Dr. Taylor said, clearing his throat.

"Dr. Taylor, my name is Dr. Robin Vastbinder. I'm an oncologist from Brooklyn University hospital."

"I still can't believe they haven't closed that place."

"I'm sure it hasn't changed much since you've left."

Robin proceeded to tell him about Nicole Johnson and the shark virus. There was a long pause on the line, then Dr. Taylor said, "I don't remember a Nicole Johnson. Could you please refresh my memory about the case?"

"She was an African American woman with Stage Four Non-Hodgkins lymphoma who left the hospital against medical advice five years ago without treatment."

"I've had several patients like her over the years, Dr. Vastbinder," he said, his voice becoming more condescending with each word. "I worked at that hell hole for over fifteen years. I've seen a lot of things. The names and cases just seem to run together."

"Well, I find it quite a coincidence that your article talks about shark viruses, of all things, and cancer treatment. And your name just happens to be all over that chart. And your patient, who supposedly had a fatal illness just died four days ago. Five years after she contracted the disease, and now we found a shark virus in her blood."

"I've told a lot of people they had five months to live and they lived for years. We don't know everything and besides I have been working with shark viruses long before I ever met the patient you're talking about. I have no idea how the virus got in her blood, but I'd sure be interested in finding out."

"I've never heard any of our staff speak about shark research done at our hospital. I've been here for five years now. I'm sure it would've come up in one of our discussions around the lunch table."

"I worked with the people at the zoo. You can check it out yourself."

Robin could feel a twinge of rage swell in her stomach. He was talking in circles. "Listen, Nicole Johnson's body and organs are missing from our morgue. The police are investigating the case as we speak. Your name is definitely going to come up and I will make sure they know everything we discussed. So, if you don't want any trouble, I suggest you make sure you tell them everything you know before they go looking."

"Are you threatening me?"

"No, I'm telling you," Robin said emphatically.

"This conversation is over," Dr. Taylor said, calmly. "Bring on the police, I have nothing to hide."

"You better hope so."

Chapter 10

Detective Frank Roberts stepped into his two toned Ford Escort, pulled out of the police station parking lot and glanced at his watch. Three hours to find some answers from Nicole's brother before he had to be back at the station to finish a report. He turned the key and the engine choked at first, then started. The city -owned car was ten years old. The gray plush seats were worn and the air conditioner barely worked. The city was too cheap to provide his precinct with new vehicles, so they just kept patching up the old ones. How in the hell could he catch a criminal in this piece of shit?

Frank pulled out a Newport from his jacket and fired it up. He exhaled a large cloud of smoke and pulled a piece of paper from his jacket. Nicole's brother lived on James Street in New Jersey. As he maneuvered around the traffic into the George Washington tunnel, the thought of the tears in Nicole's eyes the night she told him she was pregnant entered his mind. She wanted him to be the way out of the mess that she called life. But, the child couldn't be his, he thought at the time. He wasn't even sure now. The debate kept him awake last night, nibbling at his soul.

He checked the address again and slowed the car so he could examine the numbers on the homes. He spotted 576 James Street, drove to the end of the block, and parked his car. The split-level townhouse was modern with a spacious lawn. It was a lot better than Frank's apartment. Brian must've done well for himself, he thought. He sauntered up to the door and rang the bell. The door opened and a muscular black man answered. He was bald, with a bushy mustache. "Are you Brian Johnson?"

"Yeah," the man said in a deep baritone voice, interrogating Frank with his eyes.

"I'm detective Frank Roberts."

"What's this about?" Brian barked.

Frank didn't blame him for his apprehension. If Brian grew up in Brooklyn, he probably had been harassed by the police at some point in his life. It was a sad commentary on the NYPD. "I just wanted to ask you a few questions about your sister."

"What about her?"

"Have you ever heard her talk about her other son?"

"Me and my sister haven't spoke since my mother's funeral. Ever since she started pulling tricks and putting that poison up her nose, I had nothing to do with her. Broke my mother's heart."

"I'm not here to cause you trouble. But I think she has another child out there."

"She probably has a lot of children out there. I doubt any of them are alive thanks to the abortion clinic."

"No, this one is alive. I've searched every foster home in this city and he's not in their system."

"So, why do you care?" Brian asked, his nostril flaring, his forehead furrowed. "It's just another dead black person to you, isn't it?"

A nidus of rage crept up Frank's throat. He had done nothing to deserve this. He treated his sister with nothing but love and respect. "Listen, your sister was someone I really cared about," he said, raising his voice. "And I'm not doing this for me. I'm doing this for her. I know you have all that hate in your heart and I can't make it better. But if you love your sister, you'll help me. She has a son out there that I believe could be in harm's way."

"Maybe he's dead."

"Maybe he is. But what if he isn't? Are you willing to bet the life of your own flesh and blood on it?"

Brian inhaled a deep breath and then exhaled, rubbing his face. His dark brown eyes examined Frank once again, this time trying to look into his soul. "Come in," he said opening the door.

"Thanks."

The inside had African art on the walls and a sculpture of an African princess on a coffee table in front of a plush blue L-shaped couch. A big screen TV and large stereo system sat in an entertainment system on the other side of the room. "Can I offer you anything to drink?"

"No thanks," Frank replied, sitting on the couch.

"Sorry about my attitude, but it's been tough these few days."

"No problem. Completely understandable."

Brian returned from the kitchen with a beer in his hand. He stared at it somberly, then took a sip. "Everyday I would check my answering machine waiting for that call saying she was dead. Man, she was a train riding down the wrong track ever since I could remember. I tried everything. I sent her to rehab, helped her get jobs, but she just couldn't kick that shit. When she stole my checkbook and took ten thousand dollars from my account, my entire savings, that's when I washed my hands. But, Mom, she never gave up. Not even till the end. Nicole caused my mom to die with a broken heart. Even to this day I find it hard to forgive her."

"I tried myself."

"Since when is a cop so interested in a hooker?"

Frank wanted to tell him how much he loved her. How much he wished the world was a different place. But, he couldn't. He couldn't even tell his best friends. "I met her after one of her friends was beat to death by a serial killer a few years back. I saw that there was something different about her, something decent that could be saved."

"I once felt like that, but man, she broke my heart one too many times. And now, I got Jacob to raise."

"Where is he?"

"In bed," Brian uttered. "He hasn't spoken since all of this. I've been taking him to the psychiatrist twice a week and still not a word. And he has these nightmares. Boy sleeps with me every night. I don't know what do."

Frank looked away from Brian, trying to hide the pain that was about to change to tears. He remembered the day Nicole needed him to baby sit. He adamantly said no at first, until Jacob's eager eyes convinced Frank to take him to a Mets game. The look in Jacob's eyes as he reached over the railing, trying to catch a foul ball made him feel young again. His father would take him to five or six Mets games a year. Unfortunately for Jacob, he didn't get to live in a house in the suburbs. He went to a tiny little apartment in Brooklyn with his mother strung out on drugs. "Would you happen to know what pediatrician Jacob went to?"

"Yeah, the free health clinic down in Brooklyn. I had to get a copy of his shots so I could take him to daycare."

"There's probably a good chance she would take the infant there for care, wouldn't there?"

"Tough to say," Brian said, taking another sip of his beer. "My sister is pretty unpredictable. But, there's one thing that has been bothering me all this time."

"What?"

"They gave me my sister's stuff and in her pocket was a plane ticket and wallet. I figured she just lifted the contents of a dude's wallet, trying to make an extra buck."

"Where are they?"

Brian got up from his chair and left the room. He returned and handed Frank a leather wallet and a balled up plane ticket. "Bismarck, North Dakota?" Frank said, reading it.

"That's what I said. I guess the guy was here on business."

Frank examined the contents of the wallet. Inside the pouch were three credit cards and a North Dakota state driver's license. The man's name was Aaron Harris. He was a black man, twenty-five, with an obese face and deep set brown eyes. In the side pouch was a paycheck receipt from the Loventhol clinic, most likely his place of employment. "Do you mind if I take these with me?"

"Sure, what in the hell am I going to do with them?"

"Well, I really appreciate your help."

"Let me know if you find out something," Brian said, rising to his feet to walk Frank out. "I would be willing to take the other child if you find him. It sure would put pressure on my social life, but I'm sure my mom wouldn't have it any other way."

"I'm sure Nicole would like that," Frank said shaking his hand. "And by the way, would it be possible if I could come see Jacob sometime?"

"Sure, I'm always looking for a babysitter." Brian said, with a smile.

"Thanks again."

Frank pulled out of Brian's driveway contemplating why Nicole would steal the man's wallet. She was a prostitute not a thief, he thought. But, there were a lot of things he didn't know about Nicole. Things that he was glad the dream world he created protected him from. As he jumped onto the freeway, he picked up his cellular phone and called his office. He would be up late tonight doing paper work, because his next stop was the pediatric clinic. All of his life he dreamed of having a child, but knew his job would prevent him from being the kind of father he had. He had been though a divorce and several relationships, all ending in nothing but a heartache that made him bitter. Nicole was the first woman that truly understood him. She could deal with his mood swings and tough exterior. She knew him better than most of his friends. If the kid was his, he promised himself he wouldn't make the same mistake twice.

Chapter 11

Judd Isla took a deep breath through his nostrils, inhaling the thick industrial air of New York City, as he drove towards the George Washington tunnel. The antihistamines were working; it was his first clear breath since he arrived in New York. The stale stench of the congested wind made him wish his nose was still clogged. Nevin Cuff sat in the passenger's seat of the black Ford van, his face emotionless and his eyes staring sharply into the night as if he was a caged animal. It worried Judd. Nevin was young and didn't quite understand that finesse worked a lot better than force.

Thick balls of clouds blanketed the smoggy sky, eclipsing the light of the moon. A soft drizzle fell on the windshield. The road was lightly scattered with traffic. "Want a piece of gum?" Judd said, plopping a piece in his mouth.

"No thanks," Nevin said, as if Judd wasn't in the car.

"Listen, you need to lighten up. This isn't a Navy SEAL operation. We're dealing with civilians here."

Nevin was silent.

"You married?" Judd asked.

"The only thing a woman is good for is a hard fuck. They make you weak."

Judd shook his head. "Been married for ten years now," he said, reaching in his pocket and pulling out his wallet. "Three kids. Two boys and a girl."

Nevin glanced at the pictures quickly, then resumed his sardonic glare. "I'm surprised you survived this long."

"What are you talking about?"

"Having a family makes you think too much," he said, turning his head looking deeply into Judd's eyes. "Makes a man careless, worrying too much about living."

"That shit sounds all well and good in the movies, but I know that everything I do has a purpose now."

"Whatever."

Judd pressed on the gas, passing a slow moving vehicle, as he exited the two-mile long tunnel. He glanced at Nevin and realized what a monster he had been twenty years ago. "So, are we straight on the objective?"

"Yeah, we're straight. Get the boy and uncle, drug them with the sedative, and dump them in the van. Sounds like a mission for a bunch of chumps. I mean, stealing a body from the morgue, now this. What are they going to ask us to do next, pick flowers and deliver them to someone's house?"

"Just make sure we're straight," Judd warned. "To you and I, this may be bullshit. But the boss doesn't get involved in shit like this unless it's something big, believe me."

"I'll believe it when I see it. What about the cop we spotted at his house today?"

"His name is Frank Roberts. He's NYPD, from Brooklyn."

"What do we do about him?"

"We'll find out what he knows first, then deal with him."

Judd pulled out a hand held computer from his jacket. He punched in his code and the address of Brian Johnson appeared. James Street was the next exit. Driving into the tranquil suburbs of New Jersey was like going from black and white to color. The streets of New York were nothing more than macadam and glass. The only grass lawn seemed to be in Central Park. The townhouse had a spacious yard surrounded by sculptured bushes. It reminded him of home. He scanned the lawns and pictured his daughter and son riding their bikes. What he wouldn't give to be home.

The black van was almost invisible in the darkness. It was two a.m., and the streets were silent. He spotted the town house, then drove behind and parked. "You ready?" Judd asked.

"This is the first exciting thing I've done since I've been here," Nevin said, filling a syringe with a long needle full of sedative and handing Judd a smaller one.

Judd slipped a black ski mask over his face, and Nevin did the same. The black turtleneck and pants would be perfect for the dimly lit back yard. Judd exited the van with his lock picking kit in hand. Nevin scanned the area, then motioned his hand forward, as if they were going into battle. Judd slithered over the grass towards the door. Nevin went to the other side to disable the alarm. Judd slowly pulled the kit from his pocket and put a pen light in his mouth. Nevin returned and nodded his head, acknowledging the alarm was disabled. Judd carefully jiggled the lock with his tools until it clicked, and then he carefully opened the door. The basement of the townhouse was pitch black. Judd walked on his toes, carefully maneuvering around the objects in the dark. Nevin followed behind.

Judd had studied the floor plan of the house the night before. Brian slept on the second floor, the boy on the third. At the top of the steps was a nightlight. Judd pulled it from the plug. Calculating each step, they cautiously crept down the hallway, past the bathroom, past the study, finally to his bedroom at the end of the hallway. A faint light, from a clock radio illuminated the corner of the room. Just as Nevin moved ahead of Judd with the syringe in hand, he bumped the dresser, knocking an object to the floor. Brian stirred, then immediately became awake. Judd jumped on the bed and tried to hold him down. He was a large man, with thick arms and strong legs. Judd strained his muscles, trying to hold him down, but he was too strong, and pushed him off the bed.

Nevin struggled with Brian on the floor, knocking over the end table, sending the lamp crashing to the floor. The syringe in Nevin's hand slipped from his fingers and fell to the floor. Something had to be done, quick, Judd thought. The fight made too much noise. In one swift move, Nevin kicked Brian in the throat, knocking him to the floor. Brian moaned and groaned, but jumped up again, now staggering. Nevin kicked him again, this time in the face. The thud of Brian's body hitting the floor shook the house. Judd reached his fingers under the bed and found the syringe. As he stood up, he found Nevin on top of Brian, punching his motionless body repeatedly in the face. "That's enough," Judd whispered loudly, pulling Nevin off him.

"Bastard cut my eye," Nevin said.

"You inject him. I'll go upstairs and get the boy."

Judd grabbed a small syringe from the inside of his shirt and searched for the stairway to the third floor. Walking up the carpeted stairs, he could see rays of light seep through the bottom of the door at the top. He heard a window open. He rushed up the stairs and the door was locked. He kicked it opened and found a room filled with stuffed animals and action figures on the floor. But the boy was gone. He had escaped through the window. "Fuck," he said.

Running back down the steps, Judd went back into Brian's room to find Nevin trying to hold Brian down. His large rotund body was flailing wildly. The room smelled like urine mixed with feces. "What the fuck is going on?" Judd snapped.

"I gave him the shot and he freaked, started shaking all over," Nevin said, hyperventilating, "shitting and pissing." Finally the convulsions stopped and Brian's body went completely limp. His eyes fixed and dilated toward the ceiling. Judd pushed Nevin away from the body and felt for a pulse. He was dead. Fucking dead! "What the fuck happened?" Judd demanded.

"Like I said, I just gave him the shot."

"Fuck...Fuck." Judd said, kicking the bed. "Get him to the van and make sure this place is clean, I'm going to look for the boy."

Judd ran through the backdoor scanning the darkness. Thousands of thoughts infiltrated his mind as he searched the bushes around the house and proceeded up the alley. This was his first job in twenty years that went this badly. He thought about the angry wrinkles on the boss's face and how his bushy eyebrows scrunched and forehead would furrow once he found out the news. What had happened? Why did the man die? He slowed his jog to a walk and then heard heavy breathing behind a car at the end of the alley. It had to be the little boy.

Chapter 12

Jacob Johnson rubbed the tears that soaked his cheeks and held his breath. He crouched his body into a ball behind a car trying to hide from the bad men. The bad men were the reason he decided to no longer speak. It was impossible to tell who they were, and if he had kept quiet in the ventilator shaft his brother wouldn't be in that awful place. He couldn't trust anyone, not even his Uncle Brian. Jacob positioned his body around the tire and angled his head so he could see under the car. The gravel in the alley crunched slowly, as if someone was sneaking up on him. It reminded him of hide-and-go-seek, but this time, there was no "Ollie, Ollie, oxen-free." A streetlight above one of the garages cast the shadow of a man. He was a big man, with long arms that seemed as long as the octopus he saw on a Johnny Quest cartoon. He moved to the other side of the car and prayed that his mommy would come down from heaven and help him. The crunch approached. "I'm not gonna hurt you son, just come on out," the bad man said.

The bad men always made promises. They promised to stop taking his blood if he gave just one more time. The pain of the I.V. still gave him nightmares. He had bruises all over his arms and they would swell up, just like Popeye's. But, Jacob was sure spinach wasn't enough to stop the bad men. He tried eating it, but it never gave him enough strength to fight off the bad men to save his mother and brother. The bad men wouldn't even stop taking his blood when he got dizzy. They just gave him orange juice and a sandwich, and told him not to worry.

Jacob's heart raced when the crunching stopped. Where was the man? On the other side of the alley? Or did he walk right by? He turned his head quickly around and began to weep softy. The bad man appeared. Jacob eluded his grip and tried to run. Jacob remembered his mommy telling him that the bad men would fall right down if he kicked them in their nuts. He pictured himself as a Power Ranger, mustered up all the strength he had and kicked the man. Mommy was right. The bad man fell right to the ground, holding his special place.

The trees that surrounded the road looked like monsters that could reach out and get him in the darkness as he ran down the road. The air was cold against his face. The bad man followed, taking long steps, drawing ever closer. Jacob spotted a bridge. He sprinted under it. The bad man followed. There were trees and a small stream that was filled with rocks. Big rocks. Jacob made it around the corner of the small stream before the bad man. He picked up the biggest rock he could lift and waited. As the bad man turned the corner, he lofted it at his face. It connected, knocking the man to the ground. He resumed his sprint, this time through a small wooded area and climbed a tree as fast as he could.

A thin ray of sunlight warmed Jacob's face, waking him from his momentary sleep. He pulled himself to a sitting position on the branch and glanced at his red, chaffed arms from the rough bark, wondering how long he'd been in the tree. That had to be the longest he could remember, even during hide and seek on a Friday night when he could stay out past midnight. But running from his best friend was a lot different than hiding from the bad men. His best friend would never try to kill him.

Jacob looked down, then left and right, searching for signs of danger. The only sounds were of birds chirping in the distance. He was afraid to climb down the tree, but he was starved. What he wouldn't give for a piece of his mom's sweet potato pie. She made it three times a year, during the holidays, and he could eat half of a pie in one sitting. He slowly released his grip of the top branch and placed his foot on the branch below. He stopped every few seconds during his descent and listened for voices. Luckily, it was quiet. He finally reached the bottom and walked through a yard, not sure where to go. He was certain the bad men would check his uncle's house again. In the distance he spotted a white-haired lady that reminded him of Mrs. Santa Claus. Despite her kind eyes, Jacob cautiously walked to the other side of the yard.

"Are you lost son?" the woman asked?

Jacob continued to walk, trying to ignore her comforting voice. Maybe she could give him some food, he thought, trying to subdue the growl in his stomach. He fought the urge to keep going, and walked closer to the woman, interrogating her every move.

"I've never seen you around here," the woman said, moving closer. "Where are your mommy and daddy?"

Her voice may have been soft like his mom's, but he refused to open his mouth. She might figure out that the bad men want his blood and make him go back to that terrible place. His mother always told him the less you say, the better. He moved closer, then stopped, all while examining her eyes.

"Can't you speak son?" the old woman asked, kneeling.

Jacob continued his solemn gaze.

"Why don't you come inside, honey," the old woman said, slowly placing her hand on his shoulder. "I bet you haven't had breakfast yet. Do you like eggs and bacon? I even have some blueberry waffles."

The thought of blueberry waffles drenched in butter and syrup thickened the saliva in Jacob's mouth. He was sure he could take the old woman if she tried anything, so he followed behind her through the screen door. "After we eat, maybe we can find your mommy and daddy."

* * *

Judd Isla pressed a rag against his head, trying to stop the blood that trickled from his head. Nausea tightened his stomach when he realized what had happened. A five-year-old boy had kicked his ass. He fought men fifty times the boy's size, with years of hand-to-hand combat training and easily wrestled them into submission. But the boy was smart, much too smart. Nevin and Judd had been up all night driving the streets of New Jersey, searching yards and alleys to no avail. The little runt had disappeared as if he were a magician. It was the kind of night that meant a career.

The morning traffic in New York City was congested with pissed off taxi drivers swerving around pedestrians like running backs dodging linebackers. Nevin sat in the driver's seat of the black van, his face tight with rage, his eyes blank with disbelief. "So, what in the fuck do we do now?" Nevin uttered.

"I don't know," Judd replied, repositioning the rag on his head. "We wouldn't be in this mess if you wouldn't have given him so much of that drug."

"Hey," Nevin barked. "I gave him what I was told, not a drop more."

"How much medication did you draw up?"

"Eight, just like it said on the bottle."

"Eight what?"

"Eight cc's."

"I knew I should've checked, but I figured you weren't an idiot. I guess I was wrong."

"What do you mean?"

"8mg is only one cc, you stupid fuck. Now we got a dead body in the back and the boss is going to rip our skin off, inch by inch."

"Well, at least I didn't get my clock cleaned by a five year old boy."

"He surprised me," Judd said. "But it doesn't matter now. We need to do some damage control to soften the blow. First we get rid of this body. My friend in Brooklyn can help us with that. Then, we have to get to that cop. He was the last person that saw Brian Johnson alive."

"What about that doctor?"

"Oh, don't worry about that doctor. I've got something that I think will take care of her."

CHAPTER 13

Robin Vastbinder peered through the microscope in the pathology lab, amazed by the possibilities of the virus. Imagine if the virus could be mass produced, like a vaccination, and used as the standard of care in every cancer patient in the world? Cancer could be like having the common cold. The thought made her excited for a moment, until she realized that every corporation would stop at nothing to own the virus.

Orpheus entered the room carrying a stack of papers. He plopped down beside Robin, and a smile widened on his face. "This is truly amazing."

"What?" Robin asked, pulling her head from the microscope.

"I'm starting to believe this virus wasn't introduced."

"I find that hard to believe. Where in the hell would a human contract a shark virus?"

"I have no idea, but the report I got from the immunology lab at NYU shows that the virus had infected her DNA years ago, probably since birth."

"I still can't fathom how a woman from New York City could ever come in contact with a shark virus?"

"Maybe she was turning tricks at Sea World or something. Sort of a side show attraction for the adults. It's like a movie I once saw. It was a

B-movie from the sixties. You know, the one that had women with big breasts dressed in flimsy clothing."

"What are you talking about? I've never heard of that movie."

"Maybe it wasn't a movie...just one of my bad LSD experiences in college. The sixties and seventies are still a blur to me."

"So where do we go from here?"

"Well, I think we should write this case up and send it to the *New England Journal of Medicine*. Maybe we could even get a grant to study this. Imagine, the cure. This could be the cure."

"I know, but something is not right about all of this. I spoke with Dr. Roderick Taylor."

"The guy in Boston?"

"Yeah. It was really weird. He seemed like he was hiding something."

"Like what, he's a cross dresser?" Orpheus cracked.

"No," Robin said, slapping him playfully. "He was very confrontational, like he had something to hide. And that cop that was looking for his child. I have a feeling someone else knew about this."

"But, there has been nothing in the literature. I think if someone had discovered this gold mine, they would've ran with it."

"That's not true. Dr. Taylor had recently published an article on shark viruses and cancer. Now where do you think he came up with that data?"

"Shark virus, huh." Orpheus replied, rubbing his chin.

"He knows something we don't and for some reason, it's quite a sensitive issue. Listen, I've got to run."

"So do I," Orpheus said, looking at his watch. "I've got to pick my boy up from school and take him to the dentist."

Robin entered her office with a Styrofoam container that held her lunch. She opened the box and took a bite of the cold baked potato and leafed through her mail. A letter arrived that was painful for her to open. It was the remnants of her late husband's research project. He was a cardiologist who had been studying the effects of B-blockers on congestive heart failure. She remembered how his eyes would light up when he talked about his work. The night he received his five million dollar grant was the best she could ever remember. They dropped their son off at the babysitter's and got a hotel room. They ordered room service at the Waldorf and made love all night. His touch, his kiss, still tickled her soul. It had been many months since she last made love and it seemed like an eternity. She reached for a letter opener and the tears welled up in her eyes. She dropped the opener and threw the letter in the garbage can. It hurt too much, even after almost a year. When was the hurt going to stop? Why did he have to die?

Robin pulled out her appointment book and looked at her schedule. She was the attending physician on the in-patient service this week; a week she dreaded. The residents would call her at all hours of the night, keeping her awake and exhausted. But, the hard work was good. It kept her mind off things, away from the bottle and sleeping pills that had started out as a way to relax but slowly became a way of life.

The thought of getting a drink in the afternoon bothered Robin. But, a tall glass of wine was calling her, like a voice in her head that had control over her resolve. She slowly rose from her chair, thinking of a way to hide the smell from her breath, when the phone rang. She picked it up, thinking about which bar to go to without being spotted by an employee of the hospital.

"Hello?" Robin said.

"A Dr. Roderick Taylor is here to see you," her secretary said.

Dr. Roderick Taylor? What in the hell was he doing in New York City? And why was he here? "Send him in," Robin said, bewildered.

Dr. Taylor was a tall thin man, with a bony face and long fingers. His hair was thin at the top, peppered gray, and sticking straight in the air as if it hadn't seen a comb in years. His blue dress shirt was wrinkled and stuffed liked a rag into his baggy dress pants. "I apologize for not calling before I came, but this was a very spontaneous thing."

"What brings you to Brooklyn University?"

"Your phone call," Dr. Taylor said, sighing, then sitting down on the chair in front of her desk.

"Can I offer you some coffee?"

"Yes, please. Cream and sugar. I'm exhausted."

"So, why the sudden change of heart?" Robin asked, handing him the cup.

"I'm…sorry for the way I acted, but this thing has been bothering me for the past few years. I really didn't want to discuss it over the phone," Dr. Taylor said, looking reflectively at his cup. "What I'm about to tell you can go no further than this room."

"Why?"

"Because it's all just speculation. Speculation that I can't prove right now. You see, I knew about Nicole's blood five years ago. I was intrigued by all of this just as you were when I first saw her. That's when I really got involved with shark viruses. I traced her family back to South Africa. They were from a village on the coast, near Cape Town. It was amazing how they contracted the shark virus."

"How?"

"Her family members would take baby sharks and use them for medicinal purposes, like our ancestors used leeches. The bravest young men would catch baby tiger sharks as a right of passage to manhood. The medicine man in the small tribe would let baby tiger sharks bite their dying patients, and occasionally they would get better. So, I was able to exhume the dead body of her great grandmother and found that the viral genome was lying dormant in her genes. It must've been passed down through the generations."

"So, you're saying that her family had the same protein in their blood as sharks which sustained the virus, thus preventing them from getting cancer?"

"Precisely."

"You could've told me all of this over the phone," Robin said crossing her arms. "Why did you run the whole way to New York?"

"I wanted to see the body, if you don't mind. And maybe collect some samples for my work."

"The body is gone," Robin said handing him a cup of coffee. "All we have left is some blood and a few tissue samples."

"What do you mean it's gone?" Dr. Taylor asked, his eyes widening.

"We think it was stolen."

"I was afraid that might happen," Dr. Taylor said, sipping his coffee. "I sent some samples of her blood to a colleague of mine, Dr. Ethan Loventhol, who is an immunologist at Cal Tech. He told me it would be impossible to use this stuff on humans because too much of the protein would be destroyed if we tried to sustain the virus inside the serum. And because of the complexity of the protein, it would be impossible to synthesize enough in the lab to keep the virus alive to treat any tumor. We talked maybe a few more times, but nothing ever came of it until I found out that two years ago Dr. Loventhol resigned at Cal Tech and opened some alternative medicine clinic in North Dakota. I found that odd considering he wasn't much of a clinician. He was a recluse who lived in the lab. He hated people. And a few of his patients were getting better. The FDA tested the herbal extract that he supposedly used to treat these people and found it had no real therapeutic properties and that the patients had gotten better because of prior chemotherapy, not the extract. But, I didn't believe it. Why would he quit Cal tech? He was on to something. I know it."

"Any way to get the files of these patients?"

"Impossible. Dr. Loventhol won't release the results of the study."

"If he's come up with the cure, then why wouldn't he want to share the find with the world? He'd win a Nobel prize."

"He probably hasn't studied enough patients and he knew once I found out about his work, there would be hell to pay. I knew I should have never trusted him, but he's one of the best in the world at what he does. And I thought there was no way he would stoop this low."

"So, what does all this have to do with Nicole Johnson?"

"I'm not sure. But one thing I do know; Dr. Loventhol would do just about anything to achieve what he set out to do. He's that kind of man."

Chapter 14

Detective Frank Roberts leafed through the file on his desk and knew the child was alive. He had waited three hours at the county health department, haggling with secretaries, filling out paper work, to finally discover that Nicole had an infant child. But where was he? He was seen in their clinic one year ago for his immunizations, and then never returned. And now he knew the truth; a truth he didn't want to face. The kid had the same blood type as his. AB positive. What were the chances? It was his son and he had the sinking feeling he was in danger.

Frank held the phone with his shoulder close to his ear trying to reach Brian Johnson. The police station was crowded with cops, toting their guns on shoulder holsters, running from phone to phone, trying to uphold the bullshit the country called justice. Frank reclined in his chair as the phone continued to ring, until Brian's answering machine picked up. "Damn," Frank said, slamming down the phone. He reached in his drawer and searched for Brian's work number. Brian worked as an electrical engineer for a small company in New Jersey. He dialed the numbers with his pen and the phone rang nine times. A computer message picked up, the same message that was on every corporate phone in America. He shoveled through the commands and finally a person answered. "Engineering," a deep voice said.

"My name is detective Frank Roberts, NYPD. I was wondering if I could speak with a Mr. Brian Johnson."

"He hasn't shown up for work today."

"Is he sick?"

"Don't know. He hasn't called in."

He hasn't called in? Where was he? He knew Brian would never leave the city, considering the fragile condition of Jacob. Maybe he had been in a car accident? Or something else? It was the 'something else' that bothered him the most. "Are you sure?"

"Positive. Brian hasn't missed a day this year, excluding vacation."

"Thanks," Frank said, slowly hanging up the phone.

Frank searched through the stack of unfinished paper work and found his car keys at the bottom. He was at least a week behind on his paper work and still had work to do on a homicide case he got called to investigate yesterday. There weren't enough hours in the day for him, but he had to figure out a way. His son's life may be at stake. And what about Jacob? Where was he? Most likely at day-care, he hoped. Just as he was about to leave, a tall, obese, black man, with a receding hairline and mustache, stomped toward his desk. It was his boss, Captain Dennis Irwin. "Where in the hell are you going?" Captain Irwin asked, his face tight, his forehead furrowed.

"Out to get something to eat," Frank said, trying to ignore him.

"Out to get something to eat? Just like yesterday? A four hour lunch break?"

"I stayed till ten o'clock last night doing shit."

"And that's what it was, *shit*," Captain Irwin said, pointing at Frank's chest. "A millionaire was found dead, need I remind you. He happened to be friends with the mayor."

"Don't worry, Dennis, I'll get to the bottom of it."

"You better, or the bottom is where you'll be, do you understand?"

"Dennis, you really need to chill. You're going to get your blood pressure up."

"Fuck you, Frank. I'm not kidding," Dennis barked, loosening his shirt collar. "The mayor's office is breathing down my throat on this one and if my best man keeps acting like a schmuck, I'll find me a new one."

Frank twirled his keys in his hand and walked past Captain Irwin. "I'll be back in about an hour."

"If I don't have something to go on by today, it's your ass in my garbage can," Dennis yelled.

Frank exited the building, knowing Dennis was harmless. Dennis responded to stress with anger. He thought yelling and ranting got things done, maybe in the movies, but not in real life. It was a waste of energy. Frank had gotten the department out of some binds. Three months ago he broke the Linmore case; a serial killer was killing college students in Brooklyn. He even saved Dennis's job by bringing down the two dirty cops who were stealing impounded cocaine and selling it on the streets. Dennis and the mayor would have to wait on this one. His son was more important.

The engine of Frank's car stuttered, then finally started. Same old shit every day, Frank thought as he entered the George Washington tunnel and the brightness of the sun became obscured by the darkness and smog. He reached into his jacket and pulled out Brian's address, just to double check, then fired up a Newport. As he turned onto the James Street exit, an intriguing thought entered his mind. What had traumatized Jacob so much that he couldn't speak about it? Jacob was a tough kid, who had unfortunately been through a lot more than kids his age. Probably a lot more than most adults. He remembered the night Jacob called his house crying after his mother got beat up by her pimp. He rushed over to her apartment, to find her eyes black and blue, her legs cut and bruised. But, Jacob was always strong. He was the man of the family. What had happened so bad to make him silent? The thought made Frank slam his foot on the gas pedal.

The trees around Brian's townhouse seemed to tell a story Frank couldn't wait to find out. The leaves swayed slowly in the wind, casting tiny shadows across the pavement that looked like tiny faces whispering the truth with each gust. Frank could feel something was wrong. He always did. And Brian's car in the driveway confirmed his fears. Frank parked his car on the sidewalk. The engine continued to run, then sputtered to a stop. He jumped from his car and examined the area. The streets were quiet except for a few old men in the distance walking their dogs. He walked to the front door and knocked. He waited a few seconds and rang the doorbell. He lurched his head in the window, trying to see through the curtains. The maroon blinds blocked his view. Where the hell was he?

Frank scuttled around back and turned the knob of the back door. It was locked. He sighed, then decided to bend the law. There was enough probable cause to justify his break-in, he reassured himself. Or so he hoped. He ran back to his car and opened his trunk. He pulled a crow bar from under his spare tire and sauntered around back. He thought about calling the local police before prying open the door, but the thought of Jacob entered his mind. Each second he wasted was one second less from the truth. He rammed the bar into the door and pried it open. The finished basement with a pool table, stereo and small television set, was empty. He crept up the stairs, searching the floor for a blood trail or muddy footprints. Unfortunately, it was clean. He opened the basement door, expecting to find two bodies covered in blood. He inhaled a breath of relief when he saw an empty kitchen and living room.

Frank walked up the stairs and searched each room. They were empty. But, in the corner of the master bedroom, next to the nightstand, were five spots of blood. He knelt down and examined them. His inclinations were correct. Foul play. But where was the body? He was about to continue examining the room when three police officers burst through the door, guns aimed in his direction. "Freeze and put your hands in the air."

Frank calmly raised his hands. "If you let me reach in my jacket, I'll show you guys my I.D."

"Don't fucking move!" one of the cops yelled, pulling out a set of handcuffs and forcing Frank's hands behind his back.

"Reach inside my jacket. You'll find my badge. I'm NYPD."

The cop looked skeptically at Frank's face, then reluctantly pulled his badge from his inside pocket. "What are you doing here?" the cop asked, studying his I.D.

"The man and his son who live here are missing. I broke in to check things out."

"Give Brooklyn a call," the police officer said, handing a female cop the leather wallet.

The police cuffed Frank's hands so tight, his wrists burned and ached. He fell to his knees, all while thinking about what Dennis would say. He was sure Dennis would rupture a blood vessel in his forehead when he found out where he had been. The female officer returned. "He's who he says he is," she said, handing the wallet back to the other officer.

"Could you please uncuff me?" Frank barked, wincing with pain.

"Sorry, but we usually don't have cops breaking into homes around here," the cop said, loosening the cuffs. "What the hell are you doing in Jersey?"

"You see those blotches of blood on the floor?" Frank asked, pointing, then rubbing his wrist.

"Yeah."

"That's why I'm in Jersey."

Chapter 15

Frank cracked his knuckles nervously as he sat in Captain Dennis Irwin's cluttered office. Dennis paced the floor, his plump black face bloated with fury, almost about to explode, his hands and teeth clenched. "I want you to explain why the fuck you were in Jersey instead of working on the Harrison case? And why in the hell did you break into someone's house, out of our jurisdiction, on your so called lunch hour?"

"The man was a friend of mine," Frank uttered, like a child being scolded by his father. "I called his house, his work, and he had seemingly disappeared."

"Dammit, Frank," Dennis yelled, pointing. "You could've told me first what the hell you were doing. Why in the hell didn't you let the Jersey boys take care of it?"

"Instinct took over. I had to find out myself and now I think he was murdered."

"Listen, the NYPD doesn't pay you to gallivant around, breaking into people's houses because they're your friends. Do you see the name tag on my chest?"

"How can I miss it?"

"What does it say?"

"It says to quit treating me like some snot-nosed rookie," Frank said, raising his voice. "I don't deserve this shit."

"I guess you forgot your glasses," Dennis said, pointing at his chest. "It says *Captain,* and everything that happens at this precinct has to go through me."

"Whatever Dennis," Frank replied, annoyed. "I know I may have been irresponsible, but I don't have time for this. My friend and his son are missing and the boys at the Jersey lab are analyzing the blood as we speak. I know you could care less about friendships. I can see that now."

"Don't even go there, Frank," Dennis said, calming down, plopping in his chair. "This is my job and I know I may sound like a prick on this, but if I don't put my foot down on this kind of stuff, the people around here would be running the streets of Brooklyn, doing whatever they wanted. Friendship is friendship, but this is my job. Do you remember those two pricks that were stealing from right under our noses and selling that shit on the street?"

"I remember. Busted them myself. And I know you've been taking a lot of heat from the Mayor's office for it. But come on. We go way back. This is important to me. I wouldn't be acting like this if it wasn't worth it."

Dennis rubbed the top of his head, then studied Frank's face. He took a long sip of the diet Pepsi on his desk, then sighed. "So level with me, Frank. What's going on?"

Frank wanted to tell him how much he wanted to see his son, and how much he loved Nicole, but couldn't. Things around the office were already tight. The precinct couldn't afford another scandal. "The guy's name was Brian Johnson. He's from my neighborhood...."

"Frank, you're bullshitting me," Dennis said, with a whimsical smile. "You know you can't lie to me."

Frank hated the fact that Dennis could always sniff out the truth. It was his gift. Frank could easily lie to his parents or girlfriends, but never Dennis. That bastard, he thought. Frank combed his fingers through his hair and sighed. It was difficult for him to tell even Dennis, his close friend, how he felt about Nicole and her son. And how much it troubled him to keep their relationship a secret. But Dennis understood, especially after the horrible events surrounding Frank's divorce. The look in his ex-wife's eyes when he caught her with another man in a hotel room still made him nauseated. He could still see the face of the man that shattered his entire world every time he closed his eyes. He was no older than twenty-five. She threw away everything for a younger, richer man. A man that probably promised her a big house in the suburbs, not some modest row home in Brooklyn.

"So, how can you be so sure that her brother was murdered?" Dennis asked.

"When I entered his house…"

"…Broke into his house."

"Whatever. In the bedroom was a trail of blood, and the room looked as if there had been a struggle. And the little boy wasn't in daycare. Brian would never do a thing like that. And his car was in the driveway."

"So, what do you have so far?"

"Blood samples from the floor. Brian was a big man. I bet he inflicted a wound to his attacker. I know there will be more than one blood type in the specimen."

"Any motive?"

"Not yet, but I'm beginning to think that whoever broke into his home wasn't out to kill him. They wanted the boy."

"Why?"

"Think about it. This guy lived twenty-nine years, no trouble, not even a misdemeanor. But, as soon as his sister dies and he adopts her little boy, his house is broken into and they're both missing."

"Probably drugs," Dennis said, reclining in his chair. "She may have ripped someone off."

"Maybe, but the Colombians dominate Brooklyn and when they kill, there's blood and guts all over the house. It's a fear thing with them."

"What if they went for a ride and dumped the bodies in the river?"

"Possibly, but you know when I have my gut feelings…"

"Yeah, I know that *gut feeling* of yours," Dennis said, emphasizing the word gut. "Gets this department in a world of shit every time."

"But how many times have I been wrong?"

Dennis remained silent. The wrinkles on his face contoured to a reluctant brood, and then he smirked. "O.K. Frank, I'll toot your horn this one time. How can I help?"

Frank knew it was best to be up front with Dennis. He may be a son of a bitch at times, but he was always on the side of his men, Frank thought. And the longer he held the dark secret to himself, the worse the consequences when the truth finally came out. "Well," Frank forced through his lips with a sigh. "What I'm about to tell you can never leave this room."

"I'll be the judge of that."

"Dennis," Frank uttered. "We go back a long way and I wouldn't tell you this if I couldn't trust you."

"Spit it out," Dennis barked. "I give you my word that it stays right here."

"I have a son and his mother was a hooker."

Dennis's eyes widened. He jumped from his chair and sat on his desk, pounding his fingers nervously against the wood. "Damn, what the hell were you thinking? Do you know what the press will do with this? It's bad enough you were sleeping with a hooker, now this?"

"I know, I know," Frank said, burying his head in his chest. "I didn't think the kid was mine, but I checked the free pediatric clinic and we have the same blood type. What are the chances of that?"

"So where is he?" Dennis asked as he nervously loosened his tie.

"Don't know. I checked all the foster homes in this fucking city and none matched the I.D. I got from the clinic."

"He may still be out there."

"They have a computer program now that tracks the location of every orphan in this city and it's quite sophisticated. The database matches them by their footprints."

"I see," Dennis replied shaking his head. "So you've been spending your afternoons looking for your son."

Frank was about to outline his plan to independently investigate the case on his free time, when two stone-faced suits burst into the room unannounced. They looked like NYPD, but he had never seen them before. Their eyes pierced into Frank, as if they were daggers probing his brain. "Captain Irwin, my name is Harris Nolan, and this is Michael Steward. We're from Internal Affairs."

"What can I do for you boys?" Dennis asked, nervously.

"It's about Detective Frank Roberts. We found something in the trunk of his car that we need to discuss."

CHAPTER 16

Robin Vastbinder studied Dr. Roderick Taylor's face as she walked with him down the dingy hallways of the pathology department. His eyes shifted quickly side to side, like a robot with a malfunction. A layer of perspiration soaked his pale skin. He looked as if he had lost his child. Why hadn't he come forward a long time ago when he suspected that Dr. Loventhol might have been up to something? It was irresponsible, even though he had no proof.

Robin ushered Dr. Taylor into the main lab to find Orpheus placing a small piece of white, fleshy tissue into a vise with a tiny blade above it that sliced the specimen into thin fragments, like chipped ham. "Orpheus, I'd like you to meet someone," Robin said. "This is Dr. Roderick Taylor."

"I know you probably don't remember me," Orpheus said, shaking his hand. "We met a number of years back when I just started here."

"I remember seeing you around."

"Orpheus is the chief of the pathology department," Robin said

"And as you can see, that's quite a prestigious position looking at this lab," Orpheus said. "So, what brings you to New York?"

Robin proceeded to tell Orpheus about the shark virus and how it related to Nicole Johnson, as well as how Dr. Taylor thought Dr. Loventhol had something to do with the disappearance of Nicole's body. Orpheus held his chin and shook his head, as if he was calculating each word. "Sounds like we should get the police involved."

"We have no evidence," Dr. Taylor said. "It would be a waste of time."

"Why do you think Dr. Loventhol stole the body?" Orpheus asked. "Is he some sort of necrophiliac?"

"No, I think he was somehow using her blood to treat the patients at his clinic."

"That sounds pretty freaky to me," Orpheus said. "Like some Frankenstein mad scientist shit."

"I can't prove a thing, but I'd like to take a look at the samples, if that would be all right with you?" Dr. Taylor asked.

"Sure, what's left of them."

Robin and Dr. Taylor followed Orpheus into his office. Orpheus reached behind his bookcase and pulled out a metal box with a lock. He opened it and pulled out a stack of papers and slides. "I'm not taking any chances this time," Orpheus said. "This is all I have left."

Robin stood beside Orpheus as Dr. Taylor peered through the eyepieces of the microscope. The anxious flutter of his eyes changed to excitement as he maneuvered the slide across the lens. "I still can't believe the protein stayed viable in her body so long," Dr. Taylor said, smiling.

"You mean that irregular protein spike on the electrophoresis?" Orpheus asked.

"Yes, we originally thought that the virus could only kill a finite amount of tumor burden before the supply of protein would run out."

"But I thought the virus would put the code to manufacture this protein into Nicole Johnson's DNA," Orpheus said, looking into the microscope, "thus making the cell produce the virus's growth source?"

"That's what we hypothesized," Dr. Taylor said, leaning away from the eyepieces. "But when we tried it on monkeys, the virus never lived longer than three days. For some reason, which still alludes me to this day, the virus couldn't make the monkey's cells produce enough of the protein to sustain the virus."

"Did you ever try it on humans?"

"Unfortunately, we did."

"How many people did you try it on?" Robin probed.

Dr. Taylor glanced distantly at the wall and inhaled deeply. "Four."

"And you never reported any of this?" Robin asked, raising her voice.

Dr. Taylor remained silent.

"And did you ever get FDA approval for all of this?" Orpheus added, crossing his arms. "I guess you guys had a new set of rules."

Dr. Taylor's face tightened. "How many times have you told a family that they were going to lose the most important thing in their lives, Dr. Martin?" Dr. Taylor asked, his blood vessels pulsating through his forehead. "And Dr. Vastbinder, you know how long it would've taken to get this approved for use on humans. Granted, we didn't study the virus enough. Hell, the paper you read was the first ever published on the subject. But I saw a little boy who was about to lose his mother and I wanted to give her a fighting chance to the best of my ability. I'm not a criminal."

Robin leaned on the desk and brushed the hair from her face, thinking about all the people she had watched die. "No one is calling you a criminal," Robin said. "We just want to make sure that this woman didn't die for nothing."

"I'm sorry about my outburst, but you don't know Dr. Loventhol. No one does. Once that clinic was built, I knew something was up. After the experiments failed on our four patients, he said he wanted to work on things awhile by himself. I had no problem with it because I know that's how he does things. But when I called him to discuss his progress, he wouldn't return any of my phone calls. I even flew out to California, but he had moved. The next thing I know, he has this clinic in North Dakota. Who could I tell? I'd be in as much trouble as him. I would just like to find her son and test his blood. Because if he has the virus, we need to protect him and get this all out in the open so it can be studied properly."

"It's going to be tough to convince her brother to let us take some blood from her son, considering what he has been through." Robin said.

"We have to at least try," Dr. Taylor pleaded.

Robin escorted Dr. Taylor back to her office. She thought about the little boy's eyes, his distant face, and began to worry about his safety. If someone stole a corpse, then what would they do with a live specimen? She quickly picked up her phone and dialed Nicole's brother's number. It had been disconnected. She dropped the receiver slowly, becoming even more concerned. "Either he doesn't have a phone or he moved," Robin said, sitting on her desk.

"Where does he live?" Dr. Taylor asked.

"Somewhere in New Jersey. The social worker probably still has the address," Robin said, picking up the phone again. The phone rang twice, and Camilla answered. Robin's hands began to tremble and her heart quaked. The air in the room seemed to be escaping slowly, making it difficult to breathe when Camilla told her that Nicole's son and brother had been missing. Robin could barely hang up the phone. "What's wrong?" Dr. Taylor asked, concerned.

"They're both missing," Robin said, forcing the words from her mouth.

Dr. Taylor's eyes looked as if they were about to drop from his face. He combed his hands though his hair and sighed. "I was afraid this would happen. We'll have to go to plan B."

"What is plan B?"

"I know where there is a patient that was treated at the Loventhol clinic."

"Now, why didn't you tell me?" Robin asked, standing from her chair. "I've been nothing but up front with you. I expect the same."

"You don't understand," Dr. Taylor mumbled.

"Understand what?" Robin snapped. "An innocent, beautiful boy could die."

"I have given my life to this project just for one chance to see those tears go away. The tears of a mother watching her child die, the tears of a child losing his parent too young, long before they could hold their grandchildren. When I was your age, I could take the sadness as if it never happened, but I can't take watching another young person die knowing I'm this close to the cure."

The rage that streamed through Robin's veins slowly subsided as she looked in Dr. Taylor's eyes. She exhaled a long breath and asked, "Where is this patient?"

"She lives in Long Island, on Thirty-seventh Street."

"Let's go."

Robin stared reflectively out of the window of her Volvo as she drove over the Queensboro Bridge en route to Long Island. Dr. Taylor pulled a stick of gum from his coat and shoved it into his mouth as he leafed though the papers in his brief case. "What's the patient's name?" Robin asked, making a left onto Vernon Boulevard.

"Rebecca Myers," Dr. Taylor replied. "Her husband owns a big chunk of Manhattan."

"What was her diagnosis?"

"Metastatic lung cancer."

"End stage?" Robin asked.

"She's been cancer free for two years despite having mets to her bone, brain, and adrenals."

"How did you get this information?"

"A friend of mine who owns a lot of land in Boston told me about her."

"So, what the hell are we going to say?" Robin asked.

"If we can have a sample of her blood."

"That sounds like a great plan," Robin replied sarcastically. "I'm sure she's going to let two complete strangers enter her home and draw her blood. I hope you have another plan B."

"Listen, I made a badge from the Loventhol clinic and called this patient two days ago. She thinks I'm drawing routine blood work."

"Do you realize how illegal that will be?" Robin barked.

"Listen, you stay in the car, I'll do the rest. How else are we going to get proof?"

The houses that surrounded the long winding road looked like museums. They all had long driveways with large steel gates decorated with golden statues. The poorest house on the road probably had at least five bedrooms with ten acres of land, Robin thought. "What's the address?" Robin asked, slowing down.

"5555 Fulton Lane," Dr. Taylor replied, pulling out a map and pointing. "It's the next house on the left. Park across the street, I'll be back in a few minutes."

"I hope you know what you're doing."

"So do I," Dr. Taylor replied, stuffing his wrinkled shirt into his pants and getting out of the car.

The silence seemed uncertain to Robin as she tapped her fingers nervously against the steering wheel. She looked at her watch. It had been five minutes since he left. What if they didn't buy his story? She reached inside her suit jacket and grabbed her flask. The scotch burned as it went down her throat, but it relaxed the thump in her chest. She looked at her watch again, only two minutes had passed. What was he doing? Why did she let him talk her into this?

Robin took another swig of her scotch and relaxed in her seat. She almost dozed off until the image of Dr. Taylor appeared in the distance. He was carrying a small Styrofoam box in his hand with a smile on his face. "I got it," he said opening the passenger door and jumping inside. "Let's get back to the lab."

Robin arrived back at Brooklyn University hospital with a tingle of anticipation as she parked her car. The sweat that leaked from Dr. Taylor's forehead made Robin realize that her entire career could be over if anyone found out about the blood. But Dr. Taylor was right, she thought, as she exited her car and entered the main tower, it was their only chance to save the little boy's life.

Robin entered the pathology lab with Dr. Taylor following behind, carrying the Styrofoam container close to his chest. Robin quickly scanned the lab and found Orpheus in a corner, staring though a microscope as if nothing else was in the room.

"We have a present for you," Robin said, tapping Orpheus on the shoulder.

"Judging from your last gift," Orpheus said, continuing to stare though the microscope, "I'd take a Hallmark card and call it a day."

"Is anyone on the teaching microscopes?" Dr. Taylor asked, taking the top off the Styrofoam container and pulling out the tubes of blood packed in ice.

"This looks like trouble to me," Orpheus said, holding the tubes up to the light.

"Hopefully, enough to have Marty Loventhol answer a lot of questions," Dr. Taylor said, following Robin and Orpheus to another lab.

The small lab contained a centrifuge and a large microscope with five teaching eyepieces attached around a table. Orpheus dropped the test tubes in the centrifuge, spun them down and extracted cells to make a slide. He placed two drops of histological stain on each slide and slipped them under the microscope. "What are we looking at?" Orpheus asked, moving the slide around.

"This is blood from a patient at the Loventhol clinic," Dr. Taylor said. "Try to isolate one of the neutrophils."

Orpheus maneuvered the slide around until he found an image of two large white blood cells with many blue granules, surrounded by hundreds of tiny, donut shaped red blood cells. "Now focus on the neutrophil at one o'clock," Dr. Taylor said pointing.

"These are the same inclusion bodies we found in Nicole Johnson's tissue," Orpheus said, his eyes widening as he looked at the numerous tiny rods inside the white blood cells.

"Just what I thought," Dr. Taylor said with a sigh, moving away from the microscope.

"So, now what?" Robin asked, rubbing her eyes and falling back into her chair.

"I'm going to collect blood from two other patients and then we can build a case if we can prove the virus contains parts of Nicole Johnson's DNA, and get those people to testify against Loventhol."

"It looks like you have it all figured out," Orpheus said, sarcastically. "Then while we're at it, we'll solve world peace and cure the common cold."

"He's right Dr. Taylor," Robin chimed in. "Dr. Loventhol saved their lives."

"These are all very wealthy people with great reputations. If it got out that they were using the blood of a child to save their own lives, I think they would change their tunes."

"Sounds very shaky to me," Orpheus said rubbing his chin.

"It's the only chance we have," Robin said, looking reflectively though the microscope.

Chapter 17

Robin dropped Dr. Taylor off at his hotel and then merged back into traffic for the long ride home. He was going back to Boston for a few days to check on his old files and find the patients that they tested the virus on. He said he would get in contact with her in a few days, which was going to seem like forever. She glanced out of the window and saw the old daycare building her son used to go to. The memory triggered the thoughts of what Jacob was doing right now. Was he alive? Was he talking or was he still trapped in the depths of silence that held the answers to many questions? Why was he missing? And where had he gone? The thoughts raced through her mind like a sprinter running nowhere. How did it all relate? Dr. Taylor seemed to think that Jacob was in danger. But, what could she tell the police? A bunch of assumptions that would end up on the bottom pile of someone's desk. She felt helpless, as if she was watching Jacob being attacked through a glass window she couldn't penetrate; like she watched her own son die in the I.C.U.

The image of the dried blood on his tender, bruised face and the ventilator tubes that elevated and relaxed his flaccid body resurfaced, making her live through the pain again. She stayed at the hospital all night, praying and hoping he'd open his eyes and wrap his tiny little arms around her again. Just like in the morning, before work, as she got him ready for daycare. All the medical journals in the world couldn't save him. He had bled into his brain and ruptured his intestines and spleen. He lingered on for five days before she finally decided enough was enough and had them pull the plug. The EEG said he was brain dead. Her beautiful little boy was gone and she could do nothing to stop it.

The smell of sulfur mixed with mold made Robin wish she was back in Pittsburgh as she sat in traffic. In Pittsburgh, the air was much cleaner since the steel mills closed down in the eighties, and an hour wait in traffic was almost unheard of. In New York, it was a luxury. She looked around her car and pulled out a CD from the jacket and plopped it into the player, trying to remember when she was in high school, in Pittsburgh. The soft sounds of Genesis hummed through the speakers, making her remember her prom dress and how she couldn't get out of the house because her father and mother turned into the Paparazzi. Her father treated her like a tomboy, and seeing her in the elegant dress had to surprise him. What she wouldn't give to be seventeen again. The urge for alcohol slowly dominated Robin's every thought. She couldn't wait to get home and start in on the bottle of wine she opened last night. The alcohol seemed to be the only thing that numbed the suffering of the open wound that leaked from her soul every day.

The traffic started to loosen and Robin emerged from the constant horns of the city. She glanced at the digital clock of her dashboard and realized it was too late to catch the six o'clock news. They would've most likely had the story about the disappearance of Nicole's brother and son. Maybe she could catch something at eleven o'clock, she thought. As she turned off the 3rd Street exit, she noticed a green Jeep Grand Cherokee following close behind her. It had been there for at least two miles. She strained her eyes and looked through the rearview mirror. It was a white male on a cellular phone, that's all she could tell. She stopped at the light and focused harder. The glare of the sunset made it impossible to discern any distinct features.

She accelerated to sixty miles an hour, and the car followed. She made a right hand turn, the back way to her house, and the car continued to follow. Maybe he was just going her direction, she thought. It was just her paranoia, she reassured herself. She continued making left and right turns, until the car disappeared. She patted her chest, trying to relax the tension, and pulled into her driveway. Getting out of her car, she felt odd, almost childish thinking someone was following her.

She took off her jacket and went to the fridge. A half-full gallon of White Zinfandel awaited her. Just as she was about to loosen the cork, she noticed something strange. The picture of her son and husband on the end table was missing. She looked under the coffee table and found it on the floor. That seemed odd considering it was the last thing she looked at everyday before she left the house. She was certain it was in its proper place before she left this morning. It couldn't have been the wind that knocked it over, she thought, because the windows were closed.

She took a sip of her wine and dismissed her paranoid delusions. The sleeping pills were probably affecting her memory. But she was positive that she looked at the picture this morning and two delusions in one day did seem quite odd. And with Nicole Johnson's body missing, along with her brother and son, it made the notion of someone breaking into her house quite real. But for what? She picked up her purse and rummaged through the pile of junk she called makeup and found Detective Frank Roberts' card at the bottom. It wouldn't hurt to give him a call in the morning just to ease her mind.

*　　　*　　　*

Orpheus Martin pulled into the driveway of his white colonial home wondering if his wife had slept with the milkman twice as he watched his sons dancing in the yard. They were gyrating their bodies in a sort of epileptic fit while listening to a tribal sounding beat. They would occasionally throw themselves on a piece of cardboard and spin on their backs and heads. They definitely weren't from his gene pool, he thought. He recalled a video on MTV, a number of years ago, calling their moves 'breakdancing' but Orpheus was sure that the dance had gone out of style. Hopefully they would stop soon before they broke something.

"What the heck are you kids doing?" Orpheus asked, grabbing his brief case as he walked into the yard.

Marcus, his nine-year-old son, dusted off his blue Nike jogging suit and smiled. "We were cut'n it up, Dad."

"Yeah, breakin'," Rowland, his seventeen-year-old son said, smiling, exposing his braces.

"I thought that dance had gone out of style years ago?"

"It's the latest thing," Rowland replied.

"You kids don't know anything about dancing," Orpheus said, taking off his jacket. "Watch this."

Orpheus started shaking his butt, like a chicken, then did the Hustle. He pictured the big, glittering lights of a discotheque and began waving his body wildly. His boys laughed. "Dad, what do you call that?" Rowland asked, a dumbfounded look on his face.

"The Hustle, son. Watch and learn how it's really done," Orpheus said, spinning in a circle.

"You really did that in public?" Rowland asked.

Orpheus grabbed Rowland and threw him playfully to the ground and began tickling him. Marcus jumped on his back. Orpheus rolled in the grass with his sons, as his father used to do with him after work. It was the reason Orpheus woke up every morning, to see his children smile. "I don't mean to interrupt the WWF match, but dinner is ready," Orpheus's wife said sternly from the doorway.

Orpheus helped both of his sons up and put his arms around them both, leading them through the doorway. His wife, Gloria, was dressed in jeans and a baggy sweatshirt, which covered her thin muscular body. She was forty-one, but had the body of a twenty-five-year old. Orpheus still couldn't believe to this day he married someone so beautiful. He gave her a peck on the cheek and smiled. The smell of pot roast filled the house, his favorite. "Did I get any mail?" Orpheus asked, walking to the bathroom to wash his hands.

"A whole stack of bills and a manila envelope without a return address. They're on the coffee table," Gloria said from the kitchen.

Orpheus emerged from the kitchen and walked into the living room. He picked up the stack and frowned thinking about the credit cards that he needed to pay off. The manila envelope was on the bottom. It was thick, but had no return address. He ripped it open and a photo with a message on the back appeared. A sharp pain penetrated his chest when the photo came into focus. "Who was the manila envelope from, honey?" his wife asked.

Orpheus wiped the cold sweat from his forehead and inhaled a deep breath. "Just a chain letter," he said, apprehensively. God, he wished it were only a chain letter.

Chapter 18

Detective Frank Roberts slumped against the cold wall of his jail cell and inhaled a deep drag from his cigarette, trying to clear the fog that clouded his mind. It had been the worst ten hours of his life, going from office to office, answering thousands of questions that didn't make any sense. Who in the hell planted the kilo of cocaine in his car? And how were his fingerprints all over it? It could've been at least a thousand people, he thought. He had made enough enemies to fill up a landfill over the years. The mob, the local drug factions, and even people in the department. He inhaled again, flicking his ashes on the floor and rubbed his face slowly, trying to remove the bullshit that seemed to cover him every place he turned. He wasn't sure how, but when it occurred to him what he had been through the past few days, it became clear. Somehow, this all related to Nicole Johnson.

Frank pulled himself up and paced the cell, smoking one cigarette after another. In a weird sense he deserved this, he thought. He should've never doubted Nicole when she told him that the child was his. She may have been a hooker and a drug addict, but never a liar. If she was using, she never lied, despite her two trips to rehab. The white powder was her oxygen. It made her want to get up every day and go lay on her back for money. It made her forget the years of beatings and sexual advances of her stepfather.

The clang of keys reverberated through the hall and two voices approached. One was Captain Irwin, and the other was Mike Scalice from Internal affairs. Mike was once under Frank in homicide, until he kissed enough asses to move into Internal affairs. He was a short man with blond hair and dark eyes that eclipsed his boyish face. He knew Mike would love to bust him and end his career. He was that kind of man.

Captain Irwin's eyes peered through Frank like a father disappointed with his child. He opened the cell and entered. "Frank, I just can't believe all of this," Dennis said, calmly staring at the floor. "That Kilo is the same Kilo missing from our department. I know you were involved with that hooker, but just how involved were you?"

"Dennis, I've told you a thousand times, I've been set up," Frank barked. "It has to do with the disappearance of Nicole Johnson. Someone wanted me out of the picture."

"Who Frank? Your little disappearing acts this week makes it hard for me to believe that."

"And we found some interesting things on Nicole's brother," Mike said.

"What?" Frank asked.

"Well, it turns out he was picked up ten years ago for selling cocaine," Mike said, arrogantly.

"Listen, I checked his records, he was as clean as a preacher," Frank said, baffled.

"You must've checked the wrong records, Frank," Mike snapped back.

Frank examined Mike's face. The smirk irked him, like chalk screeching down a blackboard. He knew this was Mike's chance to move up in the force with an internal conviction. He was a butt smelling son of a bitch that would hold his own son hostage if it meant a promotion. "Dennis, you know me. If I was stealing from the force and dealing, do you think I would be so stupid as to bring a trunk full of cocaine to work with me in a police car? I'm a cop dammit," Frank yelled. "I would always be one step ahead of everything, just like those punks that were stealing heroin from here a year ago. You remember who busted them, don't you? Doesn't it seem like a convenient coincidence that the minute I started investigating Brian Johnson's death that all of this happened? And I just found out that Nicole Johnson's body is missing from the morgue. Why? Why?"

"Calm down," Dennis said, placing his hand on Frank's shoulder.

"You want to know why, Frank?" Mike asked, with an interrogating point. "Because maybe you got sloppy. Maybe you're too overconfident, thinking you would be the last person the force would suspect."

"You fucking brown nosing piece of shit, "Frank yelled, lunging at Mike.

"Both of you, shut the fuck up," Dennis ordered, pushing Frank back. "Listen, I don't know what to believe. But you've got a good point Frank, because Internal affairs had an anonymous tip that the cocaine was in your trunk. And I find that odd as well. But, Internal affairs is pressing down on me. And they have a lot of evidence."

Frank paced, then straightened his jacket. "I want out of here," he demanded.

"We have to hold you for another hour, then you can post bail," Dennis replied. "And I won't even tell you what I went through to get you out of here. You're lucky the judge owed me a favor."

"I also want to talk with my lawyer, none of this is gonna stick, you know it as well as I do."

"I hope you're right Frank," Dennis said.

"If you breathe the wrong way, your ass is mine," Mike said, pointing.

"I didn't know you swung that way Mike," Frank said with a smirk.

"Fuck you," Mike uttered, leaving the cell.

"You already have," Frank said through the bars.

"Would you two please grow up," Dennis barked, shaking his head.

Frank collected his keys and wallet from the desk and walked towards the exit of the precinct. He was embarrassed to walk through the front door because thousands of eyes scrutinized his every step as if he was about to take their wallet the minute they turned their heads.

He was banished from the place he spent most of his every waking moment. It felt like a punch in the face that bruised his soul. It was as if his own family had turned their backs on him, like the criminals he dragged up the steps almost every day. He could only hide his face, for the evidence against him was overwhelming. But, why? And how? Who wanted to frame him? The local mob? Doubtful. That wasn't their style. They would've come to him first and at least offered a bribe, he thought. It was something bigger, like a government official. But what would Brian Johnson have to do with the government? And what about Nicole? Did she sleep with the wrong man and the press found out? It was an election year, he reminded himself. But that seemed too much like a movie. It had to do with Nicole Johnson and the disappearance of her brother and son, he was sure of it. It was the how and why that bothered him most.

The fine mist of rain that soaked Frank's suit jacket made him wish he could've driven the piece-of-shit Ford home, instead of trying to flag down a cab. The wait seemed like an eternity until, finally, a cab stopped. He jumped inside and instructed the driver to take him home. The car sped through the myriad of traffic, like a running back fighting for the first down, until he arrived at his apartment. He gave the driver twenty bucks and exited the car. As he was about to enter his building, he spotted an unfamiliar face. He glanced at his watch and wondered what had happened to Joe, the regular doorman. This man was six feet tall, with gangly, gorilla arms and menacing eyes that seemed to watch his every move. Joe was a short fat guy from Brooklyn who couldn't keep a mouse out of the building. Who was this guy?

Frank marched into the lobby scanning the man out of the corner of his eyes. The man's face continued to track him like a laser beam. He approached the elevator and quickly turned his head, the man was gone. Frank pushed the button on the elevator and crossed his arms, wondering if it was his imagination or was something really going on. A feeling crept up his throat, making him step off the elevator. He hustled to the main office and entered. A tall, balding man with wisps of gray hair in a shirt and tie stood from his desk. It was the manager of the building, Philip Steward. "Mr. Roberts, what can I do for you today?"

"Just wondering where Joe is today?"

"He's on vacation."

"Who's the guy that replaced him?"

"Is there a problem?"

"No, I just wanted to know his name. He's doing a great job and I wanted to give him a tip."

"Let me see," the manager said, turning and opening the top drawer of a metal file cabinet. "Mitch Shannon. He's a temp, just filling in for the week. He's from the Bernstein agency. I use them all the time. I'm sure he'll be glad to hear this."

"Thanks," Frank said, leaving the office.

Frank sauntered back outside to find the man standing on the corner, flagging down a cab for one of the tenants. He tapped him on the shoulder and pulled twenty bucks from his pocket. The man turned, his eyes widened for a moment, then relaxed. "I just wanted to let you know you're doing a great job, Mitch."

The man hesitated for a moment, then grabbed the money. "Thank you sir," he said, nodding his head cordially.

Frank studied his face. He imprinted his low set eyes, heavy eyebrows and brown hair into his brain. The man's grip was firm, his eyes insincere. Frank entered back into the building and rode the elevator to his apartment on the fifth floor. He opened the door to his messy apartment and threw the keys on his bar. He fixed himself a scotch and ice, chugged it, then fished through his end table for the phone book. While scanning the pages for the Bernstein agency, he noticed the red light on his answering machine was blinking. He depressed the key, and continued leafing through the phone book. The first message was a bill collector. His body tightened, thinking about the bills his ex-wife ran up while they were separated. He'd be paying Visa for the rest of his life. The second was from

Dr. Robin Vastbinder. Her voice sounded anxious. She left her telephone number and said she would like to talk about some things regarding Nicole Johnson.

Something was wrong, he knew it. He replayed the message and jotted down the number while fixing himself another drink. He picked up the phone and dialed her number.

"Hello?" Robin said.

"Dr. Vastbinder?"

"Yes it is."

"Detective Roberts. I just got your message. What's on your mind?"

"Can you meet me at the hospital?"

"Sure. Why?"

"I really can't go into it right now, but I really need to talk."

"What time?"

"How about an hour?"

"Where should I meet you?"

"As soon as you get into the hospital, call the operator and ask to page Dr. Vastbinder."

"See you in an hour."

CHAPTER 19

The bright rays of the sun that stood just above the mountains glared in Frank Roberts' eyes as he looked up at the ancient twelve-story Brooklyn University hospital building. That building was probably as old as the city, he thought. The renovations that surrounded the main tower only enhanced the eyesore. The new white building looked as if it was sucking the life out of the dusty old one. Frank walked through the revolving doors, his mind jumbled with questions. Who was the doorman? And was he going to spend the next twenty years afraid to bend over for the soap? He pulled the address of the Bernstein agency from his pocket and mapped the quickest route to get there. That was his next stop.

Frank picked up a wall phone, all the while noticing the organized chaos of the hospital. Men in suits walked around as if they were kings and everyone else owned taxes. A young woman with frantic tears running down her cheek raced by with her little boy under her arms. A maintenance man sweeping the floor seemed to ignore everything as if he had seen it all. He dialed the operator and instructed her to page Dr. Robin Vastbinder. He hung up and waited a few minutes, then the phone rang. "Dr. Vastbinder?" Frank asked.

"Yes?"

"It's Detective Roberts."

"Where are you?" she asked, her voice cracking with anxiety.

"In the lobby."

"Be down in a minute."

Frank leaned against the wall until he spotted her emerge from the elevator. Her long flowered dress hid her slender curves he was sure she never put on display. Her long, kinky strawberry hair flowed on her shoulders, giving her a seductive, innocent look. He knew her looks should be the last thing on his mind, but it was impossible not to notice. But her distant green eyes and unsure, nervous gestures reminded him why he came.

"Detective Roberts," she said, moving a strand of hair from her face. "I'm glad you could make it."

"What's going on?"

"A lot. Have you eaten?"

"A cup of coffee is usually lunch and dinner for me."

"I'm starved. I ordered some Chinese food in the office. We can eat and talk about all of this."

Frank followed her through the corridor of the department of Hematology and Oncology until they arrived at her office, third door on the left. His office may have been only a cubicle, but it looked the same as hers; papers scattered all over the desk, a pail full of trash overflowing onto the floor. "Sorry about the mess. I've just been so busy these days," she said, moving a pile of books off the chair in front of her desk.

"No problem. You should see my office," Frank said, sitting down.

"Do you want broccoli and beef or shrimp fried rice?"

"It doesn't matter."

"Take the shrimp fried rice. I'm getting sick of it."

"Thanks," Frank said, opening up the white carton and taking a bite. "You sounded pretty upset on the phone. What's going on?"

"I think someone's been in my house."

"Why do you think that?"

"Things that I never move in my house were disturbed, and I think I was followed home last night."

"Are you sure you're not being a bit paranoid?" Frank mumbled through a full mouth of food.

"For someone not so hungry, you're practically inhaling that food."

"Sorry," Frank said, embarrassed, "I'm on the run so much, eating isn't a time to relax for me. It's functional, just like brushing my teeth."

"I thought it was kinda my imagination, but I was followed to work today."

"Did you get a look at the car?"

"It was different today, a blue Chevy pickup truck. Yesterday, a green Geo Prism."

"That's not much to go on and besides, what would be the motive?"

"Nicole Johnson," Robin said, while pacing and rubbing her arms. "This all started when her corpse was stolen."

Frank dug his fork into his food, thinking about Nicole's face, her smile, and knew Dr. Vastbinder was right. Why didn't he accept the kid? She would still be alive today, he knew it. He would've got her to the doctors earlier. And what about Jacob? He tried hard every minute of the day not to think about what had happened to him.

"Detective Roberts?"

"Sorry," Frank said, trying to rub the memories from his face. "Why would someone want her corpse?"

"Because of her blood. It somehow cures cancer."

"Really?" Frank asked, his face expanding with astonishment with each of her words.

"She has a virus that kills cancer cells."

"That would explain a lot."

"What do you mean?"

"That woman could do more cocaine and heroin than Jerry Garcia. The doctors at the E.R. once said that she did enough heroin to kill an elephant."

"I wouldn't be surprised," Robin said, tossing the half-full carton of rice in the garbage can. "She had an incurable cancer of the lymph nodes that kills most people in six months without treatment. She lived with it for five years, on top of doing all those drugs."

"So, who would want her? Some drug company? Maybe a research facility?"

"I'm not sure, but one thing I can tell you is that it has something to do with a Dr. Ethan Loventhol."

Frank rubbed his chin as Robin recanted the events of the last few days. The skin on his arms tightened and his forehead furrowed as he pictured the two doctors toy with Nicole's life without her consent. She had golden blood that thousands of drug companies would stop at nothing to obtain. And to them, she would've been just another dead lab rat if the treatment worked. Why did the name Loventhol sound so familiar? Where had he heard that name before? The wallet. The wallet with the pay stub from the Loventhol clinic.

"I found a wallet that Nicole had apparently stolen from an employee from the Loventhol clinic. I can't remember the man's name, but I wondered what the hell she was doing in North Dakota. Do you think it could be possible that they kidnapped her?"

Robin stared pensively out of the window. Her eyes peered aimlessly into the nothingness. "I'm not quite sure what they did with her blood," Robin said, somberly. "But if it can cure cancer, they would do just about anything. I sometimes wonder myself what I would do to cure cancer after all the young people I've seen die."

"Well listen," Frank said, glancing at his watch, "I've got to run. I have a few problems of my own since I went over to Nicole's brother's house a few days ago."

"What kind of problems?"

"It's a long story. Let's just say I have reason to believe there is some definite foul play going on and that my name isn't too popular over at the department because of it. And by the way, I definitely don't think you're paranoid. I would like to come over to your house and check things out, if I may?"

"Sure. When?"

"How about tonight, after I check this thing out?"

"What should I do in the meantime?" Robin asked, eyes glazed with tears. "I can't take this much longer. I had planned to sleep at a hotel tonight, just for some sort of piece of mind. I'm afraid to be alone."

"Listen, I'll take care of this, then we can go check out your house. But, you'll have to give me a ride."

"What happened to your car?"

"It's a long story."

"You seem to have a lot of 'long stories,'" Robin said, skeptically.

"I know, but that's another long story," Frank said, with a smile. "When do you finish for the day?"

"Around six."

"I'll meet you here, then we'll go to your house."

Chapter 20

Frank Roberts stood on the corner trying to flag down a cab. A fine mist of rain sprayed on his head, despite the newspaper above it, making the feeling of defeat all that much worse. The trip to the Bernstein agency was a waste of time. The temp that worked the door of his building had disappeared as if he never existed. The entire record of the job assignment had been conveniently deleted from the computer. Someone was one step ahead of him; something he thought could never happen.

The mist of rain changed to thick heavy drops that pelted Frank from wet to drenched. Finally, a cab arrived and he dove inside. His pants clung to his legs, which made them irritated and gave him a wedgy. He pulled them from his butt and relaxed inside the cab. "Brooklyn University Hospital," he uttered to the Asian cab driver that nodded his head.

Frank reached in his jacket and pulled out a cigarette. He crushed the pack in frustration when he realized the rain had destroyed all of his smokes. It reminded him of his career. All of the convictions meant nothing. He was no longer on the force. His badge and gun were gone. He was framed and could do nothing but watch his career spiral into nothing. And now faces were watching his every motion. Why? Who were these people? It had to be the mob, because no one else could make people disappear with such proficiency. But, what would the mob have to do with Nicole's blood? Maybe the black market, he thought. It just didn't seem the kind of thing they would be interested in. Too visible. Someone else had to be involved. And that someone else has to do with the Loventhol clinic.

The cab pulled into the entrance of the hospital, while Frank reached into his pocket. It was getting expensive riding the cabs around as he pulled fifteen bucks from his wallet. He walked through the entrance and rode the elevator to the fifth floor. As he got off, he spotted Dr. Vastbinder walking down the hall.

"Are you ready to go?" Frank asked.

"Give me two minutes. I just have to phone in two prescriptions and we can go."

Robin's house was a five-bedroom colonial that was ten times the size of Frank's apartment. The grass was like a golf course, and the shrubbery was sculpted like works of art. Frank followed Robin inside, surveying the walls and floors for tiny slits where a camera could be placed. Why someone would want such surveillance was beyond him. But his experience with the doorman of his apartment made him believe anything was possible.

Robin plopped her keys on the glass coffee table and walked to the fridge. "Would you like something to drink?" she asked, opening the door. "I've got wine, an old stale beer and some rum."

"I'll take a rum and coke, if you've got it," Frank said, checking under each lampshade.

"Is Pepsi O.K.?"

"Fine. So, where was the picture that was knocked to the floor?"

"Over there, on the coffee table, next to the couch," Robin said, pointing while pouring herself a glass of wine. "It was on the floor and I always look at it before I leave every morning."

Frank examined the picture and realized that she had a son and husband. Her husband was holding the infant child in his hands with a smile larger than his face. They must be out of town because she was afraid to stay home alone. Probably an ugly divorce, just like his, only this time the woman lost the kid. But, why? Was she a bad mother or adulterous? It was a difficult question, one he didn't want to ask. "You have a beautiful son," Frank said, cautiously.

Robin was silent for a moment, then she inhaled a deep breath. "The most beautiful thing I've ever seen," Robin said, with glazed eyes.

"I'm sorry…I didn't realize…"

"It's OK. It's been almost a year now," Robin uttered, staring into her drink as if the wine had all the answers. "They were both killed in a car accident."

Frank looked into her eyes and wished he kept his mouth shut. But somehow he could understand. His own son was missing. A son he had never had a chance to hold and feel the warmth of his little body against his chest. Change his little diaper and rock him to sleep. And it wasn't a car accident that kept him from his son, it was his own stupidity not to accept the truth.

"I kinda know what you're going through," Frank said somberly. "I…have a son that I've never seen. And it's my fault."

Robin's disapproving eyes scanned him from head to toe, undressing his soul. Frank knew she thought he was a monster. "How could you abandon your own son?"

"I didn't abandon him, I just never wanted to accept the fact that he was mine…until it was too late. I wish I could take back the moment she told me she was pregnant. I've laid awake every night the past week wishing I could have that time back."

"Who is the she? Your ex-wife?"

"No…she's…Nicole Johnson. The other child I told you about is my son. We have the same blood type. I found it in his birth records."

Robin's face widened, then she took a long drink of her wine, finishing the glass. "So, that's why you came to my office that day."

"Yeah, but you've got to understand, Nicole slept with a lot of men. I thought the chances of him being mine were slim. I was confused, you know, being on the force and the scandal it would've caused."

"I see. Did you love her?"

"I guess you could call it love," Frank said, turning off the lamp on the end table and unscrewing the light bulb. "She needed me as much as I needed her. I guess that's love. My ex-wife had just left me for some rich banker and she was there for me. She may have been only twenty-five, but she sure knew a lot about relationships. If she wouldn't have got hooked on that shit, I bet she would've made a great psychologist. She was the first woman that understood me and made me understand myself. I often thought, maybe...just maybe...then reality smacked me on the head."

Frank pulled the light bulb from the socket and examined the inside. It was clean. Robin's eyes enlarged, as if someone was trying to kill her, when Frank picked up the picture and pulled back the four metal tabs on each corner. "What are you doing?" Robin asked.

"Long story. Don't worry, I won't hurt a thing," Frank reassured her, carefully pulling the picture from its frame and searching the inside. It also was clean. He reassembled the frame and placed it back on the table. Kneeling down, he ran his hand under the table and on the floor, until he spotted a floor vent. "Do you have a screwdriver?" Frank asked, looking inside the vent.

"Somewhere around here," Robin said, searching a drawer next to the sink. "Will this do?" she asked, handing him a clear plastic, yellow, flat-headed screwdriver.

"That's perfect," Frank said, unscrewing the vent and putting his hand inside. He ran his fingers along the sheet metal walls and felt a round, metal device the size of a silver dollar affixed to the wall. He pulled it from the shaft and examined the magnet on its underside and the red light at the top. Probably a computer chip inside detecting the sound in the room. What else did they have in the house? A camera? The phone lines tapped? He decided to put it back; he had to find out whom he was dealing with. It definitely wasn't the mob. It was the government.

"What did you find?" Robin asked, looking over his shoulder.

"A lot of dust. I think your mind has been playing games with you."

"Listen, I know my house and where I put that picture," Robin barked, wrinkling her forehead. "I'm not crazy."

"Why don't we go have a drink?"

"I have alcohol here."

"I'd like to choke down a meal, and it would do you some good to get out," Frank said, going to the closet, grabbing her leather coat and his windbreaker.

"Maybe you're right," Robin said reluctantly, putting on her coat. "Do you like Italian? Pepe's on

Fifth has great pasta."

"That sure would be a change."

"Why?"

"It'd be the first time in a long time I didn't get my dinner from a machine."

Frank watched the rearview mirror the entire ride. It seemed no one was following them. He wanted to tell her about the device on the way over, but for all he knew the car was bugged. Robin parallel parked her gray Volvo a block away from the restaurant and locked the door. "It's right down the street," she said, pointing.

"Good, that will give us a chance to talk."

"About what?"

"Inside your vent was a bug."

"Oh my God," Robin said, anxiously.

"Relax and listen. The person that planted it must've knocked the picture on the floor. I didn't want to say anything because I think I can find out who bugged your house."

"How?"

"It's a long story, but all I need you to do is to call my house and leave a message saying that you found out some new information about Nicole and want to meet at Sharky's."

"That's on Tenth, isn't it?"

"Yeah. Tomorrow at noon. I'll be late, about twenty minutes late. Drive around for a while, act like you're lost, then park across the street from the restaurant."

"Shouldn't we just go to the police?"

"That would be a bad idea. I didn't want to get into this, but I've got as much at stake as you. If I don't find out what's going on soon, my ass will be in jail. And I'm sure the guys I busted would be glad to see me. Someone planted a kilo of cocaine in my trunk. I'm running around here on bail. Whoever planted those bugs are probably the same people that planted the drugs."

"I see," Robin said.

"Tonight, we'll eat and act natural. I'll leave when we get back, but I won't be far away. If you feel the least bit nervous, call me on my cellular phone and I'll come right over."

"I can't believe this is happening," Robin uttered, burying her face in her hands.

"Unfortunately, I can."

Chapter 21

Frank Roberts stepped into the yellow cab he borrowed from his high school buddy and realized his friend hasn't changed. An assortment of empty fast food bags and cigarette butts were on the floor and wedged between the seats. The pine tree-shaped air freshener that hung from the rearview mirror made the inside smell like McDonald's at Christmas time. Frank turned the key and the cab choked, then hummed. He pulled out of the parking lot and drove down the highway.

His first stop was a street corner, two blocks from the hospital. He parked and searched the crowded sidewalks for a homeless guy named Brooks. He walked over to a tiny park with a few trees and bushes and spotted an elderly looking white man, who probably was only fifty, lying on a bench covered with newspaper. His scraggly peppered beard hung over his dirty brown overcoat. His face was covered with dust and slobber. But Brooks knew everything that happened on the streets. He had been living on that bench for the last eight years. He drank a couple gallons of rotgut a day and still outlived his last two doctors. The stench of alcohol mixed with body odor made Frank fan his face as he jammed his finger in Brook's rotund belly. Brooks rolled over and rubbed his eyes, then stared at Frank as if he was crazy. "Can't a man get some sleep, cop?" Brooks asked, struggling to sit up.

"Brooks, when are you going to get yourself to the shelter and get a shower? That smell is enough to kill someone."

"Hey, it keeps the teenagers from fucking with me," Brooks said, pulling a bottle from the inside of his pocket and taking a swig. "So, how can I pry another twenty bucks from your hand today?"

"This will be the easiest money you ever made. But you've got to promise me you won't spend it all on wine, but get yourself something to eat," Frank said, knowing he was talking to a brick wall.

"Hey, there's a lot of nutrition in grapes. Kept me alive this long."

"Whatever you say," Frank said, shaking his head. "I want you to hang out in front of this restaurant and beg for change when I tell you to."

"Shit, I'd do that anyway. You're right, this is an easy twenty."

Frank walked towards the cab as Brooks stumbled behind. He opened the back door, ushering Brooks inside, then started the engine. As he drove down the road, a pungent aroma that smelled like rotten eggs filled the car. He fanned his hand in front of his face and glanced back at Brooks through the rearview mirror. "Did you just shit yourself?"

"Sorry. Must be a bad bottle of Mad Dog," Brooks said, pulling the wine from the bag and examining the bottle.

"Must be," Frank replied, rolling down the window. "Listen, I'm going to point out a person in front of the restaurant. I want you to shake him down for a quarter, a couple of quarters if possible."

"No problem."

Frank drove a block away from the Brooklyn University hospital and pulled out his cellular phone. He instructed Robin to call him when she was leaving the garage and to take a specified route to the restaurant. He pulled out a cigarette and lit a match, exhaling a cloud of smoke through the window. Five minutes later the phone rang. Robin was on her way. Her gray Volvo passed him. He waited a few minutes, then followed. The road was crowded with traffic, but he could still see her Volvo a block away. He swerved recklessly through the traffic, cutting people off, making right hand turns from the left lane, just to keep up with her. As she turned the bend around the corner, a blue Chevy pickup truck was following her. Frank committed the license plate to memory and followed a safe distance behind. She switched to the left-hand lane, as he instructed, and the truck followed. She parked on the left side of the street across from the restaurant and the truck disappeared.

Frank swerved his cab into an alley, knocking Brooks against the door, and took a short cut between the buildings. He emerged from the shadows of two stoic skyscrapers and pulled back onto 33rd Street. His eyes scanned the road like a computerized guided camera, searching for the truck. If it was going back around the block, 33rd Street was the only way to go. He was sure of it. As he turned the corner, he spotted a blue Chevy truck. But was it the same one? It was impossible to see the license plate in all the traffic. He decided to take a gamble and follow it. As the truck pulled around the block, the plate came into view. It was the same vehicle. The truck drove past the restaurant again, this time parking three blocks away.

"What the hell are we doing?" Brooks asked. "You damn near knocked me out cold. Who the hell do you think you are, Evil Knievel?"

"Just listen and do exactly what I say. This is really important," Frank said, parking the car a half block down the road and pulling out his binoculars. He focused the lens on the truck and a large gangly man appeared. He was dressed in a NYU sweatshirt that still didn't cover the thick muscles on his arms and chest. He wore a pair of sunglasses and a New York Yankees baseball cap. "Look through these," Franks said, pulling Brooks over the seat and forcing the binoculars to his eyes. "See that man with the NYU sweatshirt, jeans and Yankee cap?"

"Yeah, looks like a tourist to me. Easy pickin' for some change," Brooks said, looking through the eyepieces.

"You've got to get some change from him, no matter what he does. If he's who I think he is, he won't want a commotion. He should just give up the money with no problem, but drive him crazy if you have to."

"I'm good at that," Brooks replied, bumbling from the taxi. "When do I get my cash?"

"When you get the money."

Frank pulled a Newport from his coat and watched Brooks through the binoculars make an attempt at running. It was more like rambling. Frank wanted to jump from the car and choke him when Brooks stopped to beg change from the wrong man. Stupid, stupid, drunk, old man, Frank thought, pounding the steering wheel. That was the wrong person. Luckily, it must've been a ploy by Brooks not to look so suspicious, because just before the man got to the restaurant, Brooks tapped him on the shoulder and gave him the usual sob story. The man scanned the area as if to say that this was a bad time and reached in his pocket, pulling out a few silver coins. "Sorry for ever doubting you Brooks," Frank said to himself.

Brooks casually walked away, as the man entered the restaurant. A smile expanded on his face that lit up the thick shadow of hair on his face. He plopped into the cab, reached inside his jacket and took a long swig of his Mad Dog, then wiped his mouth with his dirty coat. "Easy as pie," Brooks said, handing Frank a quarter, two dimes and a nickel.

Frank reached inside his pocket and pulled out a small plastic bag with a seal at the top. "Stick them in here," Frank said, opening a plastic bag.

Brooks plopped them in the bag and reclined back in his seat. "What the hell do you want with that change? That's barely enough to buy a donut, cop."

"Long story," Frank replied, putting two drops of fixing solution on the change and pulling a glass slide from the inside of his pocket. "Here, press down on this with your finger."

"What for?" Brooks protested.

"Do you want your money?"

"All right," Brook said, reluctantly.

"Thanks. Where do you want me to drop you off?" Frank asked, handing him twenty bucks.

"You know where. I'm going to be drinking nothing but the finest today, my old friend Jack Daniels."

"If I give you twenty extra bucks and drop you off at a restaurant, will you get yourself something to eat?"

"Ain't nothing like a good clean buzz after a meal. Drop me off at the diner on 32nd. Best flap jacks in the world."

"You better eat."

"I will, I promise."

Frank turned up the next block, hoping that the next time he saw Brooks he was still alive. He fired up another Newport and choked on his first drag. Two packs a day couldn't be healthy, he thought. He reached inside his coat jacket and pulled out a plastic bag and smiled. It was time to find out whom he was dealing with. He knew he wasn't allowed back in the office, but his friend who worked at the FBI would run the prints for him. It was probably going to take a day or two because there were other prints on the change. But at least Brooks would be excluded with his prints on the glass slide.

Frank drove five miles down the road and dropped off the cab. He then caught another cab to the Federal Building and made his way to his friend's lab. He had a lot of explaining to do, but Jimmy Mickles owed him. Jimmy had enough parking tickets to paper a wall and Frank conveniently made them disappear for a little time on the government computer from time to time when he needed it. It may have been illegal, but sometimes you have to bend a few laws to keep up with the criminals, he thought. Hopefully, Jimmy would come through and the hunted would now become the hunter.

CHAPTER 22

Senator Watson relaxed in the back seat of his Limousine, sipping a half-full glass of Crown Royal and Coke while riding down Pennsylvania Avenue. He glanced out the tinted windows and noticed the sunset extend the shadows of the Washington Monument across the grass and sighed, thinking of his day. Same old stuff he had to put up with when Congress was in session: an hour and a half debate over some tiny bull-shit clause in some bill that didn't mean shit. He sometimes could barely keep his eyes open. It was the power that made it all worth it. But he knew his close friend was feeling more and more powerless as each hour passed. He was watching his wife die; a feeling he experienced a year ago when the Lord almost took his twenty-one year old daughter. Senator Watson could barely look in his friend's eyes, for it was tough seeing such a powerful man look so helpless.

How hard could it be to locate that child? He pulled his cellular phone from his coat and dialed the number of his contact. "Anything going on?" he asked, taking a gulp of his drink.

"No word, but we've been combing the foster homes."

"What the fuck is taking so long?" Senator Watson barked. "My friend is dying."

"We've run into some problems."

"Problems? This isn't some high tech mission; all you have to do is just get a five-year-old boy. I know New York City is a big place, but I've seen some of your people find people in some bumfuck country across the world. What's the problem?"

"Well, there are other people involved we have to take care of."

"Who?"

"A cop and two doctors. We have them under close surveillance."

"How much do they know?"

"They know a lot about the woman's body we confiscated, but not enough to make a stink. The cop is already taken care of."

"Who is he?"

"Just a local detective. Supposed to be pretty good, but he'll be going to jail soon."

"What about the doctors?"

"Dr. Orpheus Martin, he's a pathologist, and Dr. Robin Vastbinder is an oncologist. Both work at Brooklyn University. We took care of Dr. Martin, but not Dr. Vastbinder."

"What the hell was that shit with the woman's brother?"

"It was an accident."

"An accident my ass. Are you sure you picked the right men for this job? They seem incompetent to me. Our problems would have been solved if your pinheads hadn't fucked up. Then they let a five-year-old boy get away. I really think I shouldn't have to pay the usual fee."

"If I don't deliver the boy in one week, then we get no payment."

"This isn't fucking pizza delivery, son," Senator Watson said, raising his voice. "Someone's life is at stake. You have one week or there's gonna be a wail of trouble. Do we understand each other?"

"Understood."

"And no more killing. This all has to look legit because I have a funny feeling that once we get the boy, the secret of his blood will be tough to keep and I don't want a trail."

"There's also this Dr. Taylor character from Harvard. We didn't have surveillance in place in Dr. Vastbinder's office when he arrived, so we don't know much about him. Apparently, he used to work at Brooklyn University. That's all we know."

"Well, I would quit worrying about this bullshit and spend more time finding that kid. We're running out of time."

"I'll let you know the first minute we find out anything."

"You better or it's your ass," Senator Watson said, closing his phone.

Senator Watson reached inside the bar next to his armrest, pulled out a bottle of Crown Royal and filled the glass. No soda pop this time. It was the only way he could face his friend and his wife. He couldn't stand the way he would just sit by her bed, staring into the nothingness of the walls, looking for answers. And today, Senator Watson's visit was supposed to end all of his friend's sorrow. Unfortunately, he was nothing more than a shoulder to cry on. He inhaled another gulp of his drink and sighed, looking into the distance, as the White House appeared a block away.

The security guards outside the gates of the White House tapped on the window of his limousine and requested identification. Senator Watson rolled down the window and showed the stone-faced guard his I.D. and the gates opened. He took a last long swig of his drink, hoping it would numb his mind, and exited the car. As he walked towards the reception room, James Warren, the President of the United States, greeted him. Jim always looked like a pretty boy, Senator Watson thought. His teeth were perfectly straight and bleached. Every peppered black hair on his head was strategically placed; it was so perfect it looked like a toupee. But it was real, just like the plastic surgery that removed every blemish on his face and the personal trainer that made his body look ten years younger.

Senator Watson hated that about him ever since college. They were roommates for four years at Yale. Jim was an average student who chased skirts and smoked pot, but he could stir up a student council meeting better than anyone who ever walked the hallways of Yale. He had the chairmen of the law department in his back pocket. Senator Watson had better grades, but never had that 'thing' that separates a senator from a president. Despite the competitive animosity, Senator Watson knew Jim never forgot his friends. Thanks to Jim, he had the most powerful job in the Senate, Chairman of the Budget Committee.

"I hope you have good news," the President said, reaching out his hand.

"I wish I did, but I've got a bunch of shitheads out there searching for the stuff," Senator Watson said, following him into the Oval Office. "How is she?"

"Not good. The doctor says the cancer has spread to her spinal fluid," the President uttered, his eyes flickering with pain. "She acts a bit funny at times."

"What do you mean, *funny*?"

"Sometimes she starts talking to her dead mother or forgets Jim Jr.'s name."

"Poor Jim Jr.," Senator Watson said, firmly grabbing the President's shoulder. "I know this is killing the boy."

"I sometimes don't know what to say to him. You know he's dropped out of M.I.T. because of all of this. He just sits there day after day and watches her. It's...making me crazy."

"Don't worry, partner. The stuff that cured my baby girl is going to save your wife, I guarantee it."

"By the way, have you ever found out what this stuff is?"

"I'm not sure you want to know that information," Senator Watson said, reaching in his pocket and pulling out a toothpick.

"I want to know," the President said, looking him firmly in the eyes.

"Blood from a kid."

"From a kid?"

"He won't be harmed. It isn't like we need all of his blood, or so these doctors tell me. Just a couple pints."

"So what's so special about this blood?"

"Supposedly, he has something in it that kills only cancer cells and leaves the healthy ones alone."

"I see," the President said, looking reflectively into the distance. "So, how long?"

"No idea. My best people are on it as we speak," Senator Watson said, following him into the master bedroom. Inside was the First Lady on the bed with Jim Jr. sitting by her side, holding her hand as she slept. Her once radiant skin was pale; the flesh seemed to hang off her like a coat on a rack. Her piercing blue eyes sunk deep in her skull, making her head look like a skeleton with flesh. Multiple I.V. poles and plastic tubes surrounded her like tree branches in a jungle. Slowly she opened her eyes. "Tom Watson," she said with a smile.

"Sophia," Senator Watson said, kneeling down by her side. "How are you feeling?"

"Like I look," she said, trying to get up. "Son, would you please go get something to eat? Your sitting here isn't going to help."

"Your mother's right," the President said, walking over to his chair and leading his son out of the room. "You go."

Jim Jr. gave her a peck on the cheek, and then left the room. The look in his eyes killed Senator Watson. "Can I get you some broth?" the President asked, kneeling by her side.

"No, I just would like to rest now, if that's O.K.," she said, fixing her blankets. "That damn pain medicine makes it tough to keep my eyes open for more than an hour."

"You get some rest," Senator Watson said, kissing her on the forehead. "Soon, you'll be up and around again. We'll see to that. You just get your rest."

"Thanks, Tom."

Senator Watson followed the President out of the room, rubbing his forehead, glancing somberly towards the floor. "How long have the doctors given her?"

"A few weeks. They apparently sent her home to die," the President uttered, staring out of the window. "You know, Tom, she is the only woman I ever loved."

"She's the only woman you've only did more than sleep with," Senator Watson said, with a smile trying to break the tension.

"Tom, do whatever it takes. Stop at nothing."

"You don't have to worry about that, partner," he said, putting his arm around his shoulder. "We'll tear down a mountain if we have to."

Chapter 23

The thick rain obscured Judd Isla's view as he drove up and down the streets of North Jersey, searching for Jacob Johnson. Judd had been banging on all the doors in the entire neighborhood, posing as a child welfare agent, dressed in multiple disguises, searching for a lead on the whereabouts of the Johnson boy; no one knew a thing about him until today. An elderly man who plays gin at the local community center recalled one of his partners, Marge Henderson, telling him about a little boy who came to her house in the middle of the night. The boy was mute and African American; it was him.

Judd squinted his eyes through the windows of the Ford Explorer, looking for the address, as Nevin Cuff typed on his laptop computer. Nevin was supposed to be pulling up the file on Frank Roberts, but knowing him, he was surfing the net. Judd decided a long time ago that he would do the difficult jobs on his own. Nevin was only good for the muscle; he didn't know a thing about counterintelligence. He was reckless and it was too late to trade him in for a more experienced operative. This was supposed to be an easy job, Judd thought, as he turned the corner and glanced at the map on his lap.

"Did you find that file on him?" Judd asked, lighting a cigarette.

"What?" Nevin replied, entranced by the screen.

"The file, you fuck, on that cop."

"I'm checking out these bitches on the Internet. Frank Roberts is burnt toast."

"If he's so burnt, then how did he get away from me?"

"Because you're old and fat," Nevin scoffed. "Shit would've never happened to me."

"Believe me, this guy is good. He's not stupid and careless like you."

"See, people like you make my job hard," Nevin said, staring wildly into Judd's eyes. "We kill people. It's not fucking brain surgery. All we have to do is kill people and make them disappear. Now, if I were leading, this shit would've been over. Four bullets, four problems gone. But no, we have to follow them, check out what they ate for dinner and see what color their shit was. It's bullshit. You see how easy it was for that hooker's brother to disappear? And what do we have to show for all our surveillance? Not a damn thing. We have no idea where the kid is and we're getting shit from the top, all because you were too slow to catch a five year old boy."

"Don't preach to me. I was killing heads-of-state in every country in this world before you were old enough to suck a tit. And the one thing I learned is you must know whom you're dealing with. Anybody can be a tough guy, but they're usually dead before they're forty. And I don't think dying is something you want to do, so pull up the file."

Nevin's eyes moved back and forth as he logged onto the government computer. He placed his finger on the mouse pad and a red light beeped, then clicked. He pulled up Frank Roberts' file from the New York City police computer and his face appeared on the screen, along with pages of information. "What do we got on him?" Judd asked.

"Nothing really special. He's a company man. Busted up some internal corruption, great with missing persons. No special training. No medals."

"What about his past?"

"Ex-football star at Michigan, B student in criminology…I told you he's not Superman. I could pick out hundreds of cops on any police force in any big city and their files would look exactly the same."

"That's what worries me. He's unpredictable."

"He's nothing. He'll never beat that cocaine rap. They have enough on him to put him away for twenty years. Our man on the inside made sure of that."

"What about our man?" Judd asked, lighting a cigarette. "When have you heard from him last?"

"Yesterday. They are making plans to detain him two weeks for a minute bail violation. He'd need a miracle to clear his name in two weeks. This guy is done. Let's move on and get the kid. We only have a week left."

"Hopefully, this old woman will know where he is."

Judd made a right at the light onto Oak Street, which was four blocks away from Nicole's brother's home. He looked at the rows of oak trees that surrounded the thirty-year-old, split-level homes and banged the steering wheel in frustration, thinking about the night the kid got away. The alleys behind the houses were cluttered with gravel and old lawn equipment; he still had a bump on his shin from repeatedly banging his leg while trying to maneuver through the junk in the darkness. In the distance, he heard a soft rumble that sounded like a creek. He passed over the bridge and glanced out the window. A hundred yards up stream was the place the little bastard smashed him with a rock. He had killed some of the best operatives the KGB had and a fucking five-year-old kid gets away. Unbelievable, he thought. He would never underestimate the kid again.

"This is the place," Judd said, stopping in front of the red brick split-level home, with a manicured yard and two-car garage. "Wait here," Judd said to Nevin, leaving the car.

"How long will you be?"

"As long as it takes," Judd replied, intrusively.

"I'm going to get a quick bite. You want anything?"

"Just bring me back a burger."

"Burger it is."

Judd pulled his umbrella from the back seat and walked up the driveway. The thick raindrops changed to a drizzle as he rang the doorbell. A thin elderly woman, with white hair and a slight hunch, answered the door. She reminded him of his grandmother. "Can I help you?" she asked.

"My name is Terry Stein," Judd said, flashing his fake I.D. "I'm with the child welfare office. I was wondering if I could ask you a few questions about a boy that came to your house a few days ago."

"You mean that adorable, mute black kid?" she said, her eyes drooping with empathy. "I felt so bad for him. He just shook and shook as if he'd seen the devil."

"I heard. A shame, isn't it. Poor kid has been abused all his life," Judd said, halfheartedly. "Do you have any idea where the child is?"

"Somebody from your office came to get him."

"I know, but we've had a big mix-up since we had these layoffs two days ago and I just picked up his case. The place is like a zoo."

"I can imagine. I read about them in the newspaper. Damn politicians."

"Yeah, politicians. Listen, do you happen to remember the name of the social worker?"

"I think her name was Whitney Jiles."

"Do you remember the office?"

"I think it was in Fort Lee."

"Thanks. You've been a big help."

"I hope you find him. The poor boy, he's alone."

"Don't worry, ma'am, he won't be for long."

Chapter 24

Dr. Robin Vastbinder rubbed her eyes as she glanced at the pile of charts she still had to dictate before she went home. She had seen twelve patients in her office, rounded on five in the hospital and still had a heap of work to do. And all she could think about was the thousands of eyes that seemed to be watching her every notion. The man in the parking lot with suspicious eyes dominated her every thought. And the new nurse on the second floor tracked her every move. The five scotches and water she drank last night did nothing but intensify the paranoia. Going to work was like walking through a minefield and she was certain a bomb was about to explode.

She took her black pumps off and rubbed her feet. They thumped almost as bad as her head. She fumbled though the pile of charts on her desk and began examining Nicole's chart again. She pulled opened the drawer underneath her desk, took out a silver flask of scotch, and took a swig. The alcohol always helped the headache and the slight tremor in her hand. Every page on the chart was practically committed to memory, but for some reason she felt she was missing something. Why couldn't Dr. Loventhol let the world know about Nicole Johnson? He could assemble the greatest minds in the country to come up with a method to replicate the process. Was he so greedy that he wanted all the credit himself? She flipped to the last page of the chart and realized something. Nicole Johnson's blood was O negative, the universal donor. It would be possible to transfuse her blood into cancer patients. He probably was unable to find a way to keep the virus alive long enough to infect the mutated cells and decided to give the transfusions a chance.

She turned on the computer on her desk and looked up Dr. Taylor's number. Hopefully, he had been able to contact Dr. Loventhol and pick his brain. She had called his office four times in the past week, and unfortunately, she hadn't heard from him. It made her a bit apprehensive, considering what has been happening to her. Crossing her legs, she picked up the phone and dialed.

"Hello?"

"Dr. Taylor?"

"Yes?"

"It's Robin."

"Sorry I hadn't got back to you yet, but I did a little looking around and it was a waste of time. I was in North Dakota the past few days visiting the Loventhol clinic. That bastard finally agreed to let me come see the place because I threatened to sue. He didn't even meet me at the clinic. He had one of his assistants show me around. All I got to see was a bunch of herbs and chelation machines of the so-called alternative medicine front I think he's using. It was more like a country club than anything else."

"Did you know that Nicole's blood type was O negative?"

"I was unaware."

"I think Dr. Loventhol was transfusing her blood to the cancer patients, which decreased her viral load enough to succumb to her cancer."

"How can you prove it?"

"The only thing we have is the results from her protein electrophoresis which documents the rise and fall in the mysterious protein that no one seems to know anything about."

"That's nothing. We need patients treated at the clinic. It's our only chance."

"I wish I knew where to start."

"I have a few leads. Yesterday, I spoke with a hematologist from UCLA during a departmental teleconference and one of his patients went to the Loventhol clinic. He didn't say whether she's dead or alive, but I think we have a chance."

"What's her name?" Robin replied.

"He said he'd get back to me in a day or two. I was about to give him a call. Why don't I call you when I find out and we take a field trip?"

"Sounds like a plan," Robin said, signing a chart. "But, don't call me here, I'll give you a different office," Robin said anxiously. "Someone placed a wire in my home."

"What?"

"It's complicated, but I think you should be careful."

"Now I'm beginning to think it wasn't my imagination on the way home from the airport. A black truck seemed to be following me."

Robin felt a wave of anxiety pulse through her fingers when she realized his phone might be tapped as well. They would know everything; the discovery of the tap, their plans. And it was the 'they' that bothered her the most. Who were 'they'? Hopefully, Frank found some answers.

"Listen, I've got to go. Don't call me, I'll be in touch." Robin said abruptly, hanging up.

How could I be so stupid, Robin said to herself? Now 'they' would know and the facade would be over. She took a long swig of the flask, hoping to drown the terror that infiltrated her mind. Quickly, she glanced at her watch. Where was Frank? He said he would contact her, but how? The loneliness was tearing her soul apart. She couldn't go to the police, the FBI, or even her boss. They would all think she was crazy. She hasn't had a good night's sleep in almost a year since the accident. And now, the accident was the least of her problems. She knew that 'they' would make a move soon. Her worst nightmares couldn't fathom what the move would be.

Robin placed her flask back in her purse and walked back to the bathroom. As she put her keys in the door, she stopped, thinking about her conversation with Dr. Taylor. Maybe if she had scientific proof that Nicole Johnson's blood could cure cancer, then it would strengthen her case when they found a patient willing to let her test their blood. She walked inside the bathroom and teased her hair with a brush, trying to cover the split ends, then washed her face. She brushed her teeth briskly, covering up the smell of the alcohol, and slapped makeup on her face, trying to cover the blemishes of the hung-over mornings. Hopefully, Orpheus had enough blood samples left to mix with the blood of one of her leukemia patients, she thought as she left her office.

The ugly, speckled blue tile of the pathology department reminded Robin how cheap the hospital had become over the past few years. She had to argue an hour with a nurse at an insurance company to approve a bone marrow transplant for a thirty-five year old man with two kids. A nurse who never treated an oncological patient in her life, made life and death decisions from some book that Robin was sure the nurse didn't understand. And the hospital was countering the insurance companies with layoff and cutbacks. In a two-week span, Orpheus had lost three technicians and lab space, Robin thought, as she passed the empty room filled with dusty, broken lab equipment. She reached Orpheus's office and knocked on the door. "Come in," Orpheus uttered.

Orpheus's face had lost its usual glow; his eyes seemed distant and removed. He was sitting at his desk, index finger and thumb pressed tightly against his wrinkled forehead, reading a pathology journal. "I was wondering if I could test a theory I have about Nicole's blood?"

"There isn't anything left," Orpheus said, shortly.

"What do you mean there isn't any left?" Robin huffed, placing her hands on her hips. "Two days ago you said you had enough blood…"

"That was two days ago," Orpheus snapped back, standing from his desk, placing the book on the shelf. "I used the last of the samples yesterday, while trying to isolate more of the virus."

"Without me?"

"Do I have to consult you for everything I do?" Orpheus replied.

"On this you do."

"Well, sorry," Orpheus barked, reaching for his long, white lab coat and leaving the office.

What the hell was wrong with Orpheus? Robin thought, scurrying behind him as he left the office. "What's up your ass?" Robin asked.

"I don't want to hear about that prostitute again," Orpheus snapped back, pointing. "Not another word. As far as I'm concerned, the case is closed."

"What happened? Are you being followed or harassed? You've got to tell me. Two little boys' lives are at stake."

"The streets are a tough place, Robin. Those boys' lives were doomed the day they were born to that woman," Orpheus replied, resuming his quickened steps. "I'm not taking any blame for that."

"So, I guess they got to you, didn't they?"

"No one got to me, Robin. I just don't want people following me around. That's all. It's not worth it. Some things are better left alone."

"So, that's it? You're gonna let those people exploit those children, maybe even kill them because you're not man enough to help."

"I don't have time for this," Orpheus said, with the vessels in his brown forehead turning purple. "I've got a meeting and you're making me late."

"Fine, go to your meeting," Robin yelled, pointing. "Because if you think you can hide from all of this, you're highly mistaken. You're in this whether you like it or not."

Robin stopped and threw her arms in the air as Orpheus continued down the hallway. What had made him have such a sudden change of heart? How had they gotten to him? She was sure the samples were gone and now they had nothing. If Dr. Taylor found one of the patients treated at the Loventhol clinic, it would be impossible to prove that they were getting transfusions from Nicole Johnson. The muscles in her entire body tightened as she stomped towards the elevator. And what about Detective Roberts? It had been almost 24 hours since she had heard from him last. Was he in jail or dead? What was he doing? What was he thinking? she thought, rubbing her temples on the elevator. She may be alone.

Robin entered her office and walked over to the window. It was a cloudy day with the streets crowded with people in business suits intermingled with panhandlers. She scanned the tightly compact buildings that crowded the skyline and wished that her flask wasn't empty. Looking at her watch, she realized it was already noon and in one hour she had five patients to see and still hadn't done any of her charts from the morning. She sat down at her desk and reluctantly picked up a chart. She was about to begin dictating a history and physical into the small tape recorder when she noticed an envelope with no return address on her incoming bin on the corner of her desk. Dropping the chart, she picked up the letter and opened it. *Meet me at the Embassy Suites, on the 12th, seven o'clock. Go to room 735, and knock four times. I'll be there. Frank.*

Chapter 25

A thick wind almost blew Robin's umbrella from her hand as she entered the twelve-story Embassy Suites hotel. It had been raining non-stop for the past three days; it seemed like monsoon season in New York City. The lobby was filled with bellhops carrying luggage on gold painted racks, men in business suits laughing softly, sipping their drinks with women walking by their sides in long elegant dresses. And cute little girls and boys, with food stains on their miniature suits and dresses, running around the lobby as if it were a playground. Probably a wedding reception, she thought. For a moment, a smile broke through the wrinkles and dark circles on her face as she thought about the first wedding her son attended. His little tuxedo made him look like a little prince. He was the ring bearer and his eyes were so serious as he walked up the aisle of her sister's wedding. She remembered how nervous he was and a tear came to her eye. What she wouldn't give to have that moment back for just one second.

Robin glanced at her watch. She was ten minutes late. As she walked towards the elevator, a large man with long gangly arms and thick eyebrows seemed to be shadowing behind her. She quickly jumped on an empty elevator and rode it to the eighth floor, then walked down a flight of steps to make sure no one had followed her. In the middle of the long corridor, with soft lights at each end and a plush checkered carpet on the floor, was room 735. She knocked four times, and Frank answered. He was dressed in a dark blue sweat suit, with a New York Giants baseball cap. The room was quite large, with a small living room area and kitchen in the first room, and two beds and a T.V. in the other room.

"Did anyone follow you?" Frank asked, closing the door.

"There was a man in the lobby who may have been watching me, but I wasn't sure because I'm so damn paranoid these days. I think I gave him the slip."

"It's O.K.," Frank said, sitting on the couch, pulling a folder off the coffee table and handing it to Robin. "I think I know who's been keeping you awake at night.

Robin opened the folder and found a piece of paper with the photo of a man with thick cheekbones, short black hair and heavy eyebrows. His eyes were deep-set and intense, as if he were ready to snap at any moment. His name was Nevin Cuff. "Where did you get this?"

"Long story, but I'll need to borrow two thousand dollars," Frank said, pulling a bottle of Vodka from the bar. "Would you like a drink?"

"Got any scotch?" Robin asked, reclining on the couch.

"Beer, vodka and wine," Frank replied, pulling two glasses from the shelves.

"Vodka and tonic," Robin said. "So, who is this guy?"

"He's CIA."

Robin's stomach contracted, forcing caustic bile into her throat. CIA? They could do just about anything they wanted. What would the CIA have to do with Nicole Johnson? She wasn't a spy. "But, why?"

"Can't believe it myself," Frank said, handing her the drink and taking a sip of his. "They have no jurisdiction in the U.S., unless they're working with the FBI, and why the FBI would be involved is beyond me."

Robin reexamined the photo. "That looks like the man who was following me in the lobby," she said anxiously, taking a large gulp of her drink.

"I wouldn't doubt it."

"Where have you been?"

"Various hotels around the city. It's getting tougher and tougher to give them the slip. I know they have my place tapped, which is how I've been crossing their signals. I tell them I'm going to one place and then go to another."

"I think they've figured out we know about the tap."

"How?"

"I called Dr. Taylor today and I think they probably have his line tapped because someone had been following him as well. And I kinda told him about the tap."

"Damn," Frank said, slamming his fist on the counter. "Now what?"

"I think I know why someone would go through all this trouble. I believe they were using Nicole's blood to treat cancer patients."

Frank fixed himself another drink and looked reflectively into his glass. "Can you prove it?"

"Maybe, if we can test the blood of one of those patients and get a sample of Nicole's blood. Unfortunately, all the samples of her blood are supposedly missing. Orpheus got a case of cold feet and wants no part of this anymore."

"I still don't get the connection," Frank said, pacing. "The only thing I can think of is the government wants this boy for a reason, but I still don't understand why the CIA would be involved. They do all the international stuff, unless someone has rented them for something they didn't want the rest of the government to know."

"Someone important must be sick. It's the only thing I can think of."

"That's what bothers me the most. I wish this were the mob. At least I would know what I'm dealing with. I know they have some local people on the take, but the CIA can do just about anything. They've orchestrated so much evidence against me, there's no way I can stay out of prison unless I prove that Nicole's brother was murdered by that goon, and the chances of that are slim to none. They know everything about us, our families and friends, what school we went to. They probably even know what color we shit. Our only chance is probably the press, but this story would end up in a tabloid without any evidence."

"If Dr. Taylor comes through with a patient treated at the Loventhol clinic, that might be the first step."

"That still doesn't get me my son. And who knows where Jacob is? I've got a few leads, but I'm practically off the force and getting information has been pretty difficult, even from my reliable sources. Nicole had her problems, but she sure loved her children. That's why she humped on those streets every night, it was just that shit."

Robin looked into his eyes and saw the pain, the frustration. She couldn't imagine if someone told her that her son was alive and she was helpless to save him. "I guess you really loved her."

"I don't know if it was love," Frank uttered, staring out of the window. "I needed someone, someone who understood me, and she always did. My wife had just left me...well...I left her after I found her in bed with some big shot investment banker who would give her the big house and all that other materialistic bullshit she loved. I left that night and drove the streets. I drove those streets all night, drinking and wondering if risking my ass every day was really worth it. Then, I found her, just standing alone on the corner. It was as if she was just waiting for me. She looked like a homecoming queen in leather. I picked her up and we did nothing but talk. It was the first time I could remember that I'd rather talk to a beautiful woman than sleep with her. So, every night after work, I would pick her up and we would go eat. One thing led to another and I guess I got used to her."

"Sounds to me like you loved her."

"Maybe I did," Frank uttered, his blue eyes dimming. "In some twisted sort of way. There still isn't a day when I don't think about her and Jacob. And, well, my son...if I knew the kid was mine, I would never have abandoned him. I remember the day my own father died. I was only ten. We sat in that waiting room for hours, praying for a miracle after his heart attack, but I guess he was down too long and his brain was mush. My mom tried to make up for the loss, but everyday I went to baseball practice and saw the other kids' fathers in the stands. I knew I would never enjoy baseball again. I would hate it if my son felt like that for one moment."

"I couldn't imagine what it would feel like to know I have a child and I couldn't see him," Robin said, sprawling out on the couch, fluffing a pillow under her head. "It's the greatest thing, you know. To feel their tiny little bodies against your chest. And he had this look, I can't quite explain it, but I knew our souls were connected when he looked at me that way. I know he's gone, but I don't regret a moment we had together."

"What about your husband?"

"We had our problems, like everyone else, but I don't think I could love like that again. He knew things about me that I didn't know about myself. He wasn't the kind of man that would let you know how he feels, but he could look at you with those brown eyes of his, and I just knew. I knew it was supposed to be forever."

Frank strolled over to the phone on the coffee table and picked it up. "I'm getting some room service. What would you like?"

"Something light," Robin replied, brushing her hair from her eyes. The alcohol had irritated her stomach and the sight of food didn't seem so appetizing. "A bowl of soup and some crackers."

"You sure? I'm ordering a big steak. You need to eat."

"I don't know how you can eat a steak, after all we've been through," Robin said, sitting up.

"Food is like a drug to me, it calms me down. I'm ordering you one."

"I don't eat red meat."

"So, you're one of those people?"

"What?"

"You know, save the whales and hug a tree while you're doing it."

"No, I just don't eat red meat."

"Chicken it is."

Frank was right. The chicken sandwich eased the burning in her stomach. She finished the last bite of her meal and poured herself a glass of wine. "So, what are we going to do?"

"Well, first, I'm going back to the station and telling my boss about all of this," Frank said, wiping his face with a napkin. "My boss knows I didn't steal those drugs. We go back a long way. I know he'll help us. Then, I'm going to Pittsburgh to find this Aaron Rankin character. His pay stub was in the wallet I found with Nicole's stuff."

"So, he worked at the Loventhol clinic?"

"Yeah, and I'll break his neck if he doesn't tell me where my son is. You can stay here and continue searching for Jacob. Hopefully, that goon didn't get to him first."

Robin took a spoonful of soup and noticed a piece of bread dangling from Frank's mouth. She hoped his chewing motion would knock it loose, but it stayed affixed to his cheek as if it were riveted there. "You've got something on your cheek," Robin said.

Frank wiped his face with his napkin, only removing half of the bread. "Here, let me get it. It's driving me nuts," Robin said, reaching out her hand. His rough skin felt erotic, his lips were soft. She stared into his blue eyes that looked as innocent as a child, and a weird feeling overcame her. A feeling she hadn't had in a year. Maybe it was the alcohol or the stress, but whatever it was, she had to kiss him. He got up from his chair and went behind her, his firm hands massaging her back in a circular motion, his lips softly kissing her neck. "It's been such a long time," she said softly into his ear.

"Do you want me to stop?" Frank whispered, pulling away.

Robin's head thought no; she wasn't ready for a physical relationship with anyone other than her husband. But, the way he caressed her body made her forget about the lonely sleepless nights and the empty spot next to her in bed. She kissed him softly, and then rubbed her fingernails across the soft hair on his chest. Frank scooped her off her feet and carried her to the bed. At first, it was difficult to make love, but his soft touch made her relax. She never imagined her heart would ever let her orgasm again, but Frank seemed to hit all the right spots. She curled in his arms, with her head on his chest, and fell asleep.

Chapter 26

Frank rolled over in bed, expecting to feel Robin's warm body by his side. He methodically opened his eyes and reached out to touch her body. But she was gone. He rubbed his temples, trying to subdue the throb that pounded against his head from the alcohol and searched the living room to find Robin pouring herself another drink. "Isn't it a little early for a drink?" Frank uttered, rubbing his face.

"Best thing in the world for a hang over," Robin said, coughing.

"I think you should take it easy with that stuff," Frank said, grabbing the bottle.

"I'm not a child," Robin growled, grabbing back the bottle of wine.

"How are we supposed to get through this if you keep doing this to yourself?"

"Doing what?"

"Look, I went through this once with Nicole, I'm not about to do this with you."

"Well, maybe if you believed her, none of this would've happened," Robin barked, her temples pulsating.

Frank glared into her eyes, wondering if sleeping with her was such a good idea. Now, he felt connected, which seemed to bring out the worst in people. Her words were like tiny little daggers that pounded holes into his heart. What did she know about his love for Nicole and how difficult it would've been to marry a hooker? His career would've been over. "I don't have time for this," Frank snapped, gathering his clothes.

"Please…I'm sorry," Robin said, grabbing Frank's hands while dumping the wine down the sink. "You're right, it's just hard these days and after last night…it just brought back a lot of memories."

"I understand, but if we're going to save those children…"

"I know, I'll get myself together," Robin said.

"Here's the list of foster homes I have it narrowed down to."

"These are all over New York," Robin huffed, examining the list. "This is going to take forever."

"Is there anyone you can trust?"

"I think the social worker at the hospital could help."

"Don't tell her a thing. Just say you're interested in finding out what happened to the boy, and that you were considering adopting him."

"What do I do if I find out where he is?"

"Just call the station and ask for Captain Dennis Irwin. I'm sure after we have our little talk today, I think I'll change his mind."

"Where will you be?"

"In Pittsburgh. I'll call you when I come back. Should only be a day."

"Be careful," Robin said, giving him a gentle peck on the lips. "And about last night…"

"I know, me too," Frank replied, kissing her back.

* * *

Frank knocked on the door of Dennis Irwin's office and walked inside. Dennis was reclined in his chair leafing through a stack of papers while talking on the phone. Frank walked over to the coffee machine and poured himself a cup. He looked at the pictures on the wall and smiled. Dennis loved sports and had pictures of himself with the players of the World Champion Yankees of 95' and Giants of 91'. He remembered going to the Super Bowl with him and how drunk they got and went to the strip joints all around New Orleans. It was the biggest party of his life.

"Where have you been?" Dennis snapped. "Been trying to get in touch with you for three days."

"Long story," Frank replied, sipping his coffee. "But I think I know why someone would put a kilo of cocaine in my trunk."

"Who?"

"The CIA."

"Have you really lost your mind?" Dennis asked, rolling his eyes. "I guess you're a spy now."

"I know it sounds crazy, but I have proof. My phone lines are tapped and my apartment is bugged. They even planted taps in a doctor's home from Brooklyn hospital."

"Frank, I think you need some help," Dennis said, his eyes concerned. "Have you been using that shit?"

"Listen, I don't have time for this. I thought we were friends."

"That's why I think you should get some help."

"Do you remember me telling you about Nicole Johnson and her two sons?"

"Yes."

"If I don't find them soon, the boys could be dead. Nicole Johnson's blood cures cancer and I think someone held her and her children against their will to transfuse their blood into dying patients."

"I don't know, Frank," Dennis said, rubbing his neck. "Blood cures cancer? That sounds pretty weak to me."

"It's the truth," Frank scowled, pointing. "And they have my son. Imagine if you never got to see Dennis Jr. again?"

Dennis leaned back in his chair, his eyes distant, deep in the thought. He took a long sip of his coffee and examined Frank's face. "Do you have any evidence?"

"I can get one of the bugs in Dr. Vastbinder's house and I have prints of one of the operatives."

"How did you get prints of a CIA agent?"

"Long story, but it's legit."

"How can I be sure you didn't concoct this wild story to cover your own ass?"

"Our friendship should be enough, shouldn't it?"

"So, what if this bug thing is true? How can you link your son's disappearance to this bug?"

"I need to go to Pittsburgh for a day," Frank said.

"Impossible," Dennis said, sternly. "Your arraignment is in three days."

"It's the only chance I have," Frank pleaded. "Nicole had the wallet of a man that worked at the lab I think they held her in. It had a check stub with his address. I know I can break him down. He could link all of this together…well…enough to start an investigation. And hopefully, we'll have her five-year-old boy, Jacob. If someone could get him to speak, all of this would be over."

The look in Dennis's eyes made Frank uneasy. They were nervous and suspicious, as if he didn't believe a word Frank was saying. He understood that he was putting Dennis in a compromising position, considering what had happened with the internal investigation of the stolen drugs three months ago. The papers were watching the department's every move and the mayor's office had his ass in a vise. "Twenty-four hours, that's it. One second more and I'll put your ass under the jail, you got me?" Dennis snapped.

"I knew you'd come through. A Dr. Robin Vastbinder may be calling with the location of Jacob. You have to get there before those boys from the CIA," Frank said, getting up from his chair and placing his arm around Dennis. "You won't regret this."

"I already do."

Chapter 27

A brisk wind swept through the Pittsburgh Greater International Airport, bringing a chill to Frank's face as he picked up his overnight bag and stepped off the shuttle. It was ten o'clock at night, with a half moon in the sky, fighting to shine through the breaks in the thick clouds. He picked up his bags, strolled through the main terminal and made his way to the parking lot. He inserted the key into his Chevy Lumina rental car and jumped inside, all the while hoping he could find Aaron Rankin in 24 hours and get back to New York in time before Dennis was in deep shit. As he turned on the engine, he checked his rearview mirror, looking for any suspicious vehicles. He had taken five different cabs to the subway into Manhattan, then took another cab to the airport. It was getting tougher and tougher to hide from the CIA agents. But the fear of the ever-looming eyes of the government was not important, because nothing would keep him from his son. He glanced at his watch and realized time was short, so luck had to be on his side.

Frank drove out of the parking lot and merged onto Route 376 east. He pulled out the worn pay stub and examined the address. It was located in Swissvale, approximately thirty minutes east from his location. He lit a cigarette and clicked on the radio. Pink Floyd's *Wish You Were Here* blared through the speakers, reminding him how much he missed Nicole and his child. But to his surprise, Robin entered his mind; her smooth skin, piercing green eyes and voluptuous figure made him wish he could make love to her again. It had been awhile since he had sex, almost eight months; the longest he had ever went. And being drunk in the presence of a beautiful woman made everything so easy. Her nude, warm body soothed the pain of his ex-wife and Nicole. But, it was a heat of the moment thing, he reminded himself. What would a doctor want with an unsophisticated cop?

The road narrowed to two lanes and the Fort Pitt tunnels appeared. When he emerged from the mile long darkness, the compact skyline of Pittsburgh appeared. It was only one-tenth the size of Manhattan, but the way the three rivers met at the apex of Three Rivers Stadium made the town seem as majestic as any. He passed downtown and went through another tunnel, and the Swissvale exit appeared on the right. He checked his rearview mirror and drove off the highway.

Aaron Rankin lived on Maple Avenue, which was three blocks to the right, through two traffic lights, or so the attendant at the BP station said. Aaron Rankin probably had more rap sheets than underwear from the information he gathered from the computer at work. He had spent four years in the state penitentiary for racketeering and assault with a deadly weapon. He apparently was trying to collect money for one of the local drug dealers and shot the guy in the leg. How does a guy with a record get hired to work at a scientific lab facility? He couldn't wait to find the answer.

Frank parked beside the ten-story brick apartment building and got out of his car. He buzzed the intercom in the vestibule, outside the lobby, and a deep voice answered. "Who's there?"

"Is this Mr. Aaron Rankin?"

"Yeah, who is this?"

"NYPD."

There was a moment of silence, which made Frank nervous.

"NYPD? If you're here looking for trouble, you better speak to my lawyer, cop."

"I'd just like to ask you a few questions about your employer."

"I was fired two weeks ago."

"You're not in any trouble, I'd just like to ask you some questions. May I please come in?"

"You've got three minutes."

The door buzzed and Frank pushed it open. He rode the elevator to the ninth floor and knocked on apartment number six at the end of the hallway. The door opened and an obese black male answered. His face was twice the size of Frank's, with droopy skin folds sagging from his chin. He had a full beard and was dressed in an over stretched white tee shirt and baggy sweat pants. Aaron's eyes narrowed as he showed him inside his one bedroom, efficiency apartment. "What do you want?" Aaron asked sharply.

"May I sit down?" Frank asked, showing him his badge he lifted from Dennis's desk. "I had a long trip."

"You can do whatever you want, but now you've got only two minutes, cop."

"I came here to return something you've lost."

"What, my job?" Aaron replied caustically.

"Your wallet," Frank said, handing it to him. "It seems you had it stolen."

The man's eyes weakened and then became nervous. "You came the whole way from New York just to give me my wallet?"

"Yeah, and to find out why Nicole Johnson ended up with it."

"I don't know what you're talking about," Aaron replied, unable to look Frank in the eyes. "Never heard of that bitch in my life."

"That's funny. She's heard of you," Frank said, lying. "She said she met you at the Loventhol clinic where she was held captive."

Aaron's eyes widened. The muscles in his face tightened. "You're barking up the wrong tree, cop."

"That's not what she said," Frank scowled, getting up from his seat, moving closer to his face. "She said that you were one of the people that made her stay there against her will. And for some reason, your name is the only one she remembered."

"Well, if she told you, then why are you here?" Aaron asked, tightening his fist. "You can talk this shit over with my lawyer. Get the fuck out of my crib. You ain't got nothing on me."

Frank jumped at Aaron, catching him by surprise, and threw him to the ground. He pulled out his 9mm and rammed it into his right nostril. He didn't have time for bullshit. He pictured his innocent child lying in a crib, crying for his mother. His only child, alone, unable to protect himself from the experiments the scientists ran on him every day. This guy was going to talk. "There's a little boy in that place, and if anything happens to him, I'll make sure the only thing you see for the rest of your life is the inside of a fucking cage. Now tell me, where the fuck is he?"

"I'm not going down alone for this one," Aaron said, trying to push the gun from his face. "I only did what I was told."

"So your memory is improving."

"I'm not going back to jail for some two bit job that I got fired from."

"Well, maybe if you help me, we can prevent that."

Frank released his grip and lowered his gun, still keeping it by his side. He knew it was bad form, but he had no choice. Time was running out on his career, his freedom. And most of all, his son's life. Aaron's eyes were horrified as he sat down on his couch and snatched a pack of cigarettes from the coffee table. His hands subtly trembled as he lit a Newport, inhaled and exhaled violently. "So, what the fuck do you want to know?"

"The check stub doesn't list the address of the clinic. Where is it?"

"North Dakota, fifty miles outside of Bismarck, in the middle of nowhere. I'm surprised anyone knows the place. Supposed to be one of those bullshit alternative medicine places for cancer. One of my boys in my cellblock got me the job, said it was an easy two thousand a week, all legit. I jumped on it. Hell, I'd go anywhere for two thousand a week just to guard a hooker. But I never understood why they paid me to watch her."

"Why was she there?"

"No idea. All I know is that they took her blood like fucking vampires, sometimes two quarts a day, and all I had to do was stand guard in front of her room."

"What about her children?"

"Never saw much of them. They would let her see them twice a day, if she gave them all the blood they needed."

Frank felt the rage build inside. He wanted to add another bump to Aaron's nose, but couldn't. He needed him. "So, who ran this place?" Frank asked.

"The man who signed my checks, that Loventhol dude."

"Where can I find him?"

"Don't have a clue. No one who works there has ever seen him, not even my boss, the head of security."

"So why did you get fired?"

"I'm sure that whore told you."

"No, she didn't," Frank snapped.

"Bitch put some shit in my drink, went to sleep for a day, woke up and my wallet, truck and two thousand a week were gone. That bitch would've been dead if I caught her."

"So exactly where is this place?"

"In Minot, fifty miles outside of Bismarck."

"Do you know if her son is still there?" Frank barked, his face turning scarlet, raising his gun again.

"Calm down, man," Aaron uttered, raising his hands. "I don't know."

"If you want to stay out of jail, you'll testify against the Loventhol clinic."

"I told you, I ain't going down for this one. I'll never go back to that place. I only did as I was told. I had no idea why they made me keep her there. If I have to bring down those rich pricks to save my own ass, no problem."

"The local police will be watching your every move," Frank warned, putting his gun back in his shoulder holster. "So don't leave town. And if I find out you're lying, I'll be back…this time with a warrant, you understand?"

"Yeah, cop."

Frank left the building, contemplating his next move. He realized that going back to New York was a waste, even if it meant Dennis's ass. His son was more important and every moment he was in that lab could mean a minute less he had to live. Even if Aaron testified, it still would be difficult to prove the cocaine was planted. The CIA would make all the evidence disappear. If he could get into the lab, he could save his son and make sure he was safe in a loving family, something neither Nicole nor he could give. The other problem was Jacob. His whereabouts were just as important. But he knew Dennis would do everything in his power to help if Robin found the child before the CIA. He had to go to Bismarck, no matter what the consequences.

Chapter 28

Nevin Cuff felt a warm sensation of pleasure pulse though his body as he watched Frank Roberts jump into his rental car and pull out of the parking lot. The two-bit cop thought he could outsmart Nevin by taking back roads and switching cars en route to the airport, but he didn't. Nevin had dealt with the best spies the KGB had to offer and no cop would get the best of him. He had been staking out Aaron Rankin's home the minute Frank Roberts arrived in Pittsburgh. His reliable source in New York had come through, as usual. Every wall in the 15th precinct now had ears, which was his conduit into every futile plan Detective Roberts tried to conjure. Detective Roberts thought he was pretty sly pulling that counter surveillance bullshit in New York City. Nevin was almost impressed by Detective Roberts' clever attempt, but Frank had no idea who he was dealing with.

Nevin was glad Judd Isla was back in New York looking for the kid. He liked to work alone and Judd prevented him from doing the right thing. Detective Roberts and Dr. Vastbinder would be dead if the job was up to him. He would've loved to watch them squirm on the floor, gasping for air, as the blood trickled from their throats. But Judd had to do everything by the book, as if it were the Bible. Conformity was for the weak. It had always been the reckless that made a difference, he thought.

Aaron Rankin was scum, so it would be easy to kill him. He had gone out every night to pick up a bag of crack cocaine and distribute it to the hoards of people that stopped by his place over the past twenty-four hours. Judd instructed Nevin to sit in the Ford Explorer and play with all the high-tech surveillance equipment and find out why Frank had traveled to Pittsburgh. It was obvious Mr. Rankin knew too much. Otherwise, why would Detective Roberts risk his neck coming to Pittsburgh?

Nevin checked his watch. It was ten o'clock. The thick clouds that occluded the half moon sprinkled a mist of rain on the windshield, partially blocking his view of the apartment building. He rolled down the window and listened closely to his headset that tapped into Mr. Rankin's phone lines, and realized he was leaving his apartment to pick up his daily shipment. Business must be good, he thought. He peered through his binoculars and saw Aaron's fish eyes and fat face eating an apple while walking to his car. That better be the best apple of his life, Nevin thought, because it was going to be his last.

* * *

Robin Vastbinder crossed out another foster home from the list, almost breaking her pencil in the process. Ten down, only ten more to go, she thought. She combed her hands through her hair and sighed. It was going to be impossible to find the boy alone. She was sure the man who had been following her was a lot closer. They had the resources of the Federal government at the tips of their fingers. Her tax dollars were being used for ten thousand dollar toilet seats and CIA agents to shadow her every move. She got up from her chair and walked to the refrigerator in her office, reached in and grabbed a Coke. A half-full bottle of white Zinfandel stood alone in the back, calling her to pull open the cork and pour a glass. It was eleven o'clock in the morning and a drink and some Listerine would help her get through the clinic. But the words of Frank still echoed in her mind. She resisted the temptation and continued examining the list.

Robin was about to pick up the phone when she realized how long it would take to check the other ten foster homes. The first ten were reluctant to divulge the information; it took her ten extra phone calls and five hours to find out where Jacob wasn't. She had fought the urge to call Careen Jones, the social worker in the ER, but she was her last chance. The thought of Careen's three children being in danger made the numbers on the phone seem difficult to dial. She hung up the receiver, remembering Orpheus's predicament. What had they done to him? Paid him off? Doesn't seem like Orpheus style, she thought. She had tried calling him three times a day over the past week, without a response. What had made him forget about the two helpless little boys?

Robin picked up the phone and slowly dialed the numbers again, trying to ignore the consequences. She needed help and Careen had more information about the child welfare system in her fingernails than Robin had in her entire body. As the phone rang, thoughts of Frank entered her mind. She loved the warmth of his body that surrounded her and made her forget that her life was spiraling down a toilet. But, what kind of man was he? She barely knew him. What had he done to his wife that made her want to be with another man? She wasn't condoning the adultery, but there were always two sides to every story, or so her mother said. It was too much to think about, especially at a time when she was unsure of the next minute. One night of sex, that was it, and all it could be for now.

"Hello?" Careen said.

"It's Robin. Can I meet you for lunch?"

"Sure."

"Cafeteria, say…ten minutes?" Robin asked, looking at her watch.

"Give me fifteen, I've got a few things to finish up this morning. What's this about?"

"We'll talk over lunch."

The cafeteria was crowded with a mixture of hospital employees and patients' families walking through the line, sedately picking up cups of Jell-O and plates of French fries from the counter. Robin grabbed a juice and some chicken noodle soup, hoping that the warm broth wouldn't irritate her stomach. She paid the cashier, and then proceeded to a remote corner of the room, carefully watching all the eyes that seemed to be staring at her. There was no possible way anyone could hear her conversation, unless they sat beside her.

Careen emerged from the crowd of people surrounding the condiment stand, carrying a tray full of food. Careen liked to eat, and her rotund figure was proof. Robin waved her hand and Careen spotted her in the corner. "Is that all you're going to eat?" Careen asked, taking a bite out of her grilled chicken sandwich.

"This is plenty," Robin replied, slowly raising her spoon to her mouth.

"So what's up?"

"I just can't get that little boy out of my mind," Robin said.

"I know what you mean. I went home that night and hugged my babies half the evening. How could something so beautiful feel so much pain? I haven't heard a word about him and his uncle since I read the newspaper article."

"I heard they found Jacob," Robin said.

"Where?"

"I just heard bits and pieces from a cop, but Jacob is somewhere in the city at a foster home," Robin said, looking around, making sure no one was close enough to hear what she said.

"Robin, are you all right?" Careen asked, concerned. "You seem anxious."

"I'm fine, just been under a lot of stress lately," Robin said, taking a deep breath. "I have a listing of the names of some foster homes he might be in. It's been a chore getting information. I was wondering if you knew anyone that worked at the child welfare office."

"My old college roommate. I bet if I give her a call she can speed the process. Why are you so interested?"

"Things have been tough since…you know…David died, I thought adopting would help," Robin said, half lying, but in the back of her mind half telling the truth.

"I understand," Careen said, reaching out her hand, and caressing Robin's. "I'll give her a call and maybe by tomorrow, we can find him."

"Thanks Careen. I knew I could count on you."

Robin finished her soup and followed Careen to the lobby. Hopefully she would come through and Jacob would be out of danger for the moment. Robin stepped into the elevator and went back to her office. She took off her white coat and began sifting through the mail on her desk. Most of it was junk, except for an overnight letter without a return address. She stared at it for a few seconds, hoping it was from Frank, then opened it.

Meet me at the Pelican lounge, on Twentieth St., tonight, 8:00. I have the patient we've been looking for.

Dr. Roderick Taylor

Chapter 29

Robin tapped her finger nervously on her desk while staring at the message. It was only five o'clock in the afternoon; the day seemed longer by the second. The idea of a cool glass of wine was the answer. Time would pass faster with each sip, she thought. She finished the first glass with three gulps and relaxed in her chair, contemplating what this mysterious patient had to say. The prospect of this person testifying against the very clinic that saved their life was slim. And who would believe them if they did? Only a tabloid magazine with aliens on the cover, she thought.

Robin took two sprays of mint breath freshener and combed her hair while looking in the mirror. The once long mane of red hair had frayed with split ends, reminding her of Orpheus's afro. Why hadn't he returned any of her phone calls? It was as if he never heard the name Nicole Johnson. Maybe she didn't know him as she once thought unless he had something to hide. Without his help, it would be impossible to prove that the Loventhol clinic was involved in foul play. She picked up the phone and dialed his office. Orpheus was going to come clean or she would pull every hair from his head. The time for games was long over.

"Hello?" Orpheus said over jazz music that blared in the background.

"I need to talk to you," Robin yelled.

"Hold on," Orpheus said, turning down the volume. "You need what? Who is this?"

"I've been leaving messages for three days. I'll be down in five minutes, Orpheus," Robin barked. "And I'm not taking *no* for an answer."

Robin marched down the hallway, her eyes determined and her face twisted with anger that the alcohol accentuated. She strolled right in his office without a knock to find Orpheus staring at the wall with his eyes closed, while listening to his headphones. Robin reached over his shoulder and turned up the volume of his compact stereo.

"You must have just lost your mind," Orpheus yelled, jumping out of his chair. "You almost blew out my ear drums and that was the best part of the song."

"You must be out of your mind if you think you can close your eyes and all of this will go away," Robin snapped, her eyes fiery red, her blood vessels jumping from her skull.

"Listen Joan of Arc," Orpheus uttered, his eyes about to burst through his eyelids. "You need to cut back on the coffee."

"I've been calling your office three times a day for the last week. I'm up to my ears in shit...."

"Calm down. Why don't we go to my lab? Your yelling is waking up the entire department and god knows I'd hate to interrupt their eight hours of beauty sleep."

Robin followed Orpheus to a remote corner of one of the small labs that was empty. She entered behind him, noticing the collection of centrifuges and beakers cluttered around microscopes and specimen jars filled with organs and tissue. Orpheus pulled out a steel hair pick and lifted his Afro a few more inches, then walked over to a drawer against the wall and opened the drawer with a key. He dropped a manila envelope on the counter and crossed his arms.

"You know, my oldest son just had sex for the first time," Orpheus said with a smile. "I knew it the moment he walked in the door at three in the morning. He had that smile that only another man could understand. I was about to kill him, but instead, we ended up talking all night. I was kind of proud, you know. It was weird. My little boy had become a man."

"What does that have to do with this envelope? And by the way, sex definitely doesn't make a boy a man."

"Only from a woman's point of view," Orpheus said, handing it to her. "Open it."

Robin hesitated at first, looking into Orpheus's eyes that barely held the fear inside, and pulled a photo from inside. It was Orpheus, his hair almost hiding his face, standing in his yard, passing a football with his tall, bright-eyed sons as his wife watched. "It's a nice picture, but what does this have to do with Nicole Johnson?"

"Read the back."

Robin flipped over the photo to find a message. *HOW MUCH DO YOU REALLY LOVE THEM? IF YOU DO, YOU'LL DROP ALL MATERIALS RELATED TO NICOLE JOHNSON IN THE FIRST GARBAGE DUMP IN THE BACK OF THE BUILDING AT ONE O'CLOCK IN THE MORNING. ALL OF THEM. IF YOU GO TO THE POLICE, YOUR FAMILY IS DEAD.*

"I had no idea," Robin murmured.

"I couldn't imagine missing any of those moments with my boys. I don't sleep at night, I practically have a rearview mirror on my shoulder everywhere I go and I'm not even having sex with Gloria…well…that has nothing to do with this."

"I know what you mean. My phone lines are tapped and my house is bugged, " Robin said, leaning against the bench. "That's why we have to bring these people down."

"I wish we knew who 'these' people were? I'm sure it's not a bunch of geeked out scientists with shotguns out to get us."

"It's much worse than that. It's the CIA."

"The what?"

"I know it sounds like a crazy conspiracy theory, but it's the truth. Do you remember Dr. Taylor?"

"Guy who walks with a stick up his butt?"

"Yeah, I guess you could say that. Well, we have reason to believe that a Dr. Loventhol has some clinic in the middle of nowhere where he transfused Nicole Johnson's blood to his patients and cured their cancer."

"That sure is going to be tough to prove. We have no body or specimens left, a missing child with all the answers, and they have all the powers of the Federal government. I don't think I want any part of this."

"Do you really think you have a choice?" Robin asked. "You know too much already, they could make us both disappear without blinking an eye. Look at Nicole's brother, they still haven't found him."

"I guess I've really been in denial all this time," Orpheus said, staring somberly at the ground. "I'll get the kids and Gloria out of town, but then what?"

"I'm going to meet with Dr. Taylor tonight, and an actual patient from the clinic. We do have one friend in the police force that's on our side, and he's in Pittsburgh as we speak, questioning an employee who works at the Loventhol clinic. If we can get the patient I meet tonight and that guy from Pittsburgh to testify, then we can build a case. If they start an investigation, the CIA will have to back off or risk exposure. I'm sure that's the last thing they want to do."

"What about the boy?"

"Careen Johnson, the ER's social worker, is looking into things, but don't worry, she doesn't know a thing about this."

"So, what am I supposed to do now? Just hang out and wait for a bullet in the back of my head?"

"Hopefully, this thing will be over by tomorrow."

"I still don't understand why the CIA would be involved in this."

"Someone very important must be sick."

"But who?"

"That's the million dollar question. I'll give you a page tonight after I meet with Dr. Taylor, then we can meet somewhere."

"This is crazy."

"You're telling me."

Robin popped up her umbrella, protecting her hair from the fine mist of rain that caused the curls to wilt, and exited her car. She took a swig of the scotch in her silver flask and took slow deep breaths. She regained her composure and walked up the block, scanning her surroundings, looking for suspicious eyes. It seemed no one had followed her. She opened the glass doors to the restaurant and walked inside.

The restaurant was dimly lit with a bar and lounge at the entrance, and ten to fifteen tables scattered in the other room. Only six tables were occupied, with older men and women in business suits eating pasta and seafood. Dr. Taylor was not to be found. She glanced at her watch. It was one minute after eight. He must be running a little late, she thought. She took a seat at the bar, ordered a scotch and water, and tried to relax. A man, with long black hair and a thick mustache, who was at the other end of the bar, seemed to be watching her every move. She turned her seat in the opposite direction and glanced at him through the mirror behind the bar. His eyes were picking her apart. Maybe this was a set up. She took another drink, and noticed him getting out of his chair and approaching her. "You seemed real lonely…thought you could use some company," he said with a smooth smile.

"No…just waiting for someone," Robin replied, nervously watching his every movement.

"I guess they're late."

"They're always late."

"Can I buy you a drink?" the man asked, moving closer to her chair.

"Thanks, but I already have a drink," Robin replied tipping her glass.

"I'm not trying to pick you up. It's just nice to have someone to talk to every now and then since my wife died."

"I'm sorry," Robin said, feeling guilty for being so rude.

"Happened about a month ago. We had no children, so instead of sitting in my empty apartment, I come here every night, eat dinner, and watch the people."

"What did she die of?"

"Cancer of the breast," the man murmured. "Doctors said it was tough to treat a young woman, even when they do surgery. It was just bad luck I guess."

Robin stared into the man's eyes. They were honest and sincere. She understood his pain. She understood the sleepless nights and barren echoes inside an empty house. But this wasn't the time or place for therapy. Maybe his flight got delayed, she thought. She decided to give him till nine o'clock, then she would leave. "What hospital?" Robin asked.

"Brooklyn University."

"I work there. What doctor took care of her?"

"Dr. Davidson."

"Daniel Davidson?"

"Yeah, Daniel. Nice guy. He was really there for us."

"He does all the breast cancer. I'm part of the group."

"You must have a tough job, watching all those people die. Are you a physician?"

"If I could ever get all the paper work done I could be."

"I wouldn't want your job."

"Sometimes I don't want my job."

"Jim Erret," he said, offering his hand.

"Robin Vastbinder," she said, shaking his hand.

Robin decided to let him buy her a drink. He was harmless; just another lost soul who could truly understand how it feels to be alone. She spent the next half-hour drinking and reminiscing on life. Jim Erret talked about trying to start a new a life, but every date was a woman with his wife's face. An inadequate replacement he tried to hide behind. She understood, but after the night with Frank, the hopelessness wasn't as bad. There was something about Frank. His thick arms were like a security blanket, his eyes could light up her darkest hour. But, at times as they made love that night, she did picture her husband. Thinking about him while she was with Frank wasn't as painful as she would have thought. It may have been she needed someone, just like Jim needed her to listen to his sorrow. But somewhere in her heart, it was a lot more. A lot more than she wanted to think about.

It was nine fifteen and there was no sign of Dr. Taylor, which worried her. What had happened? It wasn't a setup or something would've happened by now. She checked the dining room again—the faces were different, but none were Dr. Taylor. Now what? She returned to the bar to find Jim still sitting in his chair, staring deep into his glass, looking for the answers that she still couldn't seem to find. "Thanks for the drink," Robin said, finishing the glass. She put on her coat, then grabbed her umbrella. As she walked towards the door, a weird feeling overcame her. The room seemed to oscillate, like a bell that had just been rung. Her feet felt as if they were sinking into the floor. She looked back at the bar, then glanced in the mirror. Her face looked as if someone had put her eyes on her forehead and her mouth became wide and distorted. Her heart was about to burst through her chest. Perspiration soaked her forehead and blouse. What was happening?

"Are you all right?" Jim asked, looking concerned.

Jim's words seemed two octaves deeper and in slow motion. His eyes looked twice the size of his face. His razor stubble became tiny bugs that swayed back and forth and crawled through the crevices in his long mustache. His nose began to vibrate. "The bugs, the bugs," Robin said, rubbing her arms vigorously until they chafed. "They're all over me."

"What are you talking about?" Jim asked, grabbing her by the shoulders and helping her to a chair. "Why don't you sit down?"

Robin closed her eyes, hoping the illusions would go away, but they got worse. The darkness had colors that changed to a horrible beast with horns and long claws. She opened her eyes and the entire room looked like a Picasso painting. "Help…please…help me," she pleaded, covering her head, trying to avoid the trails of light that looked like ghosts with bloody faces.

"We need to get this woman to a hospital," Jim said frantically to the bartender.

Chapter 30

Frank Roberts stared at the ugly green walls of his hotel room, wondering if he needed Aaron Rankin to travel with him to North Dakota. The hotel room was dusty, with an old table and chairs that badly needed re-varnishing. The bed had flowered sheets and it creaked every time he moved. But what could he expect for thirty-five dollars a night? he thought. He had to save every penny of the two thousand dollars that Robin had lent him. Thank god she trusted him enough to lend him the money because the bank froze all of his funds. He rolled over the bed and grabbed his cigarettes on the nightstand. He lit one, exhaled a thick cloud of smoke, and stared out the window. The dimly lit rays of the sun, behind the rows of the Pennsylvania mountains, relinquished its command of the day and the darkness conquered the sky. It was eight o'clock and a half moon predominated. The thousands of tiny speckles that illuminated the night reminded Frank of those summer nights with his father. They would sit on his front porch in Queens, sipping lemonade on a hot summer night, staring at the constellations and talking about life. Before his father had a heart attack, it became a contest of who could find each of the constellations the quickest. The image of his father grasping his chest while standing on the porch still haunted his every thought. He took a long look at the pack of cigarettes on the nightstand and realized that was probably his same fate, if he didn't quit soon. His father was never without a Lucky Strike in his hand. The only time Frank remembered seeing him without one was the night he watched him fall to the floor of the front porch, struggling to breathe. He died later that night and the stars haven't seemed the same since.

Frank rose from the bed and stuffed his clothes in his overnight bag. He checked out of the hotel and jumped into his rental car. He drove five miles down the road and pulled up in front of Aaron Rankin's building, hoping he was still home. If he wasn't, he would wait all night if necessary. He walked up to the stoop and pressed the buzzer. There was no answer. He pressed it again, holding the button in for a minute—still no answer. "Damn," he said to himself. Where the fuck was he? Out of the corner of his eye, he noticed a fire escape that led to the patio of his floor. He contemplated the trouble it would cause if someone spotted him and concluded he was already in too deep. He checked the streets; they were empty. He slithered to the side of the building, jumped up and pulled himself onto the first level. He tip-toed up the steps, trying to sneak by the five sliding doors on each landing and finally arrived in front of his apartment.

A thick maroon curtain obstructed his view. He tried to angle his head through the corner of the window, but only saw an inch of the room. He then glanced at the lock and realized he needed a locksmith to get inside. A feeling of desperation overcame him and the thought of breaking the window entered his mind. Instead, he tried the simple approach and opened the door. To his surprise, it was open. That was a bad sign. A convict would never leave his apartment unlocked. He looked over his shoulder, then cautiously entered. He could see the steam rising off of Dennis's face as he walked inside the living room. First cocaine, now breaking and entering; his rap sheet was growing with each second. The apartment looked the same, except the television was on, without sound. The phone was off the hook. He looked on the floor and saw tiny drops of blood that led into the bedroom. He pulled his gun from his holster and entered the bedroom.

The tiny drops collected to form a pool in the corner. He turned on the bedroom light and found Aaron leaking blood from a large gash in his throat. His face was blue and bloated. His eyes were fixed and dilated, staring at the ceiling. He quickly turned off the light and quietly left the room, making sure he didn't touch a thing, but his fingerprints were all over the place. He wanted to run down the fire escape, but held his adrenaline in check. He thought at first that it could've been a drug deal gone bad, but his intuition told him that someone knew he came to Pittsburgh.

How could they have followed him? he thought, carefully placing his steps as he went down the fire escape. Judging from the position of the body and the fact that the television set was on, someone was waiting for him when he got home. They let him relax for a moment, but made a sound. That's why the TV was on mute. Rankin was checking out the unfamiliar sound, when the assailant slit his throat and dragged him into the bedroom. No time for a struggle, he summated. The blade probably cut him so fast, he didn't have a second to yell. This was a professional job; not a gun job by some two bit drug dealer. It had to be the CIA, but how would they know?

Frank jumped from the fire escape and searched his surroundings. The night played tricks with his mind. The shadows that projected from the tall oak trees looked like people about to call the police. The brake lights from a bus that passed by reminded him of a silent cop car. He rubbed his eyes and realized the block was empty. He could only hope no one was looking out their window and spotted him as he climbed down the fire escape. He stepped inside his car, his mind reeling with jumbled thoughts. He took a deep breath and started the engine, trying to calm the visions of prison that dominated his mind. He glanced at his watch. It was nine forty-five. If things went his way, the body wouldn't be found until tomorrow. It would take at least seven hours to secure the scene, then run the prints, he thought. He had twenty hours before anyone knew; twenty hours to save his son.

The idea of flying to Bismarck was a forgone conclusion. The chances of him being trapped in the airport were almost one hundred percent. He had to drive to Bismarck, and with some luck, find the place. The ford Tempo was brand new, but he would have to change cars at the halfway point. He entered the parkway and spotted a gas station a half mile down the road. He needed a map. He rushed in, grabbed a hoagie, two packs of cigarettes and a McNally map of Central and Western United States. The Loventhol clinic was ten miles outside of Burlington, North Dakota, a hundred and fifty miles away from Bismarck. It would be a 24 hour trip. He drove fifty-five-miles an hour until he reached the Ohio/Indiana border. He stopped at a gas station, filled up the tank, and then contemplated calling Dennis Irwin. It was a risky proposition, but he had to know if Robin was safe.

He picked up the phone and dialed the first five digits. He was about to dial the last six, when he realized someone at the station was helping the CIA. How else would they know he went to Pittsburgh? It had to be Mike, that prick. He would do just about anything to advance his career and working with the CIA was a chance of a lifetime. Or maybe the station was bugged, he thought. It sounded ludicrous, but judging from his current predicament, anything was possible. He hung up the phone, then picked it up again, picturing Robin's body in some garbage dump in the middle of nowhere.

"Hello?" Dennis said.

"Dennis, it's Frank."

"Where the fuck are you?" Dennis scowled. "I have the mayor's office barking down my throat. You get your ass back here or I'll fucking drive to Pittsburgh and break your neck."

"Shut up and listen," Frank snapped. "Someone murdered the man I went to see in Pittsburgh— cut his throat from ear to ear."

"What?"

"It was professional. I'm sure the only prints in the place are mine."

"This is becoming a nightmare."

"Only two people knew I was going to Pittsburgh, you and Dr. Robin Vastbinder. Either they got to her or someone at the station has double crossed me."

"How do I know you didn't lose your temper and kill him yourself?"

"Do we really have to go through this again?"

"Yes, we do. I'm willing to go the distance, but I've got to know you're on the up and up."

"You've got to trust me," Frank said desperately. "You're all I have."

Dennis was silent for a moment, and then said, "I'll have the department torn apart. If someone is up to something, I'll find out, you better believe me."

"I only have a few minutes of change left, so listen. Has Dr. Robin Vastbinder called your office?"

"No."

"Damn it," Frank yelled. "Please check on her. There is no telling what they'll do to her and you have to find that boy. She has a list of foster homes that he may be in. It's going to be difficult because he doesn't speak."

"Why don't you come back to New York, Frank. We can work on this together. You're about to be 'at large' and I can't help you then."

"I don't need your help, just make sure Robin and Jacob are safe. I'll be fine. It doesn't matter what happens to me anymore, Dennis. I've got to save him, even if it means my life."

"Where are you going?"

"That's a long story, just make sure they're safe," Frank said, hanging up the phone.

Frank jumped on the highway, smoking cigarette after cigarette as if it were oxygen. He knew that Dennis was in a tight predicament. He was five years from a pension and had two kids in college. The last thing he needed was to lose his job. And assisting a felon was more than grounds for dismissal, it was a jail sentence. But once Dennis started looking into things, he would know the truth. He was the best detective Frank had ever met. He owed everything he knew to him. But the CIA was the mob without restraints. They could easily force Dennis's hand.

The lines of the road mesmerized him, making the trip grueling. He looked at his map and realized he was an hour outside of Chicago. Sleep was risky, but he had no choice. He was working on two hours of rest and he found himself dozing off, being awoken by the grates on the shoulder of the road. He strained his eyes and spotted a Motel Seven sign a mile off the next exit. Two hours of rest was all he needed, he thought. He drove onto the off ramp, his body aching, his hands chaffed from gripping the steering wheel so tightly, and parked in the lot. As he grabbed his overnight bag and exited his car, he realized that his chances against the government were slim. It was at least a forty-point spread that he was sure he couldn't cover.

Chapter 31

Robin's head thumped. Her skin tingled and eyes felt as if ten-ton bar bells were holding them shut. She tried to lift her arm to her face and wipe the thick sleet that held them shut, but her hand was stuck firmly against her abdomen. She wiggled her arms violently, but the more she fought to break loose, the tighter the restraints seemed to be. The three minutes of fight drained what little energy she had left. She fell to the floor and forced open her eyes. She was in a padded blue room constrained by a white straight jacket. What she once thought was just a bad dream was a reality. What had happened last night?

The last she remembered was the bar, then time lapsed from her mind like a clock without a face. Think, think, she kept telling herself. But nothing was registering. A faint remembrance crept in her mind; the distorted ceilings and walls, the faces that seemed to be melting from people's heads, and she realized that she had been drugged. It had to be LSD; it was the only substance she knew that would create such delusions of time and space. She tried to rise to her feet, but couldn't stabilize her body against the wall. She slid down the soft wall and sighed. Now what?

Who had put the drug in her drink? And where was Dr. Taylor? It was a set up. How could she be so stupid? The man, Joe or Jim Ferrt or Erret was the culprit, she thought. He knew his sad sack story about his wife would touch a nerve in her riddled soul. He probably worked for the CIA and knew that her family was killed just a year ago, she surmised. Now, she was in a Psych. hospital, committed against her will. They knew they would check her old records from Brooklyn University and paint a picture of a woman tormented by the death of her child and husband.

Robin guessed they gave her a huge dose of Haldol because her mouth felt dry, muscles felt tight and vision blurred. It was the drug of choice for acute psychotic behavior. Fortunately, the effects lasted only four hours. She angled her shoulder against the wall and pulled herself to a sitting position. Now what? she thought. Dr. Taylor was most likely either dead or in a similar predicament. Frank was in Pittsburgh and Jacob was still in danger. The straight jacket held two lives captive: Jacob and her own.

The sound of keys jingling approached the room. The door creaked, then opened. A heavyset man with three chins and two guts entered first. His eyes examined her every move. Then, a short man with a large nose spread across his face and a receding hairline, emerged behind the beast. He wore a blue suit jacket with a gray turtleneck and clicked his pen annoyingly while looking at her chart. "Robin, I'm Doctor Womack. How are you feeling today?" he asked with a condescending smile.

"I'm not crazy," Robin snarled, rising to her feet. "I was drugged."

"Just calm down," Dr. Womack said, stepping back.

Robin noticed the fear in Dr. Womack's eyes and realized she better gain her composure. They would never believe she wasn't insane unless she controlled the fury that stirred in her heart. "I'd like to talk about last night," Dr. Womack said. "Do you remember what happened?"

"I was at a bar and some stranger slipped a *Mickey* in my drink."

"Your drug screen only showed high amounts of alcohol and a trace of sleeping pills," Dr. Womack said, flipping through her chart.

Alcohol? No LSD? What was going on? "Did you check for LSD or Peyote?" Robin asked.

"We checked for everything," Dr. Womack said, ignoring her. "So, you don't remember what happened after that?"

"No," Robin replied dropping her head.

"You were screaming at the top of your lungs, saying the walls were melting and that the CIA was doing it to you. It took three security guards to put you in the straight jacket. Then you starting spitting on everyone, saying that they were causing the murder of a child."

The drug must have meshed reality with delusions. Her friend in college once told her of the 'bad trips' she had when monkeys flew around her room. It had to be LSD or some derivative, and someone must have tampered with the blood. "Why don't you test my blood again?"

"Our lab is impeccable," Dr. Womack said. "That won't be necessary."

"I'm telling you I was drugged. I'm not crazy. You've got to believe me," Robin pleaded.

"Why do you think someone would drug you?"

Robin knew if she told him the truth, she would not only propagate the illusion of her mental illness, but also provide more information than he needed to know. "Maybe I wasn't drugged," Robin said, pacing. "Maybe I was just drunk."

"So, you don't believe someone is out to get you?"

"I don't know what happened last night."

"The man that brought you here said you talked about killing yourself."

"I don't remember ever saying that," Robin uttered, knowing there was nothing she could say to convince the psychiatrist otherwise.

"I've been reading your chart extensively and I'm under the impression that you've been under a tremendous amount of stress over the past year."

Robin remained silent.

"And you have been under treatment for severe depression."

"My depression has been under control."

"How much would you say you drink a week?" Dr. Womack asked, writing in the chart.

"A few glasses of wine," Robin replied, starting to pace.

"Have you ever heard voices?"

"I know where you're going with this Doctor Womack," Robin fired back. "No, I've never heard voices, no I've never had delusions of any kind. First of all, I'm much too old to be a Schizophrenic. Second, if you think this is severe depression with manic or psychotic delusions, you're highly mistaken. And thirdly, if I were psychotic, would I have so much insight about the condition?"

"I see you're a physician," Dr. Womack said, rubbing his chin, looking at the chart. "Oncology?"

"Are you listening to me?" Robin snapped. "I need to get out of here. I'm not suicidal, nor am I a threat to anyone. You can't hold me here."

"I think your insight, Dr. Vastbinder, is from the high doses of Haldol we gave you every four hours. I'm sure you don't realize how close you came to killing yourself."

"What are you talking about?" Robin asked, alarmed. "I didn't overdose."

"The man said he stopped you from cutting your throat with the glass you broke in the bar. You have ten stitches in your hand."

Robin rubbed her fingers against her palms and felt the tiny nylon threads in her hand. That bastard must've staged this whole event, she thought. She may have been drugged, but there was no drug that could convince a mentally sane person to kill himself. "I didn't try to kill myself," Robin said, becoming more frustrated with each word. "Why am I even wasting my breath? I could tell you that I'm in a padded room and you wouldn't believe me."

"I'm here to help, Dr. Vastbinder," Dr. Womack said. "I know you don't believe me, but it's true. I'm not sure how much insight you truly have, but you must look at the facts. You have been through a tragedy. It's not very uncommon for severely depressed people to have periods of psychosis."

"When do I get out of here?"

"If you stay calm for the next four hours we'll transfer you to a regular floor."

"I don't mean out of this room, I mean out of the hospital," Robin said, wishing she could scratch the itch on her face.

"Let's see how things go," Dr. Womack said, closing the chart. "We'll talk more once you get to the ward."

Robin slumped down the wall and pouted like a child denied candy. She watched them leave, feeling helpless and defeated. The forces beyond her control had won. She was trapped in the place she once enjoyed working in medical school. A prisoner of her mind that Dr. Womack would never believe that was as sound as his. And with Frank in Pittsburgh and her in a mental jail, the little boy was prey for the lions hiding behind the mask of the government. She rolled on her back and stared at the ceiling. The prospect of being trapped in a psych. ward made the walls seem to inch closer each second. The forced heavy doses of medication would cloud her resolve a little more each day. And as each moment passed, it was one less that Jacob and his baby brother had left to live. She was certain that it would take billions of virus to treat an adult with cancer—which meant a lot of blood the children did not have.

Chapter 32

Orpheus Martin stared at the empty walls of his house wishing he could hear the animated sounds of his wife and children. The silence was so loud that the funky music of George Clinton couldn't drown it out. He hated the wrestling and fighting between his two sons, but now he longed for it. His family was now safely in Florida with her parents. He tried to convince his wife that they needed a vacation, but she saw right through him. She bantered with him for two hours, but he never broke down. He didn't want her to know more than she needed. But the look of desperation in her eyes made him realize she knew enough. He got up from his couch and turned off his stereo. George just wasn't doing it for him today.

He walked into the kitchen and opened the refrigerator. He had taken the day off and didn't have the luxury of the cafeteria. *If you want to call it a luxury*, he thought. Nothing to eat, he thought scanning the fridge, unless he wanted to break out a pot and pan; a dangerous proposition considering he was the only person alive that could burn water. He went to the cabinet above the sink and found a box of graham crackers and called it lunch. He picked up the cordless phone and dialed Robin's house again. The phone rang once, then the answering machine clicked on. Where the hell was she? This was the fifth time he called her home this morning. He had called her office four times and paged her three. No answer. Thousands of scenarios swirled though his mind, none of which were optimistic. He decided to try her office again.

The condescending tone of her office manager made Orpheus want to strangle her. She acted as if it was an honor to have a few minutes of her time. She wouldn't even be in the position if it weren't for doctors. He had a difficult time pumping her for information, but finally she broke. Robin was in a mental hospital in Brooklyn. But why? He knew things must've been hard for her, losing her entire family, but something wasn't quite right. She was committed, unable to leave without the consent of a psychiatrist. There was only two reasons that someone could be held against their will: if they were a threat to themselves or someone else. It didn't make sense that Robin would try to kill herself, considering she fought so hard to save those children. And if she tried to harm someone else, she'd be in jail, not a mental hospital. Something was wrong.

It had to be the same people that sent him the manila envelope, the CIA. He knew he had no chance of proving it and the police wouldn't be any help. He walked upstairs, passing the school photos of his sons from grade school to junior high. He chuckled, thinking about how many teeth they missed and how they protested to having an Afro just like dad. The Afro only lasted until second grade; his wife made them get a haircut. As he reached the top of the stairs, a harrowing thought overcame him. Nicole Johnson's son. With Robin in the loony bin, the child had no chance. They would get to the boy much sooner than later. He galloped into his bedroom and searched his lab coat for the number Robin had given him. He had to call Careen Johnson and find out the location of the kid. He picked up the phone and dialed.

"Hello?"

"Is this Careen Johnson?"

"Yes it is."

"Dr. Orpheus Martin from Pathology."

"What can I do for you?"

"I was wondering if you found out anything about Nicole Johnson's son?"

"Popular boy," Careen said. "Where's Robin? I've called her office all day."

"She's sick," Orpheus said, thinking about Robin being in the psych. hospital, trapped against her will.

"Is she O.K.?"

"She'll be fine. She wanted me to find out where the boy is. She's really concerned about him."

"Cute kid. Spoke with his social worker yesterday. He's at a foster home in Queens."

"Do you have the address?"

"Sure, but she won't be able to see him unless she goes through the welfare office."

"I know this sounds out of the ordinary, but she really wants to see the boy," Orpheus said, cautiously. "You know her situation?"

"I understand," Careen said, softly. "I don't know how she does it."

"Neither do I."

"I don't think the foster home would have a problem. The address is 471 East 11th Street. You tell her I hope she feels better and to give me a call when she gets back to work."

"I will, and thanks."

Orpheus plopped on his bed and massaged his eyes. He had to get Robin out. That was his only choice. By the time she would be released, who knows what would happen to her. And no one will ever believe her story. How to get her out? he wondered, concentrating on the ceiling. Walk right through the doors with a sawed off shotgun and demand her release? Sneak her out through the back doors? He let out a long sigh, realizing he was headed for prison, when it hit him. He went into the closet and looked for a suit. He frowned when he realized his wife had put his three new suits in the cleaners and he didn't have a clue where she put the tickets. In the back was a suit jacket he hadn't worn in twenty years. It was blue with green stripes and wide lapels. He knew he would look ridiculous, but it would fit the role perfect. He grabbed a bow tie and got dressed. Hopefully, it would work.

* * *

Robin stabbed her fork into the dry piece of sausage, took a bite, and then pushed her breakfast away. The room was as big as a closet. It reminded her of her dorm in college: only a bed, dresser and desk. But it was much better than the padded cell. At least she could look outside and see the city. The streets were filled with pedestrians walking like a herd of trained animals stomping the pavement. The traffic was so congested, the road looked like one big vehicle moving one mile an hour. Robin hated the fact that it took her an hour to travel ten miles, but today, sitting in traffic would be heaven. She would love to take a deep breath of the smog-filled air again while eating a greasy hot dog in the middle of the afternoon. It seemed that would never happen again.

Robin opened the door of the stale smelling room and walked down the hall. She walked up to the nurse's station and tapped on the window. A thin, African American woman with thick curly hair opened the door. "Robin, what can I do for you?"

"I'd like to make a phone call."

"You'll have to wait till were done with group," the nurse said, looking at her watch.

"This is worse than a prison," Robin said, throwing up her hands. "I've been in here for almost two days and haven't been able to make a damn phone call."

"Group is only an hour," the nurse said, wrinkling her face, putting her hands on her hips. "You've waited this long."

"Whatever, "Robin said, storming away. Now how would she get in touch with Dr. Taylor? For all she knew, he could be dead by now. She had to have the phone, no matter what the cost. She stomped back to the nurse's station and pounded on the door. "Listen, I have to let my partners know where I'm at," she yelled. "There are patients in the hospital today that won't get seen because they don't know I'm sick."

The nurse stared at Robin as if she was about to shoot fire from her eyes, then sighed. "Five minutes," the nurse barked, opening the door.

Robin walked inside and quickly picked up the black phone. She dialed Dr. Taylor's number at home and bit her fingernails, all the while wondering if Dr. Taylor was still alive. The muscles in Robin's hands almost crushed the phone, but relaxed when she heard his voice on the other side of the receiver.

"Hello?" Dr. Taylor said.

"Listen, I don't have much time. Did you send me a letter?"

"Why would I send you a letter? I'll be in New York City tomorrow. Well, I hope. Things have become quite crazy these days. There are a lot of new faces in my hospital that seem to be reappearing everywhere. I'm almost positive someone followed me home from work."

"Don't say another word. You need to stay where you are."

"Why?"

"I just don't feel it's safe to travel."

"Are you O.K.? You sound a bit shaken," Dr. Taylor said concerned.

"I'm in a mental hospital. I was set up. I can't talk much more about it. I'd probably leave Boston if I were you."

"What are you talking about?" Dr. Taylor replied, with a crack in his voice. "Mental hospital? What in the hell is going on?"

"I've got to go. I'll try to contact you again."

"Before you hang up, I want you to know I have friends that will help us, friends that are untouchable. Don't you worry, Loventhol will be stopped. And I hope whoever is listening can hear that."

Robin hung up the phone and ventured to the recreation room and sat down in front of one of the two television sets. A pool and ping-pong tables were in the middle of the room with card tables on the sides. Three male patients were playing gin rummy in the corner as two female patients played ping-pong. They all looked over forty and their faces appeared as if someone had removed their souls. Had to be the heavy doses of medication, she thought. She picked up the remote and flicked through the channels. Her heart skipped a beat when a picture of Frank appeared on the screen. She turned up the sound and leaned closer to the screen. Frank was a wanted man. What happened? His face flashed off the screen and the female news anchor appeared. She had missed the story. Slamming the remote on the table, she reclined back in the chair and rubbed her temples. Combing her hands through her hair, she tried to remember the detective Frank told her to call. Dennis something, she thought. The past two days had drained her. The antidepressants made it difficult to stay awake, let alone think. She stood from her chair, jogged back to the nurse's station, and pounded loudly on the window. "I need a newspaper," she said.

The same nurse emerged from behind the door. "I think we have yesterday's, but group..."

"Listen, I need a newspaper and now!" she barked. "I've got five minutes, don't I?"

The nurse hesitated at first, then went inside and handed her a *New York Times* and said, "If you keep up this behavior, we will be forced to send you back to isolation," the nurse snapped, handing Robin the paper.

"I'm sorry, but you could never understand."

Robin leafed through each page as quickly as she could. Finally, in the local section, a picture of Frank appeared. His piercing blue eyes looked innocent and helpless. His face was tethered with his usual scruff. She read through the article underneath and realized the CIA was now in control. Frank was not only framed for possession of cocaine, but murder as well. She started to hyperventilate, then took slow, deep breaths. If the nurses saw her, they would force her to take a high dose of Xanax, which would cloud her already twisted thoughts. She returned to the couch and sat down. The article had taken all the strength to fight that she had left. The boy would soon be in the hands of the CIA.

She picked up the paper and noticed a quote from the Captain of Frank's station. Dennis Irwin, that was his name, she thought. He was her only chance. She buried her head in her hands and felt the tears leak in between her fingers. She wiped her face and was startled by a heavy hand touching her shoulder. She looked up to find a muscular African-American male with an empty stare on his face. "You O.K.?" he asked sitting down, continuously clicking a pen.

"I'm fine," Robin said, snorting back the tears.

"Damn government, isn't it?" the man said in a monotone voice, shaking his head.

"What?" Robin sputtered, flabbergasted. Who was this guy? How did he know?

"CIA has been following me for years. This seems to be the only place I can hide from them. You look like you have the same problem."

Robin smiled and slowly got up from the couch. At that moment, she understood why the authorities would never believe her. This guy was truly nuts. "I think it's time for group."

"Are you sure you're O.K.?" the man asked, holding up the pen. "Because I can help you. You see this pen?"

"Yeah," Robin said, slowly walking away.

"If I click it enough, it sends off a signal through the streetlights," he said, handing her the pen. "Confuses the hell out of them."

"I can't take this," Robin said, handing it back.

"Please," he said, holding up his hands. "I've always got a spare. Those agents are a tricky bunch. I have to keep changing pens to keep them on their toes."

Robin glanced at the pen for a moment, then plopped it in her pocket. "Thanks," she said, smiling nervously, then walked towards the group therapy room. What a nut, she thought. Unfortunately, that was what the psychiatrist would think of her if she told them her story. It was going to be impossible to convince the police. They'd throw her out of the station the minute she mentioned the word CIA. She pulled the pen from her pocket and smiled. Maybe it did have some magic powers, she chuckled to herself. She put the pen back in her pocket and made her way to the group therapy room at the end of the hallway. She was about to open the door, when a thin, gray-haired nurse tapped her on the shoulder. "Robin," she said in the comforting voice that Robin had come to hate. "You are being moved."

"What?" Robin replied, astonished and worried at the same time. "To where?"

"A Dr. George Clinton, from Brooklyn University, has come to get you. He said you are a personal friend and a patient of his and pointed out the fact that your insurance doesn't cover your stay here. Do you know Dr. Clinton?"

Who the hell was George Clinton? The only George Clinton she ever heard of was from one of the groups Orpheus always listened to. *Parliament*, she thought to herself. That was the name of the group. It had to be him. "He's been my therapist since the accident," Robin said, dropping her head to hide the smile on her face.

"He's come personally to pick you up," the nurse said, putting her arm around Robin. "Why don't we go get your things?"

"Thanks."

The metal door closing behind Robin's back sounded like chains being broken. But who was in the lobby? Maybe it was another clever ploy by the CIA. It was too late to turn back. She followed the nurse onto the elevator and rode it to the first floor. Please be Orpheus, she thought over and over the entire ride. Out of the corner of her eye, she saw a large Afro. The heaviness in her chest subsided. She let out a long cleansing breath, then fought back the laughter that rose to her face. It was the first funny thought she had in days. Orpheus had on the worst suit she had ever seen. It looked like he had just stepped out of his seventies prom picture. The blue suit, with wide lapels and green stripes, was accented with a thin blue bow tie. His pants were bell-bottoms. She knew the staff wouldn't give it a second thought—a lot of psychiatrists were quite eccentric. She walked through the door to find Orpheus with a serious look on his face, signing the forms for her release. "Robin, why haven't you been to our last two sessions?" Orpheus asked, scolding her like a parent. "You should've called. I was worried."

"I'm sorry," Robin replied, fighting to keep a straight face. "I've been through a lot. Can we go?"

"Of course," Orpheus said, leading her towards the door. "I appreciate your cooperation. I believe continuity of care will be preserved quite well once we get back to Brooklyn."

Robin followed Orpheus outside of the building, then burst out in laughter. "You look so ridiculous."

"What are you talking about?" Orpheus asked, insulted. "I graduated from college in this suit. Still fits like a glove. And besides, it was the only suit I had. My wife took my other three to the cleaners a day before she left."

"I was just kidding," Robin said, hugging him. "How did you pull that off?"

"It's amazing what you can do with a computer these days," Orpheus replied, holding up his fake ID and medical license. "I conned them with the professional courtesy thing. I explained to them how devastating to your career this would be and how I was a personal friend. And besides, your insurance didn't cover your stay. It's the first time having no coverage really helped someone. I know where the boy is."

"Where?" Robin asked anxiously, the smile clearing from her face.

"At a foster home in Queens. How did you end up in that place?"

"I'll tell you on the way."

CHAPTER 33

The rays of the afternoon sun blinded Judd Isla as he drove over the Queensboro Bridge en route to Queens. He glanced at his watch and realized it had been an entire day since he heard from Nevin Cuff. Fucking bastard, he thought, as he maneuvered around a taxi entering the right hand lane. He knew the moment he agreed to let that self-proclaimed cowboy go to Pittsburgh, someone would end up dead. Why didn't he follow orders? He was supposed to make Aaron Rankin develop a bad case of amnesia. Murder was only reserved for overseas work. Nevin was too stupid to realize that if the FBI got wind the CIA was operating in the states without authority, someone was going to pay. And that someone was going to be him.

The thick smog and smoke of the streets caused Judd's sinuses to go berserk. He reached in his pocket and pulled out his steroid nasal inhaler. Taking two quick puffs, he felt a sense of relief, not only from his congestion, but also from the fact he would soon be leaving New York. Despite the few glitches caused by Nevin, everything was going as planned. Dr. Vastbinder wouldn't see the light of day for weeks, and once she did, no one would believe her story. There was no need for blood, just deception. Nevin had never learned that, he thought. Dr. Vastbinder really believed he was a lost soul who sat at a bar every night, hoping for the pain to go away. He should've won an Oscar for that performance.

He would've burst into tears if he had to. And the Peyote derivative, which caused her violent hallucinations, was virtually undetectable in any drug screen. She never suspected for one second that he slipped the powder in her drink.

The CIA was the last of Detective Frank Robert's problems; he had every cop in the country after him. No one likes a bad cop, he thought, especially the politicians. Dr. Roderick Taylor was no longer a factor, considering Nevin was on his way to Boston to have a little chat with him. And Dr. Orpheus Martin would never risk his family's lives, he was sure of it. And now, he finally knew the location of the boy. All he needed to do was pick up an operative from L.A. and the circle would be complete.

Judd glanced at the piece of paper on the armrest of his black Ford Bronco and realized he was a block away from the diner he was supposed to meet the operative. He swerved around a bus and spotted a parking place on the right side of the street. Stepping out of his Bronco and walking into the café, he noticed ten bar stools crowded around a counter and seven booths lining the windows that were filled with overweight suits slopping down the greasy spoon menu. The operative from LA was supposed to be in the third booth. He counted the booths and spotted a thin, bald black male in a blue Nike sweat suit. He walked over to the booth and offered him a cigarette—the signal. The man reached out his bony hand and grabbed one from his pack. "Where are you parked?" he asked, lighting it and exhaling a cloud of smoke.

"Right out front," Judd replied.

"Let's go."

Judd walked out of the cafe, the man followed behind. He opened the door of the Bronco and they both jumped in. "Judd Isla," he said extending his hand.

"Mike Young," he said shaking his hand.

"Have you been briefed?"

"I have all the identifications," Mike said, showing him his wallet. "My name is Sean Patterson, I live at 555 53rd St., Brooklyn. I am Jacob Johnson's father."

"Do you have the form with the blood type verification?"

"Yeah," Mike said, throwing his cigarette from the window. "So, what do I do with the kid once I get him?"

"You're his father, right?"

"Today I am."

"Tell him where he's going to live...you know...something about a big yard and how'll you'll play catch with him."

"What's so important about this kid anyways?"

"That's classified," Judd said, officially. "All I can say is this kid is very important to national security."

Judd dropped Mike off at the child welfare office and drove around the block. He approximated it would take at least a half an hour to fill out the paper work and then the kid would be the property of the government. Then he could leave the smog filled streets of New York for the comfort of home. He couldn't wait to hear the sounds of his own children playing in the yard. Three more years of this shit, he thought, and then he would have the desk job he so desperately wanted. Life on the road was draining his soul. He missed most of his son's basketball games this year. He knew it had to kill his boy not seeing his dad in the stands. This was his last job. The brainwashing of the CIA had made him forget what life was truly about. He had no idea what they were going to do with the child, but the years of obedience made him not care. The boy was just another objective.

As he circled the block again, a thought entered his mind. The boy was as old as his youngest son. He couldn't imagine giving his own son to the government to do with what they pleased. But this was his job, the career he had chosen twenty years ago. The boy may have been through the worst trauma imaginable, but he had to tuck his feelings behind his thick skin. The needs of the country came before the needs of a single boy. For all he knew, the boy could be the son of a terrorist who carried the plans to make a nuclear device. But somehow, he doubted it. How dangerous could a five-year-old boy be?

Judd glanced at his watch. Twenty minutes had passed. It was time to pick up Mike, and then get the boy. He double parked in front of the building and entered. He was about to open the door when Mike appeared. "How'd things go?" Judd asked, showing Mike to the Bronco.

"We can pick him up at a foster home three miles from here."

"Did they give you any problems?" Judd asked, opening the door of the Bronco.

"No. They were happy that the boy could be reunited with his family," Mike said, lighting a cigarette. "When does my flight leave for LA?"

"At six o'clock. I'll be jumping on a plane with the boy myself. We're going to North Dakota of all places. Hopefully, Agent Cuff will be done with his work in Boston so we can be done with this mess and go back to work overseas where we belong."

* * *

Nevin Cuff tried to stay a safe distance behind Dr. Roderick Taylor's gray Volvo wagon, but the heavy Saturday night Boston traffic made it difficult. The cars were bumper to bumper, like a herd of steer grazing a pasture. "Where the hell is he going?" Nevin thought out loud. Dr. Taylor maneuvered between the traffic like a mouse struggling though a maze, until finally he stopped at a coffee shop two blocks away from the Bull Finch bar, the place the TV show *Cheers* is based on. Nevin parked his car a block away, pulled out his laptop computer, and put a CD ROM disc in the drive. It was the disc he picked up from the locker at the bus station that contained a report from an operative in Boston.

Dr. Taylor had been a busy man the past two weeks, Nevin thought as he scrolled through the information. He had been to New York City for two days then back to Boston. The wiretap placed a week ago proved he'd spoken to Dr. Robin Vastbinder twice. He probably knew way more than he needed to and now it was time for him to die.

Nevin continued scrolling through the information, glancing out his window between sentences, keeping a close watch on Dr. Taylor's vehicle. He wanted to throw the computer out of the window when he realized that Dr. Taylor was now aware of the wiretap. That fucking walking corpse would purposely make statements on the phone about his plans for the day and disappear for ten to twelve hours, Nevin thought. "That fucking bitch," Nevin said, slamming his fingers on the keyboard. She must've told him when she called him from the psych. hospital. None of this would've happened if he were the lead on this objective. Dr. Robin Vastbinder would be so dead that it would seem she never had existed.

The operative may have dropped the ball on the tap, but at least he found Dr. Taylor, Nevin thought reading the end of the message. He was hiding in a hotel room in South Boston. Luckily, the operative finally figured out his scam. He was quite clever for a civilian, Nevin thought. He would dress up like a woman and leave his apartment. Then he climbed back in through a basement window and continued the facade. The operative should never have underestimated him. He was staying at a dive hotel about five miles from where he was located. Nevin quickly started his car and pulled away. Dr. Taylor was about to have a one man surprise party that would end his life.

Nevin arrived at the three-story hotel, a dive with dusky bricks about to fall from the building and a sign that was half lit, and parked his vehicle a block a way. He popped his trunk and got out of his car. He clicked opened a silver brief case and grabbed a black container, the size of a pill bottle, and walked toward the hotel, looking for signs of Dr. Taylor. He checked in and went to his room. Dr. Taylor's room was one floor above. He scanned the hallway, sneaked up the stairwell, walked casually to the door and looked around. The corridor was empty. He picked the lock and slowly entered. Pulling a flash light from his jacket, he scanned the room. There was a suitcase on the bed with a briefcase beside. He thought about inspecting them, but decided Dr. Taylor would be home soon. He walked inside the shower and waited quietly.

Dr. Taylor was about to ingest one of the most poisonous and untraceable drugs the CIA used, INH. It was safe for the treatment of tuberculosis in small doses, but if a large enough dose were given, it would kill in a few hours. Dr. Taylor was going to ingest an INH cocktail at gunpoint. It was virtually untraceable. He wanted to blow his brains through his ears, but Judd wanted no evidence of foul play. At first he was pissed, but when he realized he would at least get to kill someone, he couldn't wait to get on the plane to Boston. Stakeouts really sucked, he thought.

The thought of waiting in the shower all night made Nevin want to forget about orders and put a bullet in Dr. Taylor's head. He slumped in the tub, pulled out his cellular phone and read his email messages. He was about to doze off when he heard footsteps approach the hotel room. Finally, he thought. The footsteps got louder with each second and his fingers began to tingle, anticipating the kill. He was about to position himself in front of the bathroom door, when his cellular phone buzzed against his chest. He thought about ignoring it, but only one person had the number, Judd Isla. "Hello?" Nevin whispered.

"Abort the objective."

"What?"

"Don't kill him," Judd barked. "We have other plans for him."

Chapter 34

Robin Vastbinder rolled down the window of Orpheus's blue Audi and enjoyed the cool wind that caressed her face. It had been two days since she felt the warmth of the sun on her cheeks and smelled the fresh smog she once hated. But the few moments didn't last. It was going to be difficult to get Jacob from the foster home. She had no adoption papers and it would take months to get them. And since she'd been committed, it would be impossible. The notion of the CIA getting the boy made her nauseated. "Orpheus, can we stop at this liquor store?" Robin asked, pointing.

"It's two o'clock in the afternoon," Orpheus said, his eyes picking her apart.

"Please."

"No way."

"I'm not asking you," Robin said through clenched teeth. "I'm telling you. I need a drink."

"Calm down," Orpheus said, his eyes about to jump from his face. "We'll stop. But I think this is the last thing you need."

"I just need to relax for a moment and figure out how we're going to get Jacob out of there."

Orpheus reluctantly pulled over the car and opened the door. "Maybe you really do need a few days in that nut house."

Robin jumped out of the car and ran inside. She bought a pint of scotch, a metal flask, and ran back to the car. She filled up the flask, spilling a puddle on the floor, and took a long swig. She inhaled a deep cleansing breath as the alcohol relaxed the tight muscles that strangled her neck and shoulders. "Give me a swig of that," Orpheus said.

"It's two o'clock in the afternoon," Robin snapped back sarcastically.

"It's been a bottle of scotch kind of day," Orpheus replied, taking a swig and wrinkling his face. "Are you sure that isn't lighter fluid?"

"I'm sorry it's not single malt, but that's all they had," Robin replied, taking another drink. "So, how are we going to get this kid?"

"Hey, I used up all my ideas getting you out," Orpheus replied, shrugging his shoulders.

"What if you pose as a child psychiatrist from Columbia with a radical new therapy for Post Traumatic Stress syndrome in children?"

"Maybe, but this is a child we're dealing with. I'd need release forms and clearance from the Department of Welfare. The police would love to throw an educated black man in prison. Then I'll be in some cell with a fat guy named Bubba who hasn't been with a woman in years and wants to take a slice out of my black ass."

"Don't worry, you won't be alone. We'll all be in prison or dead before this thing is over."

"How long do you think we have?"

"If we know where Jacob is, I'm sure they do by now," Robin said, staring pensively out of the window. "You know how much blood it would take to cure a 70kg adult?"

"I estimated the viral load would have to be enormous," Orpheus replied, rubbing his chin. "It would be like bleeding the kid to death. There's no way they could transfuse back the blood they removed in enough time to save the child's life. And even if he did live, they'd never let him leave. He'd be a slave until they figured out how to replicate the protein."

"How could they do that to a child?"

"Hey, I'm not surprised. I'm sure you've heard of the Tuskegee experiment? A lot of young black males died of syphilis because they withheld treatment of penicillin."

"What the hell are we going to do?"

"We better decide soon. The place is just around the corner."

What to do? What to do? Robin kept asking herself. As the car turned the corner, fifteen row houses appeared. She counted the houses and spotted 816 on the corner. As they parked, she noticed a thin black male about to walk inside. A familiar face stood in front of the building. His eyes scanned the area, then he jumped back into his red Ford Bronco. She blinked twice to refocus on his face, and then she realized it was *him*. The pockmark on his cheek looked like a crater on the moon when the drug distorted her mind. And his heavy eyebrows, black balding hair with brown deceptive eyes that looked so desperate at the bar that night. It was the CIA. But why did the other man go inside? She could only think of one thing. "Get into the other lane, quickly," Robin barked.

"Why?"

"Just do it!" Robin yelled, pushing the wheel.

Orpheus swerved to the right, almost wrecking into a taxicab, passed through a red light and barely avoided an oncoming Honda Civic. "Are you trying to kill us?" Orpheus snapped. "Speed Racer was a skinny little white boy…without an Afro."

"Listen, you have to drive me around back. We may be able to get lucky."

"What's going on?"

"They're here," Robin said, taking a drink of Scotch. "Two of them. One was black. Probably posing as his father and has all the paper work to take Jacob out of the place."

"What are you planning to do?" Orpheus asked, concerned.

"I want you to find a Captain Dennis Irwin. He's at the 15th precinct in Brooklyn. Tell him what's going on. It's our only chance."

"Why don't you come with me?"

"Just do it and drop me off around back."

"Listen..."

"We don't have time for this," Robin interrupted. "Drop me off around back and go."

Orpheus swerved into the alley behind the houses. A small yard was fenced in around the back of each house. "Slow down," Robin said, scanning the yards for the boy. Hopefully, he was outside. It was the middle of the afternoon. Every five-year-old boy had to be playing outside on a sunny spring Saturday, she thought. Three yards were empty; the fourth had a little boy playing catch with his father. "Stop the car and let me out," Robin said.

"Are you sure you know what you're doing?"

"No. Do you have a cellular phone?"

"Yes. The number is 555-1854."

"1854...got it. I'll call you when I can."

"Be careful."

Orpheus sped away as Robin ran from yard to yard, unable to approximate which was 816. They all looked the same. Two yards to her left, she spotted the outline of a black child. His narrow little face, full lips and desolate, silent eyes stared at the sand box as if the yard were empty. She sprinted towards him, stopped at the fence and closed her mind of the consequences of her apparent actions. The child's life was in danger.

Robin leaped over the fence and rushed towards the sand box. The boy's eyes widened as she scooped him up into her arms. He fought, kicked and struggled, but she held him close to her chest. She fought the pain he inflicted with a bite to her chest, and kept running. She jumped over a hedge and ran through the adjacent yard. Quickly, opening the latch on the fence, she ran down the alley until a sharp pain radiated through her chest and she dropped the boy. "I'm not here to hurt you," Robin yelled, holding his shoulders firmly as he struggled to break her grip. "Some very bad men are here to get you and if you keep fighting me, they'll get us both. You've got to trust me. I'm all you have."

He continued to kick and fight, bruising Robin's shins and feet. But, she fought through the pain and held her grip. "Please Jacob, I need you to calm down. I can't do this without you. I know you don't trust anyone, but you have to trust me. Please."

Jacob gradually slowed his resistance. He examined her eyes as if he could look into her soul and grabbed her hand. Robin pulled him along through the yards, maneuvering around lawn equipment and swings set until she reached the street. A myriad of people filled the sidewalks. Young couples holding hands as they moved in and out of the panhandlers begging for change, businessmen on cellular phones choking down hot dogs discussing their next millions, and old men and women walking the streets trying to occupy their time. Robin glanced at the road. She almost lost her breath when she spotted a red Bronco turn around the corner, stop, and a man jump out. She grabbed the boy and fought her way through the crowd. She looked over her shoulder and spotted the CIA agent. She doubled her pace, almost tripping over the feet of a woman in her way. Looking back, she noticed the man was gaining on them. She crossed over the sidewalk and headed for the road. The light to her right was yellow; the light ahead was still red. She dragged the little boy behind her as his little feet fought to keep pace. She was halfway across the road when the light turned green. Three cars skidded to an abrupt stop as she feebly raised her hand, trying to stop the three lanes of traffic. Finally, she made it to the other side. Out of the corner of her eye she could see the man stop at the corner. The oncoming traffic had saved her for the moment.

Robin frantically scanned her surroundings. Her eyes moved back and forth, up and down, until she spotted the entrance to a subway. Looking back down the street, the Bronco reappeared. She sprinted until her lungs burned, practically dragging the boy on the ground. One block away, she thought to herself. Around the corner, the Bronco reappeared. Its engine roared down the road, weaving in between the traffic and stopping along side the sidewalk. This time, two men got out. She kept running and reached the entrance. She skipped down the steps and reached the bottom. Frantically, she combed through the lint in her pocket and found enough change to go through the turnstile. Looking back, she saw the two men reach the bottom of the steps. She picked up the boy, his face frozen with fear, and sprinted towards the subway train. The men jumped through the turnstiles and followed. The door slowly opened as passengers exited. She fought through the crowd and jumped aboard. The men were a hundred feet away, knocking over people as if they were bowling pins, fighting to get to the train. The doors were still open as the men continued to approach. She went to the back of the train trying to hide behind an obese man with a long beard, decorated with tattoos on his arms. The doors weren't going to close in time, she was sure of it. She held her breath and held the boy close to her chest, praying that God would protect them. The doors moved as the men reached out their hands to stop them. Robin felt her muscles relax as the doors sealed shut. The men were trapped outside. Tears poured down her face as she squeezed the boy close to her heart.

The subway had many stops, which made it difficult for the men to follow her. But where should she get off? Brooklyn? Hopefully, Orpheus had convinced Captain Dennis Irwin to help. It was a slim chance considering the story sounded outlandish. But he had to know Frank would never steal drugs and murder someone. The click of the tracks against the wheels of the train reminded Robin of the clock that ticked against Jacob and her own life. She glanced down at Jacob; his eyes trembled with fear as he clung to her side. It was the same look he had the first time she saw him in the E.R. He may have only been six, but he knew that the chances they would get away were unlikely. She could see it in his eyes.

The subway stopped. It was time to get off. The doors opened, Robin grabbed Jacob and walked up the steps. She carefully examined the streets. Not a cop in sight, she thought. By now, the police had to be aware she was on the loose and the only cop she could trust was Captain

Irwin. Glancing at her watch, she realized it was six o'clock. She spotted a pay phone on the other side of the road and dialed information. Obtaining the number to the police station, she punched the buttons, examined her surroundings, and waited for the phone to pick up. An operator answered and punched her through to Captain Irwin's office. A sinking feeling overtook her when she realized he was gone for the day. She was out of change, but luckily remembered her calling card number, which she hadn't used in a year, and called Orpheus's cellular phone. The phone rang fifteen times. No answer. She tried his home, and then tried the cellular phone again, this time letting it ring twenty-five times. No answer. Where the hell was Orpheus?

CHAPTER 35

After five 'rot' dogs from a convenience store, two packs of cigarettes, and a grueling twenty-three hour drive, Frank Roberts was an hour from Minot, North Dakota. His butt had felt as if someone had rubbed sandpaper against it. His neck was as tight as an over-stretched rubber band. The road had hypnotized him; he could see yellow lines every time he closed his eyes. The two hours of sleep he had planned turned out to be only forty minutes. The image of his son slowly dying in front of his eyes made him jump awake every ten minutes. His eyes felt swollen, his body fatigued, almost ready to drop, but he fought through it all. He was only an hour away.

North Dakota was unlike any other place he'd ever been. It reminded him of upstate New York, but it was a lot flatter with long stretches of nothing but mountains and sagebrush. The air smelled as if it had been filtered. The sun seemed to predominate the sky. He reached inside his pocket and grabbed another Newport. His throat was raw, but the need for nicotine made him ignore it. The only thing that tempered the boredom was cigarettes and visions from the past. He had relived his childhood, the pain of watching his father die and the empty seat at his high school football stadium. And all those fans at his college football games, especially his ex-wife. Those days, she begged to be by his side. He was a football star, which was the top of the food chain in college. He could've had any woman he wanted and, unfortunately, he chose a trophy that fit nicely on his arm at the frat parties. Their relationship was never the same since the day he blew out his knee, ending his chance for the NFL. Luckily, he graduated with honors in criminology and easily got a job on the force. But that wasn't enough for Cindy. She wanted the big lights and fancy cars. That's why she left him for the rich banker. Poor bastard, he thought. Her love was only as deep as his pockets.

The last ten minutes were grueling. The road no longer appeared as black bituminous pavement with yellow lines, it became a jumbled blur. A half-mile down the road he spotted a gas station. He pulled in, barely able to steer the car and parked. He pulled out his map and examined it. He looked up at the sign near the gas pump and realized he was in Minot. But, where the hell was the Loventhol clinic? He walked into the station and found a burly man with a full beard, dressed in a grease-stained Chicago Bears tee shirt, standing on the other side of the counter. "I'm lost, I was wondering if you could help?" Frank said, picking up a pack of cigarettes.

"What are you looking for?" the man asked, ringing the items up.

"The Loventhol clinic."

"That herbal cancer place?"

"Yeah."

"It's about forty miles from here. Make a left out of the park'n lot and drive till you see a sign for Farley's Tackle and Bait; at that sign you'll make a right and it's ten miles down the road…can't miss it. It's in Burlington. Most of those folks stay in Minot and make the drive to the clinic every day. You don't look like you're all that sick considering what I see passing through my store."

"Well, I will be if I don't get there soon," Frank replied, looking away from the man's face.

"The place hasn't helped a person in these parts. Too damn expensive and I still can't see how a bunch of herbs and oils can save anyone from cancer. Bunch of bullshit if you ask me. If it was me, I'd save my money and get out a fishing pole and a six pack and let the good Lord take over."

"I'll keep that in mind. Thanks."

The remote location was perfect, Frank thought. The wheat fields that stretched miles beyond his view were like a blanket of gold swaying in the brisk wind. The mountains surrounded the terrain like the borders to the ends of the earth. The road was so flat that Frank thought Columbus might have been wrong. Frank stuck his hand out of the window and enjoyed the cool wind that tickled his fingers. It was the kind of breeze that made him forget for a moment that he had no idea how he was going to get inside the complex and find his son. The chances that his boy was readily accessible were slim. He had to be hidden in some remote location that he didn't have the time or the patience to find.

Minot looked like New York City compared to Burlington. There was a small plaza with a Denny's and a Best Western. It was probably the only franchise restaurant in the entire town. Frank pulled into the parking lot of the Best Western and entered the building. The lobby was occupied with elderly women with wrinkled, tan skin and polyester pants and children, who looked malnourished, with baseball caps covering their baldheads. He was sure most of them were dying and the clinic was their last hope. But, with Nicole dead and Jacob missing, their only chance was his son: a thought that made a chill tingle his body.

Frank approached the counter, his mind churning with discombobulated thoughts of how he was going to get into the lab. He was sure the security was pretty tight, considering they used criminals to guard the premise. He paid the sixty dollars a night and grabbed the key to his room. As he walked down the hallway, past the ferns and cheap paintings of birds and flowers on the wall, a man emerged from the room beside his. He was in his fifties with a frail frame that barely held on the flesh and a face that sunk into his skull. Frank stared at him for a moment and then realized this was his chance. "Excuse me," Frank said, stopping him in the hallway. "You here for the clinic?"

"I'm not here for the farmers' conventions," the man said, breaking a smile.

"I was wondering if I could ask you a few questions," Frank said.

"Shoot."

"Have they helped?"

"I'm pretty much past help," the man said somberly. "The treatments sure do wonders for my quality of life, though. Before I came here I could barely get out of bed. Doctors wanted me to go through another round of chemo, but I declined. I figured I'd try something else because that shit just made me sicker, and they only gave me a ten percent chance of surviving. I heard about this place from a friend and decided I had nothing to lose."

"Do you think it's worth the cost?" Frank asked, trying to figure out if the thousand dollars in his wallet would get him in the door.

"A hundred thousand dollars is a lot to part with, I must admit. But, my family has all the money they need. I wish it was enough to give me back my health."

"I heard about this place from a friend also. He said it worked wonders for him and I figured I'd at least check it out before shelling out that kind of money. Do they offer a tour of the facility or something before you commit?"

"I'm sure they have something considering how much cash this place costs. I'll be leaving at eight o'clock for Aloe Vera juice and therapy," the man said, scanning Frank. "You don't look like the typical patient."

"I'm in remission," Frank said, feeling guilty for lying to the dying man. "But the doctors say it won't be for long."

"Well, the best of luck to you. Name's George Babinchick," he said extending his hand.

"Jeffrey Coors," Frank replied, extending his hand, thinking of his favorite beer.

"Same family that makes the beer?"

"I wish."

Frank plunged his plastic card in the door, then opened it. The room had a musty smell mixed with industrial cleaners trying to hide the odor. He plopped on his bed and lit a cigarette. He clicked on the TV and the Mets were playing the Braves and losing by three runs in the ninth, with two outs and nobody on. It was the same feeling he had the moment he found Aaron Rankin's body in Pittsburgh— desperate and hopeless. The CIA or police would find him in a day or two. Hopefully, that would be long enough to find his son.

Chapter 36

The digital clock on the nightstand beside Frank's bed seemed to move as if the seconds were hours. It had been the longest night of Frank's life. He stared at the shadows on the ceiling and thought of his son, Jacob, and Robin. Were they still alive? The thoughts swirled endlessly around in his head like an angry ocean on a brisk summer night. Unfortunately, bad luck seemed to follow Robin around like a lost tourist. It was almost comical how much tragedy had consumed her life. She was the kind of woman who had everything, a promising career, a beautiful house: everything his ex-wife dreamed of. But the thought of what those brainless goons from the CIA would do to her made Frank consider going back to New York. He could only pray that Dennis Irwin would look after them. His son was his only responsibility at the moment.

But, the image of Robin's face dominated his every thought. She was the kind of woman that would've laughed at his advances five years ago. She had a classic beauty, like Rita Hayward, that complimented her brains. He could tell by the way she made love that her heart usually only belonged to one man. Money didn't matter to her like it did to his ex-wife. What would a woman like that want to possibly do with him?

Frank tried to fall asleep, but every unfamiliar creak and pop jarred his eyes open. He was a cop fallen from grace: every precinct in the country would like to take a bite of his ass, he thought. He imagined the smile on a local policeman's face as he broke into his room and put a gun to his head. It would make the security guard, dressed as a cop, a legend. The cop could walk in the local barbershop and brag to his cronies about how he busted the big city cop. It would only be a matter of hours until someone knew he was in the area. He was sure the computers in Minot worked just as well as the ones in New York City. It would be a big game on the Internet: catch the cop. He closed his eyes and slipped into a half sleep, waiting for the door to break open.

The rays from the sun leaked though the blinds and brightened the darkness behind his eyelids, awakening him from a restless sleep. Frank stretched and rubbed the thick sleet from his eyes. He lit a smoke and pulled himself to a sitting position. The jolt of nicotine made the rusty cogwheels in his brain start to churn. He looked at the clock and realized he only had ten minutes to meet George Babinchick. He rushed around the room, washing his face, and then changing into a sweatshirt and jeans. A soft knock vibrated the door as he put on his shoes and stumbled trying to answer it. "You ready?" George asked, carrying a folder full of papers.

"Sorry, I'm running a little late," Frank replied, tying his sneakers.

The Loventhol clinic looked more like a health club than a health care facility, Frank thought. The building was all glass, with a rock waterfall in front, artistically trimmed bushes and plush grass. A sports complex, comprising of a tennis court, miniature golf course and Olympic size swimming pool, was behind the building. Frank followed George into the lobby, noticing the marble floors and works of art on the wall, and realized how rich these people had become from the blood of Nicole. The thought brought a rage through his bones that he fought to subside. "I'll show you to the main office, then I've got to go," George said looking at his watch. "I don't want to be late for my chelation therapy."

Frank followed George through the glass doors and found three secretaries typing on computers and answering phones. "Why don't we meet for lunch?" George offered about to leave. "We'll meet at the cafeteria, say twelve o'clock?"

"Twelve o'clock it is."

Frank approached the desk to find a voluptuously shaped woman behind it. "May I help you?" she asked, typing on her computer.

"I'm here for a tour."

"Who are you with?" the secretary asked with suspicious eyes.

"I'm not with anyone. Just here to see if this place is worth the kind of money you people are asking."

"Are you interested in treatment?"

"Yes. I was just diagnosed with lung cancer three months ago," Frank said, realizing that the lie could someday become the truth if he continued smoking two packs a day.

"Have you had any form of treatment?"

"That's why I'm here. Chemotherapy is pretty rough and I've heard some good things about this place."

"I think we could arrange a tour," the secretary said, looking at her watch. "Could you wait here for a moment?"

"Sure."

The secretary disappeared into the back office as Frank sat down on a soft, green couch against the wall. On the coffee table was an assortment of magazines with pictures of plants. There were journals that contained information on alternative medicine and the so-called cures they promised. The glass doors opened and a guard appeared. His somber brown eyes, pale skin marked with a tattoo on his arm, and sagging breasts made him look like a sumo wrestler in bad need of a bra. Frank was sure he hadn't seen his penis in years. His thin eyes examined Frank for a moment, then looked past him at the clock on the wall.

A thin, bubbly woman dressed in a business suit emerged from her office. "Are you Mr. Coors?"

"Yes," Frank replied, standing up.

"Jenny Howard," she said extending her hand, "Director of public relations. So what is your diagnosis?"

"Lung cancer," Frank said nervously.

"What kind?"

"The worst kind," Frank said, lowering his eyes.

"Small cell?"

"Unfortunately," Frank replied, relieved that his lack of knowledge didn't blow his cover. "My doctor said I have about six months without treatment. I wanted to explore any other possible options before I took that poison they call chemotherapy."

The woman's eyes seemed to melt with concern. She smiled and said, "Well, that's why we're here. To give people an alternative which we here at the Loventhol clinic feel is much better than mainstream medicine can offer. As you know, there are no guarantees, but we have quite a few success stories. Why don't you follow me?"

The fake smile and rehearsed lines made Frank want to laugh at her every notion. She was a walking commercial that the plastered-on makeup couldn't hide. She led him through the doors and back into the lobby. She smiled and the guard buzzed her through the metal doors. A long hallway appeared, with large glass windows displaying four rooms. Frank looked up at the ceiling and noticed a camera in the corner. He wasn't sure if it was his imagination, but it seemed it followed him down the hallway. On top of each one was a tiny plastic box that blinked a red light. It was a motion detector, the same they used in banks. It was quite sophisticated, which further strengthened the notion that his son was in the complex. But where?

Frank planted his hand on the glass and looked in the first room. There were six people inside sitting in recliner chairs that sat next to a large box-shaped machine with a control panel on the front containing a digital display. A small wheel, surrounded with tubing filled with blood, spun slowly in a circle as the three men and one woman sat comfortably reading books and magazines. They looked similar to the dialysis machines his aunt had used when her kidneys failed. "This is the leukemia center where they take their blood through that machine," the woman said pointing. "And it removes abnormal cells from their blood. We've had a few success stories. Our most famous is Senator Tom Watson's daughter. We completely cured her of acute leukemia after she failed a bone marrow transplant twice. I wish everyone had her success."

"So, how many people have been cured?"

"Like I said before, Mr. Coors, there are no guarantees. It's impossible to predict who will be cured and who won't. But, we've had many success stories," she reminded him like an infomercial. "The people we usually see are at the end of the line. We are their last hope."

The next room looked very similar except it was dark with screens on every wall. It looked like a miniature Imax theater with a vibrant sky and slow moving clouds on the ceiling. The rays of the sun barely penetrated the mountains as it set in the distance. The waves of the ocean gently crashed against the sand, reminding Frank of the vacation with Nicole in the Bahamas. The people in the relining chairs had headphones on which probably had the sounds of the ocean mixed with soft comforting music. The look on their faces projected a peace that the cancer couldn't dim. "This is our relaxation therapy room," she said. "We believe in whole body treatment and our patients seem to respond well. I love to come in here myself after a rough day."

"So would I," Frank said, wishing he could forget the turmoil of his every second and layback in one of the recliners.

The next two rooms were clones of the first with similar machines but with different functions. Jenny Howard informed Frank the first was used for chelation therapy, which removed heavy metals from the blood, possibly slowing the progression of the cancer. The other room removed an array of toxins from the blood produced by the cancer. Frank followed Jenny through the double doors into a lobby and then stepped on the elevator. The building had five floors and a basement that probably wasn't accessible without a key to stop the elevator. That had to be the logical place they held his son, he thought. But how to get a key? What if he wasn't in the building at all? What if they had him at another place that would take days to find and weeks to get into? His son was nothing more than a dollar bill lying in a crib. They didn't want to teach him how to throw a baseball or pee standing up, or explain to him why the sun sets or how all those little people fit inside the radio. Hopefully, fate would be fair, just this once.

When the elevator stopped, Frank followed Jenny into the cafeteria. His stomach ached from all the cigarettes, but he decided to eat just to look natural. He grabbed a tray and followed Jenny to the line. "I think you'll find the selection unusual, but after you get used to it, you'll never want to eat supermarket food again," Jenny said, picking up a glass plate and walking over to the salad bar. The main entree was a soybean casserole with organically grown sweet potatoes and what looked like a cooked piece of bark for a side. It would be the last thing he would want to eat if he only had six months to live. The thought of choking down dry bark made him nauseated. He decided to try something safe, like salad. Unfortunately, the lettuce was replaced with a green leaf that looked like a palm tree. The tomatoes were the only things that resembled the salads he ate at Denny's. Faking a smile, he proceeded to fill his plate with food he pictured growing in the woods of his backyard. It wasn't food, it was weeds, he thought.

"I see you loaded up on the palm leaves," Jenny said examining his plate. "You'll love them, trust me. What this diet will do for your cancer is amazing. It not only makes you feel better, but it doesn't have any of that junk in it that you buy at the supermarket. I wish I could join you for lunch, but I've got some things to do in my office. If you decide that this place is right for you we can get the paperwork started later and we'll have you receiving your first treatment by tomorrow. Why don't you join George for lunch? He's over in the corner of the dining hall," Jenny said, pointing. "I'm sure he'll answer a lot of your questions. He's one of our success stories."

"Thanks," Frank said forcing a smile and walking into the dining area. In the corner of the room that contained couches surrounding the tables instead of chairs was George Babinchik waving his arms.

"How did your tour go?" George asked.

"Interesting place," Frank replied, fighting to swallow the bitter herbs that covered his plate. "The lady tells me that you're a success story."

"For a while," George replied, looking reflectively at his glass. "For the past ten months I've been getting better, but for some reason, the treatments don't seem to have the same effect."

"You mean those chelation treatments you were talking about aren't working any more?"

"Not those, the extracts from the shark's blood."

"I haven't heard about those."

"That's because they are fifty thousand a piece and you need two a week for six months. And the supply is so small. It's from a species of great white shark off the coast of South Africa. It has seven gills, instead of the normal six that most great white sharks have."

What a bullshit story, Frank thought. Those treatments came from the suffering of Jacob and Nicole. He pictured Jacob's terrified face as he winced with pain as they jammed the needle in his arm. Each second fueled his rage stronger than the one before it. They were probably using his son's blood by now with Nicole dead and Jacob missing. If George only knew his comfort came from the suffering of an infant. "Seven gills, huh?" Frank said, skeptically.

"Sounds crazy, but I have never felt so good since I've been sick after one of those treatments."

"Who knows, maybe it's some type of lag effect thing," Frank said. "It may start working again."

"Hope you're right," George said. "I keep feeling weaker everyday."

"You probably live in that relaxation chamber," Frank said, with an idea brightening in his brain. "I bet one night in that thing would cure my five months of insomnia."

"You think you're interested in having the clinic take over your treatment?"

"It's my last chance."

"I'm really not supposed to be doing this," George said, lowering his voice and leaning forward. "But, I think I could arrange it if you keep it quiet."

"Sure."

"Since I've invested so much money in this place they've pretty much let me use the facility when ever I want. If you promise to give me back the key card first thing in the morning, I'll let you use it tonight. But, you've got to be out of the place by four in the morning."

"I don't know what to say," Frank said, holding back a smile.

"Hey, I know what you're going through. Trust me. You can't put a price on a good night's sleep."

Frank followed George to the garbage area and placed his tray on the rack. They were going to meet for dinner and the access to the compound he needed would be in his hands. He felt guilty for a moment thinking about the desperate hope in George's eyes, but it quickly dissipated when the image of his son entered his mind. It was sad that George was probably going to die soon. But, George had watched his children grow. Frank's son could possibly never know what it would be like to play catch in the summer time or enjoy hide and seek until the darkness draped the neighborhood. George's key card was his son's last hope of the life he deserved.

Chapter 37

Dr. Noah Jenkins slammed his pen against the table when he saw the latest test results from the infant's blood. He had been in his lab every night till midnight trying to synthesize the protein contained in the infant's blood, but it was too complex. The virus constantly mutated, like the AIDS virus, producing a slightly different protein each time. The infant had enough blood to save the First Lady, but he would die. And the virus could possibly be lost forever if the other child is not found. The thought made the kink in his neck strangle him more and more each minute. He had slept two hours a night and ate one meal a day for the past month as Dr. Loventhol ate caviar and drank cognac. Dr. Loventhol acted as if the situation were an inside joke in which only he knew the punch line. His lack of concern made Dr. Jenkins want to peel off his skin.

Dr. Jenkins rubbed his eyes and sighed. He picked up the test tube filled with the cancerous blood cells from a mouse, put two drops of the synthesized protein mixed with some of the virus from the infant's blood, and jiggled the tube. He placed it into the incubator, went back to his lab table and peered deeply into his microscope. The mouse's cells that he incubated for the past three days were not infected by the cancer-curing virus. He pushed the microscope from his face and slammed his hand on the table. The most powerful woman in the world and ten million dollars were slowly dissolving away like the dying cells on the microscope. And the most powerful men in the country wouldn't take 'I can't' for an answer.

The constant phone calls from Senator Watson had strangled his every notion. It kept him awake at night, tormenting his every moment as Murray Loventhol made his celebrity appearances at the lab once a week.

Noah was about to pull a rack of test tubes from the incubator when the image of Murray Loventhol's face infiltrated his mind. He closed the steel door and walked over to the phone. He pounded the keys as if he were banging on finger drums and waited for Murray's answer. "Do you know what time it is?" a groggy voice barked.

"I thought it would be a good idea to make you know what it feels like being awake for the tenth night in a row till three o'clock in the morning," Dr. Noah Jenkins snapped.

"This better be important," Dr. Loventhol said, sharply.

"The protein doesn't work."

"Did you match it with the spike in the protein electrophoresis report I sent you?"

"It matches perfectly, but it doesn't work. It could be as simple as one amino acid, but when you have a million combinations to choose from, the chances of finding the right one are about as good as winning the lottery."

"I told you I'd be there in the morning."

"I need your ass in North Dakota now," Dr. Jenkins barked. "I suppose you don't realize that we have a week. Even if I get the protein, it will take at least a month before we could transfuse the blood into the First Lady to be effective. We need the boy."

"They'll find him."

"When?" Dr. Jenkins shouted. "When she dies? I'm not taking this one on my own, Murray. This will all be gone if they don't find that boy soon."

"Relax, Noah," Dr. Loventhol said. "You need to spend more time in the relaxation center."

"You think this is all a game, but when they shut this place down along with our careers, you'll be sitting in some jail cell, praying to see the light of day."

"We have many options," Dr. Loventhol said, confidently.

"Like what? Use the infant?"

"If necessary."

"But, he will die."

"Who would you rather die? The most important woman in the country or some insignificant child of a dead hooker? We'd probably be doing the kid a favor considering what he'd have to endure if his mother were alive. Do you think in the animal kingdom a lion is concerned about killing the cubs from another pride? It is the survival of the fittest and the weak always die. It's the way it has been since the beginning of time. And with the President's help, we'll save millions. One life is definitely worth the sacrifice."

"Have you lost your mind?"

"Have you?" Dr. Loventhol snapped back. "You knew from the start, Noah, that some choices had to be made when you signed on to work on this project, so don't think for a moment you're not as deep into this as I am."

"So, when do we send the child to Washington?" Dr. Jenkins uttered with a regretful sigh.

"One of Senator Watson's associates will be calling me in the morning. I'll let you know what we're going to do when I arrive late tomorrow morning."

"We have another problem."

"You must be talking about Detective Roberts?" Dr. Loventhol said calmly.

"He's in Burlington."

"I've already spoken with security. Don't worry, he won't be a problem. I'll see to that."

Chapter 38

Dr. Robin Vastbinder stared into the depths of the rubble of the abandoned building and realized that following the tug of Jacob's hand wasn't such a good idea. Jacob knew Brooklyn, but his silence made it difficult to fully trust his judgments. Robin followed him through alleys, under bridges and in between buildings, fighting her fears of the darkness. The dimly lit street lamps merely illuminated inches of the cracked pavement. The lights from the dusty, chipped away, condemned buildings were small fires or flickering light bulbs that highlighted the black brick that was once red. It was a place that she had seen only in her nightmares, but Jacob acted as if it were his front yard.

The air felt coarse against Robin's lungs as she struggled to keep up with Jacob. A five-year-old boy had the endurance of ten adults, she thought. Her legs burned, muscles ached and feet throbbed. She pulled on Jacob's arm, trying to slow him down, but he continued dragging her along. She gathered enough strength to plant her feet and Jacob's skinny legs finally came to a stop. "Where are we going?" Robin uttered between breaths.

Jacob's fearful eyes remained cold and determined. He tugged on her arm again and stared deeply in her eyes as if he knew they were headed for a safe place. Robin inhaled four deep breaths and continued the jog. The ten-ton balls that seemed to be shackled to her ankles loosened as

Jacob slowed and entered one of the buildings. The stairs creaked, almost about to buckle, with each of her steps. The darkness was as thick as mud. Jacob pulled her to the end of the corridor and into the last room on the right.

He opened the door and inside was a dusty mattress and a wooden nightstand that had only patches of varnish left. The cracked wood floors were black, with dips spread randomly around the room. The air smelled like garbage mixed with dust. Jacob released his tight grip on her hand, walked over to the nightstand, and opened the drawer. He pulled out matches, two candles and lit them both. He walked over to the black, film-covered window and stared at a small open field across the street. His face looked as if he were an old man reliving a life that seemed to pass him by before he was ready.

Robin walked over to the window and tried to think of her next move. It was much too dangerous to go out into the night and try to find a phone booth. She had already tried ten times to get in touch with Orpheus, but to no avail. The thought of him dead or in jail made her want to pull her brain from her skull. And what about Frank? Where was he?

It was a question that plagued her mind every second for the past 48 hours. He could be dead, she thought. But, something inside her could feel he wasn't. He was too smart to let that happen. It was a connection that she hadn't felt since her husband died. What was it about him? He was good-looking, but not very sharp around the edges. But there was honesty in his eyes that brought a comfort that she hadn't experienced in a long time. The chaos that surrounded her every second seemed to be calmed by his smile. But, what if he was really dead? She could never make it alone. She reached in her pocket and pulled out her flask of scotch and took a long swig. The alcohol would numb her fears. It always did, she thought.

"I wish I had your strength, Jacob," Robin said, taking a drink and pacing. "You just seem to take it all in, as if this is the way it's supposed to be. Not a word. You take the easy way and I don't blame you."

Jacob stared at her for a moment and then resumed his sullen gaze out the window.

"I have no idea what we're going to do in the morning. I don't even know if we'll make it through tonight," Robin said, leaning her head against the wall and crying. "The entire city is probably looking for us as we speak and they have no idea about the truth. But I know how you feel. I know what it's like to lose someone you love so much. My son wasn't much older than you when he died. My husband and I just celebrated our ten-year anniversary before the accident. I haven't taken off this tennis bracelet he bought me since the day he died," Robin uttered, twirling the chain reflectively between her fingers. "For the first week I thought he was coming home from a long day at the hospital, but once I realized that it was forever, I knew I would never wake up without that hopeless feeling again. I've got to give it to you kid," Robin said tipping her flask, "You would be a great psychiatrist. I could talk to you for hours and you would never give me some antidote that was supposed to make me feel better."

The alcohol began to saturate Robin's brain, making the stress a little more bearable. She walked over to the window and stabilized her arm against the wall beside Jacob. His thin little eyes stared pensively at her face as if to say he understood, then the muscles of his face relaxed and he sighed. He gazed back out of the window and his mouth opened. "We'd play football every Sunday out there."

Each sound from his mouth sounded as if it had been amplified a thousand times. His voice was soft and innocent. His gestures were subdued, like a broken down football star recanting tales of his glorious past. His face looked as if he had lived another life, an existence that couldn't be tarnished by his everyday struggles. A thick tear ran down

Robin's face as she kneeled and leaned towards Jacob. "I bet you were the best player."

"My boys used to call me Flash because I could run faster than anyone," he said, dropping his head. "Wish I could play again."

"You'll get to play again," Robin said, placing both hands on his shoulders.

"Maybe in my dreams. Why do you drink so much?"

Robin glanced down at the flask and became immediately embarrassed. "I don't know," Robin replied searching for words. "I guess it makes things easier."

"My momma used to drink a lot," Jacob said, turning his face away from her, then staring ponderously at the floor. "She also put a bunch of flour up her nose. Said it helped her to breathe better, but my best friend Jimmy said that it was cocaine and once she started she would never stop. He sure was right. I guess she did it to forget about all those boyfriends she had. They would come over and give her a lot of money and stay overnight, and then in the morning they were gone, just like my dad. Mommy said that it was her job having boyfriends. She said she was doing a lot of good for the world. She made sad men very happy just by them spending the night. We were able to move out of the dirty old place into a nice place with all the Captain Crunch I could eat. So, that was O.K. with me. I could watch any video I wanted at anytime."

"What about your Dad?"

"I met him once. Brought me Wolverine."

"Wolverine?"

"He's an X-Man," Jacob said, as if Robin was from a different plant. "Don't you know who the X-Men are?"

"I can't say I do."

"Wolverine was the best X-Man because he could make all the bad men go away."

"Why haven't you spoken all this time?" Robin asked, softly.

"Don't know," Jacob said. "The bad men can be anyone. My mom told me not to trust anyone except for Frank."

"Detective Roberts?"

"He was the best boyfriend my mother ever had," Jacob said, his eyes brightening. "He'd stay more than one night all the time. And sometimes we'd go see the Mets."

"Your mother must've really loved him," Robin said, finally reaching out her hand, overcoming her inhibitions and caressing the little boy's hair as if he were her own. He moved away at first, but for some reason he trusted her. The muscles in his face and arms relaxed and he sat on the bed.

"She did; because she stopped sniffing that stuff and all her boyfriends didn't come around anymore. You're nice, like Frank."

"I would never let anything happen to you."

"You promise?"

"I promise," Robin replied, pulling him close to her chest. She held him tighter and nothing seemed to matter. It didn't matter whether she lived or died, her life was now about him. He would live to see his grandchildren if it took her last breath. "Do you think anyone will find us in here?"

"Most people who sleep in here don't wake up till noon. They drink all night and most of them are old and crusty and smell like poop. Nobody comes down here. My mom calls this place the forgotten world."

"Good. We need to get some rest. We have a lot to do in a few hours."

Robin wasn't sure what 'a lot to do' meant, as she brushed a layer of dust from the mattress. Captain Irwin had to be in his office before seven o'clock. But what if he wasn't? It was possible. Then what? She cuddled beside Jacob and stared into the darkness.

Chapter 39

The warmth of Jacob's chest against Robin's heart made the two hours seem like seconds. She glanced at her watch and realized it was time. She gently stirred Jacob. His face grimaced at first then he opened his eyes.

"It's time to get up honey," Robin said, softly.

"Where are we going?" Jacob asked, stretching, rubbing his eyes.

"I know a man who can help us."

"Are you sure he's not a bad man?" Jacob asked, a wave of fear oscillating through his eyes.

"Frank said he was a good man," Robin reassured, rising from the bed.

"I can't go back to that place," Jacob uttered through tears. "I hate needles and that's all they like to do at that place. Put needles in my arm. Makes me sick and dizzy."

"I would never let anyone do that to you again," Robin said, caressing his hair. "Trust me, we'll be safe."

The early morning sun brightened the streets making the decrepit neighborhood look a thousand times worse as she looked out of the window. It was as if someone had built run down buildings in a landfill. The heat from the sun made the air pungent with a stale odor that reminded Robin of a fraternity house after a puke-filled party night. She was about to reach for her flask when she realized her purse wasn't beside the bed as she remembered. She glanced over in the corner of the room and found Jacob on the floor looking through her stuff. "It isn't polite to look through people's things," Robin scolded.

"My uncle said if you leave something out that you don't want someone to find, don't be surprised if they look at it," Jacob said, gazing at the pictures in her wallet. "Is this your son?"

"Yes, it is," Robin said, walking over to his side.

"Did you love him?"

"Very deeply," Robin replied.

"I bet you miss him, just like I miss my momma and brother."

"I sure do."

"I didn't like my brother when momma brought him from the hospital. He was smelly and cried a lot. He made mommy act real mean. I thought she didn't like me no more but she told me she did. And Sean was pretty cool after a while. I could make faces and he'd laugh. He even watched cartoons with me. Well, I think he watched them. He would just stare at the T.V. and make weird faces. I guess that means he liked them."

"He probably was just happy that you liked them. It made him happy."

"You think so?" Jacob said, excited.

"I know so," Robin said, patting him on the back. "Is there some place you think we could eat and use the phone?"

"Two blocks up that street," Jacob said, pointing. "They have chocolate donuts with sprinkles."

The streets were lightly scattered with homeless people lying on the street corners waiting for the morning traffic to wash windows. The worn down buildings looked as if a gust of wind would powder the chipped away bricks into invisibility. Jacob grabbed her hand and led her into a tiny coffee shop that probably hadn't changed since the fifties. The floor had broken tiles and an inch of dust. A creaky ceiling fan whirred above. An Asian man was behind the counter wearing a New York Mets sweatshirt. He smiled, then went back to the coffee machine and poured water into the top. She scanned the place, looking for any suspicious stares and found two elderly African American men sipping on coffee. They looked up for a moment, and then went back to drinking their coffee. She ordered two chocolate donuts with sprinkles, an orange juice, and a cup of coffee, then made her way back to the telephone in the back of the shop.

She plopped the change into the pay phone, all the while watching Jacob sit at the booth picking the sprinkles off the donuts and drinking his juice. She dialed and waited for an answer. "15th precinct," a woman said.

"May I please speak to Captain Dennis Irwin?" Robin asked, quickly.

"Who should I tell him is calling?" the woman asked.

"A friend of Detective Frank Roberts."

"I'll see if he's available."

Soft elevator music purred over the line when the secretary put her on hold. The thought of Captain Irwin declining to speak with her made the anxiety that much thicker. What would she do then? It would be impossible to hide for another day. And going to the police station would be impossible. The CIA agents were always one step ahead and they had to be watching the station. The music stopped and the sounds of the chaotic police station returned. "Captain Irwin."

"A very good friend of yours said you could help," Robin said, anxiously.

"Who is this?" Captain Irwin asked, sharply.

"My name is Robin Vastbinder."

"I know who you are," Captain Irwin interrupted. "Some doctor with an Afro named Orpheus Martin said you'd be calling."

"Is he O.K?"

"He's here at the station, no one will get him. Are you and the boy all right?"

"A little shaken, but O.K."

"I'll come and get you myself. These walls seem to have ears since that idiot Frank decided to drive to Pittsburgh and kill some drug dealer."

"He what?" Robin replied, shocked.

"I don't believe a word of it. And I didn't believe his crazy story until today. Once we get the boy and enough evidence, we can notify the Feds and see what's going on at that so-called clinic. So, where can I meet you?"

"I'm in Brooklyn, on 27th and 4th."

"I'm leaving right now. Whatever you do, don't leave."

Robin sat down at the booth and took a sip of her coffee. She wanted a bite of the donut, but her stomach felt as if someone had dumped nuclear waste down her throat. A swig from her flask would cure that, she thought. But, it was empty and Jacob's tiny little eyes reminded her that the alcohol wasn't the answer. She reached inside her pocket, pulled out a Xanax, and washed it down her throat with coffee. It would help with the tremors from withdrawal once they started. How did this happen? she thought to herself. It was like a beast that slowly crept up on her without her realizing for one moment it was there.

"You better eat your donut," Jacob said, finishing the last of his orange juice. "You're just like my momma…never wanted to eat nothing."

"I'm just not hungry right now," Robin murmured, staring at her Styrofoam cup.

"Don't worry, the bad men aren't going to get us," Jacob said, grabbing her hand. "I've got superpowers, just like Batman. My momma said I was the man of the house and could take care of anything while she was gone at night."

"I know you'll protect us," Robin said, hugging him. "I know you will."

If that were only true, she thought as she pressed his head against her chest. The uncertainty of the future made her mind twirl with doubt. What about Jacob's brother? The thought of an infant lying helpless in his crib made her skin tingle, her heart race. And Dr. Taylor—her only chance of validation of the atrocities that occurred at the Loventhol clinic—was either dead or out of the country. He was alone with the entire world after his blood. She glanced out of the window, making sure she wasn't followed, all the while wondering if tomorrow would ever happen.

Chapter 40

The walls of Frank Roberts' hotel room had become bars of plaster and wood studs that entrapped his every notion. He tried sleeping, but every voice in the hall was like an alarm clock he couldn't turn off. He stared at the clock and out the window, waiting for the cover of darkness to liberate his son. It was as if time was suspended and every second was a thousand hours. As he rose from his bed and washed his face, he realized that as each hour passed, the more prepared the people inside the lab would be.

He looked at his watch and the grumble of his stomach overtook him. It was time to eat. Frank locked his door, scanned the hallway, and examined the faces of all who passed him by. Every eye seemed to interrogate his every thought. He felt a wave of anxiety that chipped away at his confidence like a knife skimming his flesh. The thought of eating became almost an afterthought, until he realized he would need his strength for tonight. He carefully walked up to the counter of the restaurant inside the hotel and ordered a hamburger and fries. Beside the counter was a newspaper machine. He dug inside his pocket and pulled out fifty cents. He removed a *USA Today* and glanced at the front page. His throat tightened when he read "First Lady with Cancer" on the front page.

Everything that once was a cloud of deception to Frank became clear. Why else would the CIA be involved? In the middle of the page were all the community service activities she accomplished over the past three years and it was all geared toward children. If only she knew that the magic potion that could save her life came from the blood of a child.

Frank crept back to his room and forced down his hamburger and fries, all the while wondering how he was going to snatch his boy from the millions of forces that would try to stop him. He took a gulp of water and the image of Robin entered his mind. Waves of guilt crept up his throat, along with his dinner. She could be dead for all he knew. Part of him wished he had never left, but who would save his son? Dennis would protect her, he reassured himself. Dennis may be a son of bitch at times, but he was loyal.

There had been many times when the rest of the force thought he was a renegade, especially when he broke the embezzlement case against those two scumbags who were stealing drugs from the evidence room. The entire precinct treated him as a traitor when the investigation started, but not Dennis. He defended Frank even though he got heat from the mayor's office. He wanted to call him, but that would put him in a compromising position. The last thing he wanted to do was ruin Dennis's career. He was retiring in two years. Frank lay in his bed and closed his eyes. It was five o'clock; only six hours to his son, he thought.

Frank was almost asleep until he heard a thump at the door. He jumped up from his bed, grabbed his gun and slithered to the doorway. He peeked out of the keyhole and was relieved when he realized it was George. He opened the door to find him with a smile on his face. "I brought you dinner," George said, handing him a paper bag.

"Thanks, but I already ate."

"You can eat it later. You'll love the steamed Tofu with seaweed and bean sprouts. It's seasoned Cajun style."

"I'm sure I will," Frank replied, a bit nauseated from the smell.

"Here's the key card," George said, handing it to him. "I told the security guards that you'd be coming by tonight, so just slip them each a few bucks and you can spend as much time in the relaxation chamber as you want. I'm sure after a night in that place you'll definitely want to become a patient here."

"I'm sure I will," Frank said, putting the card in his pocket.

"If you need anything, just give me a yell. Maybe we can do breakfast?"

"What time?" Frank asked, faking interest.

"I'll stop by around seven?"

"Sounds like a winner," Frank said closing the door.

Frank walked over to the window and glanced at the sun as it peered above the mountains. He stared at the bag of the so-called food and felt a tinge of remorse. George was an honest, kind man despite being dealt a deck full of shit with his disease. Frank was sure if he had a terminal illness he'd be bitter. But not George. It was a shame he had to deceive him. He lit another 'nail in his coffin' and exhaled violently. The guards knew he was coming and hopefully, they wouldn't have a clue what his agenda was. No one in this part of the country read the New York newspapers, he hoped. But it didn't matter; if he has to kill one of them to get to his son, it will be their fault for getting in his way.

It was time, as Frank looked at his watch. It was eleven p.m.; the longest six hours of his life. He smoked cigarettes the entire time as if they were oxygen and lay in his bed, reliving his entire life. He thought about how it began and became such a twisted joke that he wished he could escape. The past was nothing; it was the now and forever he was concerned about. If only he could see his son, just once. His life would be complete knowing that his only child wasn't being punished for his mistakes. He could never forgive himself for letting Nicole leave because of his superficial insecurities. He gave up the chance to finally feel complete for the first time in his life. He rose from his bed and rubbed his face. It was time to break into the lab and make up for the past.

Frank packed his gun in his leg holster and left his room. The night air smelled like fresh cut grass mixed with spring water. The half-lit moon had the same uncertainty he felt. Was it half black or half white? He jumped in his car and drove down the road. The guards would either let him in with open arms or attack him at the door. He guessed the latter. Most of them were criminals, which meant they were suspicious by nature. The doors by the tennis court were his best bet, he thought. And he could take the stairwell to the lobby. He parked next to the door and exited his car. Getting in would be easy, he thought…it was the escape he was worried about.

Frank ran the bar coded I.D. card though the port beside the door. It clicked, and then opened. He walked casually through the dimly lit hallway as if he belonged and entered the cafeteria. The lights were still on, but it was unoccupied. He strolled past it, down another corridor decorated with water paintings of mountains and prairies and walked through the glass doors at the end of the hallway, which lead to the lobby. Multiple ferns surrounded the leather couches and plush blue carpet and two security personnel appeared, watching a television behind a marble cubicle. One was obese, eating a hotdog; the other was muscular with a balding forehead. They looked as if their minds were some place else instead of watching reruns of a sitcom from the eighties, trying to make the shift go faster. The heavy-set man looked up, his eyes suspicious and uncertain, and asked, "How did you get in here?"

"Mr. Babinchik said I could get a few hours in the relaxation chamber," Frank said, sliding a fifty-dollar bill across the counter. The muscular man examined his face and then grabbed the fifty. "What's your name?" he asked.

"Jeffrey Coors."

The man glanced at a piece of paper and nodded to the obese guard. "Four hours," he said, looking at his watch. "That's it."

"Thanks," Frank said. "I haven't had a good night's sleep in weeks."

"Follow me," the obese guard said, grabbing keys from the drawer below the cubicle.

"I really appreciate this," Frank said.

"Fours hours buddy, that's it," the obese guard reminded. "The guys on the next shift are a bunch of pricks, if you know what I mean."

"That's plenty of time," Frank said, leaving the lobby and approaching the elevators.

Plenty of time for what? There were five floors in the building with many rooms. He needed a blueprint of the building, but where could he get one? He stepped on the elevator and realized he would need help. But from who? The fat piece of shit was going to become his friend whether he liked it or not.

The guard led him to an elevator and pressed the button. Frank examined the keys on the panel. Five floors with a basement, he thought, which probably couldn't be entered without an elevator key. But who had the key? If they were smart, only a select few, he thought. The elevator hummed, then a ding sounded above. The doors opened and the relaxation chamber appeared. The soft sounds of chamber music purred overhead. The domed ceiling, with it's slowly moving clouds and birds, looked as if heaven were on earth. He wanted to rest his head for a moment, but a rush of adrenaline reminded him this might be his only chance.

The guard walked over to a panel by the wall and punched in a sequence of buttons. The glass door clicked, then opened. "I'll be up to get you when your time is up."

"Thanks again," Frank said, sitting on the chair. "Hey, these headphones don't seem to work."

"Are you sure they're plugged in?" the guard asked, with a sigh, walking back into the room.

"Positive," Frank replied, fiddling with the plug and reaching for the gun in his ankle holster.

The guard walked over to his side, a bit annoyed, and inspected the headphones. With one quick motion, he grabbed his gun, and pressed it tight against the guard's cheek. "If you even breathe the wrong way I'll give you a lobotomy."

The guard slowly raised his hands as his face expanded with terror. "Take it easy."

"Where is the maintenance office?"

"Second floor."

"How many guards are in this place?"

"Six?"

"You better hope so," Frank barked, pushing the gun into the guards face. "Because if there's one more than six, you're worm food."

The deep folds of the guard's face trembled as Frank pushed him to the elevator. The guard pushed the second floor button and the doors closed. "Where are the rest of the guards?"

"They're all over the place," the guard forced through his teeth. "The other four make rounds. They could be anywhere."

"You know if you somehow alerted them, this bullet goes into your brain."

"What's your angle, buddy? I mean there's no money in the place, nothing of value."

"A child."

"A child? There's no one in the place except for us."

"I beg to differ."

The elevator stopped, the doors opened. Frank peered through the door and saw an empty hallway with a glass door on each side. He forced the guard out of the door all the while checking the corridor for the other security guards. He entered the doors labeled MAINTENANCE and examined the dark room. "Give me your flashlight," Frank demanded.

There was a desk with a computer and two file cabinets on each side. In the corner was a series of shelves with five rolls of paper neatly stacked in slots. Frank dragged the guard across the room and pulled the blueprints from the slots. "Open them," Frank said, nudging the guard down in a chair.

Frank inspected the blueprints and sighed. There was over a hundred places they could be hiding his son, he thought. He wanted to scream in frustration, until he realized the basement floor was not marked on the blueprints. "Do you have the keys to the elevator?"

"No."

The guard's eyes were uncertain, as if he were hiding something. "Let me repeat the question," Frank said, cocking his gun. "Do you have the keys to the elevator?"

The guard's eyes flinched, his breaths quickened. He reached down to his side and pulled a set of keys from his chain and laid them on the desk. "That's what I thought," Frank said, snatching them off the table. "Which one is for the elevator?"

"The small circular one," the guard said pointing, his hands trembling.

Frank put the keys in his pocket and examined the blueprints. The closest exit from the basement was through a ventilation duct that led to the entrance closest to the rear of the building. Hopefully, he would get to his son before security figured out he was in the duct. "What kind of car do you drive?"

"A blue Nissan Sentra."

"Where are you parked?"

"Outside of the main entrance."

"Give me your keys."

The guard slowly reached in his pocket and reluctantly passed over his keys. "Let's go," Frank said, pulling the guard by his shirt collar.

Frank dragged the guard to the elevator, reached in his pocket and pulled out the keys. He inserted them in the slot. "How do you get to the basement? It's not on the panel."

"Once we get to floor B, wait for the ding, then turn the key."

A soft ding hummed above and Frank turned the key. The elevator sunk a few seconds, then the doors opened to a cement corridor with a metal door at the end. This was the place. The place where Nicole had lived out the last of her days. Part of him wanted to kill the guard the minute he got inside, but the thought left him once he inserted the key in the door. His son was inside; he could feel it. Nothing else mattered, nor would anything stop him. The door creaked, then opened. A few dim lights outlined the shadows in the room. In the distance he could see a glass window that looked like a mini-nursery in the corner of the room. The smell of baby powder filled the air. He jogged over to the room, feeling as if a thick steel ball was lodged in his throat. He quickly opened the door and a crib appeared. He crept closer expecting to hear little delicate breaths, but it was quiet. He looked around the room and felt a presence in the darkness. He snatched the guard and pressed his gun close to his chest. "I'll kill him if anyone moves," Frank yelled when he realized someone else was in the room. A click resonated from the corner of the room and lights came on. A cold round piece of steel pressed firmly against his head. The crib became visible. It was empty. Four men surrounded him, holding pistols close to his head. Their eyes were cold and empty. "You can kill him for all I care," one of them said. "But I guarantee you can't kill all of us. Drop the gun."

Chapter 41

Robin Vastbinder glanced at her watch and resumed her vigilant gaze out of the tiny coffee shop window, wondering where Captain Irwin was. It had been an hour since they last spoke and he still hadn't shown up. She tapped her fingers nervously on the table, embedding thousands of tiny sugar crystals into her fingertips, wishing she could taste a drop of scotch. She reached into her purse and grabbed a Xanax to abate the withdrawals and stared into Jacob's eyes. They were strong and fearless. He picked at his third jelly donut as if that were the only thing that mattered. His eyes were well beyond his years. It gave her the strength to forget about the scotch and the man from the CIA. He was all she needed.

Robin once again stared from the window, examining every vehicle and pedestrian that passed by, looking for a heavyset black man driving a blue Ford Tempo. The sky was overcast with rays of the sun fighting to break through the thick clouds. The streets were clumped with a melting pot of pedestrians stomping the pavement without a care or concern. It was a typical day in New York, at least for them, she thought. In the distance, a blue car appeared. She strained her eyes and focused, searching for the make of the car. It was a Ford Tempo and inside appeared a black male. The car parked and a large, muscular man, with heavy eyebrows and balding forehead appeared. He looked like an out of shape football player with his large arms and potbelly. He examined the streets and then entered the donut shop. The thick cloud of stress in Robin's chest subsided when she realized it was Captain Dennis Irwin.

"Captain Irwin?" Robin asked, rising from the booth and grabbing Jacob's hand.

"Call me Dennis," he said, shaking her hand warmly. "This must be Jacob."

Jacob moved close to Robin's leg, his eyes flickered with caution. "It's O.K. Jacob, he's not one of the bad men," Robin reassured, putting her arm around him.

"I won't bite," Dennis said, kneeling down, reaching out his hand.

"You wear bad man clothes," Jacob said feebly.

"Don't worry, honey. I wouldn't let him get near you if he were a bad man."

"My car's outside," Dennis said, leading them out of the coffee shop. "We need to get on the move."

The inside of Dennis's car smelled of stale cigars and coffee. The vinyl seats were worn and cracked. Jacob jumped in the back and put on his seat belt, all the while watching Dennis. Robin reached back from the passenger's seat and caressed his face. "Everything's going to be just fine now, you wait and see. I promise you'll be back playing football in no time."

"I hope so," Jacob uttered.

The engine started and hummed down the street. Dennis maneuvered between the traffic as if he were late for work. "Where are we going?" Robin asked.

"To a hotel by the airport."

"We aren't going back to the station?"

"Not a safe place," Dennis replied, his face wrinkling. "This shit has gotten crazy. I swear the walls are alive. Not even the mafia could tap a police station. This is someone big."

"It's the CIA."

"That's what I was afraid of," Dennis said turning the steering wheel, shaking his head. "That's why I've got this guy from Washington involved. He's a friend of mine from college. He's meeting us out here."

"Have you heard from Frank?" Robin asked.

"Not in the last forty-eight hours. He's got every cop in the world on his ass. I'm surprised they haven't picked him up by now. But, that Frank, boy I gotta tell you, if anyone could do it, he can. He may suck at that paper work, but I've never met a better detective in my life."

"Where was he going?"

"No clue. Probably trying to get to his boy."

"He went to North Dakota."

"He went where?" Dennis asked, almost swerving off the road.

"That's where his son is. The Loventhol clinic."

"That'll be the first place I'll have my friend look. Those bastards," Dennis said, clenching his teeth. "They must have a lot of people in the right places to get away with this bullshit."

"How about Dr. Martin?"

"Don't worry, he's safe. A little disgruntled, but safe. He's at the station. What's the deal with his hair? Doesn't he know the Afro died with bell bottoms?"

"He's trying to keep the seventies alive," Robin replied with a chuckle. "So can this guy really help us?"

"If he can't, it's over."

"Did Frank ever mention a Dr. Roderick Taylor?"

"Is he a player in all of this?"

"If we could get him to testify, it would break the case open. He knows everything about Dr. Loventhol's research. He could produce the data we would need to link the children and Nicole Johnson with Dr. Loventhol."

"Call him," Dennis said, handing her his cellular phone.

Robin quickly dialed the numbers. The phone rang five times, then clicked. There was a ton of static; he must be in his car or in the basement of a building. But she could still hear his voice.

"Hello?"

"Dr. Taylor?"

"Who is this?" Dr. Taylor snapped.

"Dr. Robin Vastbinder. Thank God you're safe."

"I read the *New York Times*," he said excited. "Are you O.K?"

"I've got some help. We can put this all to an end."

"Are you still with the boy?"

"Yeah."

"This has to end," Dr. Taylor said, his voice quickening. "I can't even go to work. I've been stuck here for a week. I'm afraid to go to the police. These men have been following me."

"This is a lot bigger than we thought. Dr. Loventhol has people everywhere."

"Are you sure it's safe?"

"No, but it's the only chance we've got. I'll call you in an hour. Maybe the FBI can send some people up to get you," Robin said, looking into Dennis's eyes.

"I think we could have someone up there in an hour," Dennis said. "Let's see what my friend says."

The sound of planes boomed in the distance as Dennis pulled into the airport parking lot. The once bright sky was now dark and swelled with rain. A few thick drops splashed on the windshield and then thousands of them pelted the roof like a machine gun. The motel looked more like a house with ten rooms connected. The main office was an A-frame with chipped white paint and fading shingles. Dennis got out of the car as Robin went to the backseat and helped Jacob out of his seat. She looked into his eyes and realized that he was still on the edge a bit. But who could blame him? Robin thought. She didn't feel comfortable herself, but it was a lot better than sitting around waiting for them to come.

Dennis went back inside the car, reached inside the glove compartment, pulled out an umbrella and handed it to Robin. He then reached for a newspaper and put it over his head. "We're going to room six," he said.

Robin grabbed Jacob, popped open the umbrella and walked towards the door. Dennis knocked twice and the door opened. Robin almost lost her breath when she realized who was inside the room. She felt as if someone had thumped her with a bat on her back, taking the air from her lungs faster than she could breathe. It was worse than any hangover she could imagine. It was the two men that had been following her. She grabbed Jacob and tried to force open the door, but the tall gangly CIA agent slammed it shut and pulled out a pistol. "I have no qualms about killing you now," Nevin Cuff said, "so I'd take it easy if I were you."

"You son of a bitch," Robin yelled, lunging at Dennis, trying to scratch out his eyes. The agent wrestled her to the floor and put a gun to her head. "One more scream and you're dead," Nevin said calmly, cocking back the trigger.

"You're Frank's best friend," she whimpered, with tears staining her face. "I trusted you."

"I'm sorry," Dennis said regretfully, hiding his face. "I had no choice."

"That's right," the gangly agent said, "I hope you don't ever forget that because if you do, you'll be in prison the rest of your pathetic life. I'm sure all the people you put behind bars would love to make you their bitch."

"You've got what you wanted, now leave me be," Dennis barked.

"You're not done yet," Judd Isla added. "You need to take a little trip with us and bring back the other fugitive. You'll be a hero, captain. Two felons in one day. Too bad they'll both be dead."

Chapter 42

Dr. Orpheus Martin tried to sleep on the thin cot, but the springs pressed against his back, making each muscle go into spasm. The cushions from the mattress were as thin as a wafer, Orpheus thought, as he rolled over trying to get comfortable. It was bad enough to be cooped up in a ten by ten room with metal bars for windows. The least they could do was provide a comfortable bed. The fourteen hours inside the cell had become a marathon of suffering. Where was Robin? Where were the boys? Was his family safe? The questions mounted, making the smell from the tiny toilet that much worse.

Captain Dennis Irwin had become a ghost since he arrived. They spoke for about an hour, and judging from his eyes, the country was about to know how the government was spending it's hard-earned tax dollars. But that was ten hours ago and time had been a procession of doubt that made it difficult to relax. He picked at his mane of hair, pulling out tiny pieces of lint from the cot, all the while wondering if his friends were still alive. Captain Irwin had to believe the story, he thought. It did sound a bit outlandish, but he had to believe him. He was Detective Roberts' best friend, he reassured himself. But something was wrong.

Orpheus stood from his bed and stretched. He closed his eyes and rubbed his face, wishing he could call his wife. She was probably up all night worrying about him. But she had to be a strong woman to put up with his ass. He knew he was difficult, but his heart was always true, especially when it came to the boys. What he wouldn't give to play football with them again. He paced the cement floors until the annoying sounds of the drunk in the next cell returned. The smell of alcohol mixed with body odor made him nauseated. And his singing was much worse. He was trying to sing the Temptations, but it sounded more like a wounded penguin on crack cocaine. "I'll give you ten bucks if you just shut up," Orpheus yelled, grabbing the bars.

"Make it twenty," the drunk said with slurred speech.

Orpheus quickly reached in his pocket, balled up a twenty and threw it into his cell. Unfortunately, the drunk didn't stop singing. "That was only a down payment," the drunk said laughing.

Bastard, Orpheus thought, clenching his teeth. Just when he was about to lose his mind, the sound of hard-soled shoes resonated in the distance. A tall white man with short red hair and long arms appeared before his cell.

"Orpheus Martin?" the man asked, looking at a piece of paper.

"Get me out of here," Orpheus said, grabbing the bars.

"You're free to go."

"Where is Captain Irwin?"

"He had to go," the man said, handing him a sealed envelope. "He left you this."

Orpheus stuffed the envelope in his pocket and walked over to the drunk in the cell next to him. The drunk cracked a toothless smile and began to hum. "Give my twenty back," Orpheus demanded. "Give me the keys to his cell."

"Relax. Let's go…before I change my mind," the police officer said, pulling him by his arm.

"You're lucky, old man," Orpheus yelled.

Orpheus followed the officer through the pit of cells, each containing a variety of vagrants, from prostitutes to streets thugs, and rode the elevator to the main floor. He went to the desk, signed a document and got back his cell phone. "Where are my suit and hundred dollars?" Orpheus asked, smiling.

"We may need you for questioning, so don't go too far, if you know what I mean," an officer warned.

Orpheus shrugged sarcastically at the threat and left the building. The thick rain soaked his dress shirt and pants, but it felt good. The air smelled like springtime; a lot better than the drunk that took him for twenty dollars, he thought. He walked over to a coffee shop across the street, grabbed a cup of Hazelnut cream, and sat at a table in the corner. Where the hell was Robin with that boy? Hopefully, at Disney World, he thought. Fat chance. He reached inside his pocket and pulled out the letter. Captain Irwin must've had something very urgent happen to leave without telling him. He ripped opened the end and blew the envelope open.

Have gone to get Detective Roberts. Contact Agent Dan Johnson. He's someone you can trust. Tell him they are about to move the infant to Washington D.C. The Presidential compound. I've been in contact with him since this started. He will help. (703) 555-6924.

Presidential compound? What the hell do those children have to do with the President? Thousands of disjointed impulses surged through his brain. He chugged his coffee and went outside. His hands trembled as he dialed the number, thinking about the scenarios. If the White House was involved, the possibilities were unlimited. The President had a blank check of power that he could cash in any place in the world. "Dan Johnson," a heavy voice announced from the other side of the receiver.

"Is this Agent Johnson?"

"The only one in this office. How can I help you?"

"Captain Dennis Irwin of the NYPD told me to get in touch with you about Detective Roberts."

"You must be Dr. Orpheus Martin."

"How did you know?" Orpheus replied.

"He told me you'd be calling."

"How can I be so sure I can trust you?"

"You can't. But, judging from your predicament, I'm all you've got. No one at that station can be trusted. What did he tell you?"

"Something about moving the infant to the Presidential compound."

There was silence on the other side of the receiver that weakened Orpheus's confidence. "This is a lot bigger than I thought," Agent Johnson said with a sigh. "I want you to go to the Federal Building and wait. I'll arrange to have you transported to Washington."

"Why?"

"If this thing is as big as I think it is, it'll be the only place you'll be safe."

Chapter 43

Senator Watson pulled out a can of snuff and shoved a thick finger full in between his cheeks and gums as he peered from the windows of the White House. He sighed and then walked over to the President sitting at his desk in the oval office. The President was leaning back in his chair, away from the piles of papers on his desk and stared at the wall. The President's eyes flickered with a fear Senator Watson had never seen in his friend. It was as if he'd been emotionally impeached. The President's body was in the chair, but his soul was light years away. Senator Watson was sure he'd give up his job if only she could be well.

The President let out a long sigh and then swiveled around in his chair. "Where in the hell is this Loventhol character?" he asked anxiously.

"He's coming to Washington. They found both children. One is on his way. He'll be accompanying the other."

"How long?" the President snapped. "I just spoke with the doctor that transferred her to the compound and she barely made the trip. She has all those tubes in her arms and mouth. I can't take much more of this."

"We'll leave for the compound in ten minutes."

"What if this leaks to the press?"

"Don't you worry...this is *National Enquirer* material. Boy's blood cures cancer? I'm sure every scientist in the world will believe that. They spend billions every year for research and two children from a hooker can cure the plague of the twentieth century? That's a ten billion dollar a year business. Sometimes I think a cure is the last thing those boys want," Senator Watson said.

"What if something goes wrong and the children die?"

"Then so be it," Senator Watson said emphatically. "What kind of life would they have had anyways? Heck, we probably saved the prison system two more inmates."

"But, you know how Sophia feels about children."

"I know, but what she doesn't know won't hurt her," Senator Watson said, expelling the tobacco from his mouth into a tissue and dropping it into a wastebasket. "Do you really think if we were in their neighborhood in the middle of the night that they would think twice about pulling out a gun and blowing off our heads? I'm sure they wouldn't worry about what their momma told them about right and wrong."

"I'm with you Tom, but this has to stay under the bridge."

"My people from the CIA will make sure it will. You can believe that, partner."

* * *

The clouds looked like large pillows that blanketed the sky to Robin Vastbinder as she sat in the back of the private jet, holding Jacob in her arms. It was the kind of jet she pictured a famous rock star flying in; the seats were leather with a full bar and tiny kitchen in the back. A large screen hung from the ceiling, which probably showed the latest movies. It would be a trip to dream about in any other circumstance, but the CIA agents sitting across from her with their eyes focused on their every move made her realize this was no vacation.

Captain Irwin sat across the aisle, his eyes distant and somber. Frank better hope that the rest of his close friends aren't like Captain Irwin, she thought. "So, what have you done with the others?" Robin barked.

"Does it matter?" Nevin Cuff replied.

"Why can't you leave them alone? You've got us," Robin said, placing her arm around Jacob.

"If you must know, Dr. Martin will not be harmed…well…at least not by us," Judd Isla said, tossing a peanut in his mouth. "I don't know what they'll do with him in prison for aiding a felon."

"What about Dr. Roderick Taylor?" Robin asked, the rage mounting with each word.

"He's no longer a factor," Nevin Cuff said calmly.

Robin buried her hands in her face, fighting the tears. She refused to let them see her cry, but the feeling of desperation over took her and tears dripped down her cheeks. It was the first time in her life she really knew how her terminally ill patients actually felt. At times they became only faces to her, to protect her own sanity, but now she understood what a death sentence really meant. They were going to kill them both, eventually. She was sure of it. And as the plane angled towards the ground, the realization of her mortality became apparent. The somber look of desolation in the eyes of her dying patient was no longer something she could escape from; it was now her existence. It was an emptiness that only time could fill. Unfortunately, time was something she didn't have.

The screech of the landing gear made Robin's heart pound in her chest. Tears leaked down her face as she looked into Jacob's tiny brown eyes. They were distant, yet strong. He reached up to her face and wiped the tears from her eyes. "Don't worry, Miss Robin. I ain't afraid to die. You shouldn't be neither. I'll get to see my momma and you'll get to kiss your little boy."

A quell of strength over took Robin with each of his words. She was about to fall apart, but Jacob was as brave as a warrior going into battle. She hugged him, almost squeezing the life from his lungs and kissed him on his cheek. "We're not going to die."

The tiny airfield was no larger than a baseball field. It contained a small control tower and a one-lane runway that a row of tiny lights barely lit. It was in the middle of nowhere, surrounded by cornfields that extended far beyond view. The two men grabbed her by the arms. She thought about a struggle but knew it would be worthless at the moment. She decided to bide her time, wait until she spotted a weakness and at least break Jacob free. They escorted her out of the plane and onto a helicopter that rose into the half moonlit sky. After a ten-minute ride, the helicopter landed on top of a building. The two CIA agents snapped handcuffs to Jacob's and her wrists, almost cutting off the circulation, and pushed them into a six-story, glass building. They guided them down a set of stairs and onto elevators. Judd Isla pulled a key from his jacket and inserted it into the elevator, which made the descent to the basement a thousand times faster. The elevator came to an abrupt stop and the door opened.

The walls of the basement were cinder block, the floors a smooth cement. A musty smell tingled Robin's nose as she was forced down the long corridor, past four metal detectors, and into a full lab, with hundreds of beakers and pipettes sitting on a long bench with four microscopes and tissue incubators in the corner. Three computers were in the middle with printers at each side. Robin tried to break free from the grasp of Nevin Cuff, but he pulled on her handcuffs, almost ripping her shoulders from their sockets. Behind the computers were three figures; two appeared to be male and one female. One looked familiar. She strained her eyes and the face of an older man came into view. Perspiration rained from her forehead, making her vision almost double. She rubbed her shoulder to her face to clear the sweat and felt as if the floor had been pulled from under her. It was *him*.

The peppered gray beard, with the receding hairline and the arrogant smile; it was Dr. Roderick Taylor. But, how? He was supposed to be dead. Maybe they forced him to work on the project, she thought. But, judging from the confident, almost dominating look in his eyes, he was the leader. "Dr. Vastbinder," Dr. Taylor said, "I'm glad you'll finally get to see the greatest breakthrough in the history of medicine."

"Who are you?" Robin asked, fighting to break away from the CIA agent.

"Who am I?" he said pointing at himself sarcastically. "I'm Dr. Marty Loventhol."

"So, who is Dr. Roderick Taylor?"

"Let's just say he's my alter ego. He's the honest clumsy professor at Harvard that keeps me out of jail if things just happen to go wrong."

"Why? Why would you do this to children?"

"None of this would've ever happened if that whore didn't escape."

"But, you know that eventually Jacob and Sean would die from the transfusions if you didn't figure out how to replicate the protein."

"Maybe, but it doesn't matter. Do you know how many lives I've saved? Twenty five and counting, and if the children die, I have enough of Nicole's and Jacob's blood on reserve to continue my work until I find a way to replicate the proteins to keep the virus alive in a different host."

"I thought you were a doctor."

"Someone has to lose for mankind to advance. You know that as well as I do. Some of the greatest discoveries in history were the result of others dying. Look at the work the Nazis accomplished on twins during the Holocaust. Ask yourself, how many times did you wish for the magic bullet after watching all those people die? Think about the thousands of children that die from cancer each year. Imagine if the sacrifice of two meaningless lives could save them. Imagine if you never had to tell a husband or a wife that the one person that mattered to them most was going to die," Dr. Loventhol said, pacing. "Imagine that?"

"Not like this," Robin yelled.

"Then how?" Dr. Loventhol barked, "I couldn't sit back and watch all those people die when I knew a transfusion could save their lives. I don't need to answer to you doctor, I answer to those who now will get another chance."

"Maybe you don't have to answer to me, but someday, you're gonna have to answer to yourself, knowing what you did."

"Enough talk. I've got a life to save, Doctor. Get the boy ready for the trip to Washington," Dr. Loventhol said to the woman in a lab coat as he walked towards the exit. "The infant is already there. Hopefully, his blood will be enough. I'd hate to lose them both."

Chapter 44

Frank Roberts slowly opened his eyes and pulled himself to a sitting position. He looked around in the dark empty room and realized he probably had been unconscious for some time. His head felt as if it were between a vise-grip. He could taste bitter blood in his mouth. The last thing he remembered was getting jumped then pistol-whipped. Where the hell was he? It was a tiny room with only a small amount of light that seeped through the cracks of the door. He rose to his feet, stumbled over to the door and carefully turned the knob. Of course, it was locked. He felt around the room and bumped into a table with an inch of dust. There were four other wooden tables in the corner. It must've been some type of storage room, he thought. Now what?

He listened closely for a minute and heard voices outside the metal door. It sounded like three men. He was about to turn on a light when an idea popped into his mind. He lay back on the cold linoleum floor in the fetal position and let out a loud groan. The voices silenced and the door opened. The light switch clicked and the room illuminated. Frank didn't move. Three large men rolled him over. "Time to wake up Mr. Coors," one of them said laughing. "How stupid do you think we are, Frank Roberts, big shot NYPD detective?"

Frank remained silent and motionless. One of them kicked him in the ribs sending a jolt of pain through his chest. He fought the urge to jump up and fight despite his agony. He was sure they each had a 9mm. Focus on something else, he kept telling himself, forget the pain. The heavyset guard, who he beat up in the relaxation chamber, appeared. His pudgy eyes were poised with revenge. The guard smacked his night-stick off his lower back sending jolts of pain through his legs. Fight the pain. Fight the pain. He fought to think. It was apparent they thought he was unconscious, because they stopped beating him. He closed his eyes and let his body go limp.

Frank carefully cracked open his eyes for a moment and then quickly shut them, obtaining a quick peek of his surroundings. Two of the three men were on each arm, dragging him down the dimly lit hallway. One of them was in front. He quickly glanced again, and saw the man to his right had his gun holster unsnapped on the inside of his hip. That was his chance. He was about five feet from the elevator. Who knew how many people were upstairs, he thought. With one swift move, he grabbed the revolver, and fired a shot at the neck of the man to his right. He immediately dropped as blood gushed from his throat. He then quickly fired a shot into the chest of the guard to his left and one at the knees of the heavyset guard in front. All three men moaned in agony, then two of them stopped. The only one alive was the heavyset guard he met in the relaxation chamber. Frank ran to the man's side and pressed the gun to his head. "I guess it's me and you again, isn't it?" Frank said, panting. "Give me your piece."

The guard reached inside his holster and threw his gun to the floor. Frank picked it up and stuffed it under his shirt.

"Where is my son?"

"He's gone," the guard pleaded.

"Where?"

"I don't know."

"Do we have to go through this again? Because if we do, this time, I'm just gonna kill ya because the way my back feels right about now I think you deserve it."

"You've got to believe me. I don't know," the man yelled, holding his leg. "They took him to the helicopter pad on top of the roof. That's all I know."

"Are you sure?" Frank barked, twisting the butt of his 9mm in the guard's wound.

"Positive," the guard uttered in agony.

Frank jogged up the hallway trying to remember the room they had held his son. Maybe the fat piece of shit was lying and he was still there. Just as he turned the corner, the sound of multiple footsteps resonated through the cement walls. It was coming from the corridor around the corner. He stopped and looked around. There were three doors. He tried to open the one to his left, but it was locked. The second door opened into a small maintenance closet, which was crowded with brooms, mops and buckets. He ducked inside, kneeled on all fours, and peeked through the grates at the bottom of the door. He estimated that it was three people, judging from the sound. Three sets of legs came into view. He angled his head to see their faces and then felt a wave of nausea permeate through his stomach. One of them was Robin. How did she get here? When he realized who was holding a gun to her back, the will to fight almost escaped him like air from a balloon. It was Dennis Irwin. The other man was tall with long, thick arms dressed in a security uniform. What was Dennis doing in North Dakota?

He inhaled three deep breaths, raised his pistol, and rushed through the door. The security guard quickly reached for the pistol on his hip. Frank fired two quick shots. Blood rushed from the security guard's chest, staining his blue shirt, and he fell to the ground. Dennis was about to pull his gun when Frank pressed his 9mm to Dennis Irwin's head, with all the memories of the super bowl, his wedding and Dennis's son's baptism racing through his mind, bringing a tear to his eyes. "Give me one good reason why I shouldn't kill you," Frank snapped.

"Take it easy, Frank," Dennis pleaded. "I know I deserve to die, but hear me out."

"Why?"

"Those guys from the CIA knew about me, Frank."

"Knew what?"

"You remember that internal investigation on that missing cocaine money? You thought the two cops you busted were behind it, you were wrong. They were only the front men—it was I that put them up to it."

"Why Dennis?" Frank asked, shaking his head.

"I keep asking myself that everyday. I guess I got sick of the criminals living the life instead of us. Those boys from the CIA found out about it and threatened to bring me down. Could you imagine what my son would think? He's just starting the force. It would ruin his life. I could never look him in the eye again."

"How could you look me in the eye, you fucking piece of shit," Frank snapped. "You're helping them kill my son."

"I can't, but I can make things right…if you give me a chance."

"Why should I?"

"The longer you sit here and bullshit, the less time we'll have to get to the helicopter pad on the roof. They're taking Jacob to Washington."

Frank looked into Robin's eyes. They were worn and marked with bruises. "Let's go, Frank," Robin said anxiously.

"Are you really going to trust him after what he's done?" Frank asked.

"Please, Frank, we're wasting time," Dennis pleaded.

The muscles in Frank's arms tightened as he fought back the urge to pull the trigger. "Give me your gun."

"I might need it," Dennis said slowly handing it to him.

"How dumb do you think I am? Give me the fucking gun," Frank said, snatching it from his hand.

Frank grabbed Robin's trembling hands and shoved his gun in Dennis' back. "I may be able to forgive you someday, but if it comes between you and my son, I'll kill you without thinking twice, so don't think I trust you."

"I wouldn't blame you," Dennis said.

Frank was about to push the button on the elevator, but realized that they probably had guards on every floor waiting for the doors to open. "Let's take the stairwell," Frank said pulling Robin by the arm.

"They're probably waiting for us," Robin snapped, pulling back on Frank's arm.

"We'll have more room to work with," Frank barked, tugging her arm again.

"We don't have time for this," Dennis exclaimed.

"Most elevators have drop ceilings. I bet all three of us can fit," Robin said, pointing at the silver doors.

Frank looked at Robin as the frustration mounted in her eyes. Women, same old shit, he thought. Think they know everything. He looked back at Dennis, who shrugged his shoulders and said, "Best idea I've heard all day."

Frank pushed the button and the elevator door beeped. The up arrow flashed red then the doors opened. Frank entered and looked up at the ceiling. "I guess my mom was right about a woman's touch. Dennis, if you want to kill me here's your chance."

"Shut up and lift her up," Dennis said, grabbing Robin by the waist.

She pushed up through the Formica and the tile moved. She grabbed onto one of the steel beams and pulled herself inside. Dennis planted his foot in Frank's hands and pulled himself up, and then Frank grabbed Dennis's hand and followed. The shaft was dark and smelled of musty oil and dust. There was barely enough room for Frank on the top as he placed his arm around Robin, trying to balance himself on the ledge. Dennis's fat shoulders were pressed against his chest like a pillow of flesh. It was impossible to see inside the elevator, but as it started to move, Frank realized it was going to stop on every floor. It rose slowly and the large metal gears at the top came into view. It stopped and the door opened. The sounds of two voices muffled below. They became louder as they entered. It seemed as if they were taking forever, until the doors closed and rose to the next floor.

"What are we going to do when this thing gets to the top floor?" Robin asked, looking around.

"I don't know. It's your idea," Frank said.

"I was hoping you had a plan," Robin said.

"If I had a gun, maybe I could help," Dennis interjected.

"Would you please give up on the gun, Dennis?" Frank said.

"I could get rid of some of those security guards if you give me the chance," Dennis said.

"Yeah, right," Robin said, rolling her eyes. "I guess you forgot about that hotel thing."

"I know you don't trust me, but I just want to make things right between us."

"You get no gun, that's it," Frank snapped.

The elevator stopped at every floor, each time voices entered, then they left. Finally, they reached the top floor that led out to the roof. Frank put his hand over Robin's head, and tucked his head between his knees as the metal gears approached their heads. Finally the elevator stopped. "Take this gun," Frank said, handing it to Robin.

"I don't know what to do with this," Robin said, handing it back. "Maybe we should give Dennis a gun."

"And get shot in the back?" Frank said. "No way. Just point the thing and fire."

Robin's hands trembled as she grabbed the gun. The thought of killing another human never crossed her mind two weeks ago, but she thought about the look in Jacob's eyes as they pulled him out of her arms. Nothing was going to keep him from her, she thought. "So what do we do?" Robin asked, flustered.

"Shh," Frank said, putting his finger to his lips.

The voices returned. There were two of them. It had to be quick. They couldn't have a second to react, Frank thought. No more time for plans. He jumped through the drop ceiling and landed inside. Two men appeared dressed in blue security uniforms. Their eyes expanded with surprise. Frank fired once, connecting with the first guard's knee, then fired again, striking the other guard in the shoulder. Outside, two men in suits fired twice. Frank ducked behind the wall as the bullets whizzed by his ears. "Don't come down," he yelled to Robin. He picked up the two guns of the security officers as they moaned in agony. "Don't be stupid," Frank said to them both, "because the next shot will be at your heads."

Frank peeped his head from the elevator. Five more shots clanked inside. He quickly fired back, this time getting a good look at the assailants. The long gangly arms, unibrow, and melon head made him realize that it was one of the CIA agents that had been following him. Nevin Cuff was his name, if he remembered correctly. The other had to be Judd Isla. In the distance, he could see the helicopter's engine firing. He had to make a move. He picked up one of the security guards and used him as a shield. To his surprise, the agents fired, dropping the guard to the ground. Frank fired again, this time connecting with Judd Isla's chest, dropping him face first on the roof. Nevin Cuff scampered forward and aimed his pistol right at Frank's head. Frank tried to adjust his aim quickly, but it was too late, Nevin Cuff had him right in his sights and was about to fire. Frank braced for the impact, when a shot raced past his ear. It came from the elevator. Who the hell fired it? Nevin Cuff fell to the ground as his gun dropped from his hand, but he wasn't dead. Frank looked back and saw Robin holding the pistol in her hands, her eyes trembling with fear. What a lucky shot, Frank thought. When he turned around, Nevin Cuff charged him with eyes red with fury. Frank raised his pistol, but wasn't quick enough. He felt his body lofted in the air, then slammed to the cement, sending a surge of burning pain through his back. Frank prayed Robin wouldn't try to fire again, because this time, she could hit him. She ran over to his side and jumped on Nevin Cuff's back. He shrugged her off his shoulders with one quick swipe as if she were a bug. Frank fought to breathe as Nevin's hands tightened around his neck. Frank kicked his legs and bruised his hands punching the agent's face. Despite his efforts, the agent wouldn't let go of his grip. Frank became lightheaded as the energy slowly crept from his body. The clouded night sky faded in and out. He could feel himself floating away, until suddenly, the grip loosened. He saw a large body fly past his head and slam Nevin to the cement. It was Dennis.

His thick arms pinned Nevin to the ground. Nevin rolled back on top and punched Dennis in the face. Frank coughed twice trying to expand his lungs, and rose to his feet. The lack of oxygen had left him dazed and disoriented. Just as Frank regained his bearings, he saw Nevin reach for the gun that Robin's bullet had knocked from his hand. Frank tried feverishly to stumble over to Dennis's side and kick the gun from his hand, but the weapon discharged, ramming a bullet into Dennis's chest. Nevin quickly rose to his feet, and swung around about to fire his pistol again, this time at Frank's head. Frank dove to the ground, expecting never to see his son again, but another weapon discharged, sending a stream of blood from Nevin's face. He fell to the ground and his body went limp. Frank looked behind to find Robin holding a pistol, her hands trembling as tears poured from her eyes. "Nice shot," Frank said, grabbing the gun from her hand. "That's two in one day. I'm starting to think you picked the wrong profession. "

The helicopter's blades began to spin and Frank sprinted to the pad. He climbed up the metal steps and aimed it at the pilot's head. "Touch one more control and you're dead," he said.

The engine powered down as the pilot raised his hands. "Robin, how's Dennis?" Frank yelled.

"He's dead," she said, somberly.

Frank tried to block the past from his mind, but the good memories erased the hate. Why Dennis? Why did he let the money get the best of him? He buried his pain and opened the helicopter door. Inside was Dr. Roderick Taylor, with wrinkles of fear tethered across his face. Jacob's eyes widened with joy and he leaped out of his seat into Frank's arms. "Momma said you'd find me," Jacob said, almost choking Frank to death.

"Your mom was always right," Frank said, hugging him back. He placed Jacob on the ground and pressed his gun against Dr. Taylor's face. "Take me to my son or you're dead."

"Take it easy," Dr. Taylor said, scrunching in his chair.

Frank grabbed Dr. Taylor by his coat and pulled him out of the helicopter, almost throwing him to the ground. "Where is my son?"

"In Washington," Dr. Taylor uttered, holding up his hands.

Just as Frank was about to pistol-whip him, Robin ran over to the helicopter pad and climbed up the steps. "The rest of the guards are coming," she said, frantically.

The metal door slammed open and three men appeared with 9mms pointed at Frank's head. Frank grabbed Dr. Taylor and pushed his body in front of him.

"Get in the helicopter and put this gun on the pilot," Frank said to Robin and Jacob. "One move and the good doctor here is dead."

The men continued to take careful steps towards the helicopter pad. "Call off your dogs or you're dead. And don't think I wouldn't do it after what you've done to my son."

Frank could tell by the look in Dr. Taylor's eyes he never fathomed the thought of death. "Put down your guns," Dr. Taylor said reluctantly.

The security guards stopped and threw down their guns. Frank pressed the barrel of the gun tight against Dr. Taylor's face, contemplating his next move. How the hell was he going to get to his son? The President of the United States was untouchable. But, as he was about to pull Dr. Taylor into the helicopter an idea popped in his mind. "Tell them to go to the lab and get us two lab coats."

"Why?" Dr. Taylor asked, his voice cracking with fear.

"Just do it!" Frank yelled.

Dr. Taylor complied with the order and the two guards left. They returned with two jackets, covered by plastic as if they had just come from the cleaners, and carefully handed them to Dr. Taylor. Frank snatched them from Dr. Taylor's hands and threw them in the helicopter. "Let's go for a ride," Frank said, shoving him inside.

Chapter 45

The soft whirr of the helicopter calmed the pounding in Frank's chest. Jacob sat by his side on the seat, staring somberly into Dr. Taylor's empty eyes, probably wanting to ask him why he hurt his momma. It seemed to have no effect on Dr. Taylor as he stared out of the window, acting as if nothing else existed. Frank put his arm around Jacob trying to make up for the past, but it didn't work. At one time, Jacob would run a thousand miles an hour to the door of his apartment just to greet Frank. But the distance in Jacob's eyes made Frank realize he was the closest thing to a father the boy ever experienced and Frank had broken his heart. The Mets games and movies, the trips to the museum, all were just an illusion to Jacob, Frank thought. He was sure Jacob would never trust another person again.

The helicopter ride was only ten minutes to the crude airport. But the jet was as plush as a hotel room. There was a bar in the back, with couches on each side. In the rear of the plane were chairs with seat belts for the landing. How many trips did Dr. Taylor take posing as Dr. Loventhol on this plane from Boston? All paid for from the blood of Nicole and Jacob. The thought made him want to shoot Dr. Taylor between the eyes before the plane landed. But he couldn't; he was the cornerstone of saving his son.

Frank leaned forward in the couch, holding the gun at Dr. Taylor's head. Robin was in the cockpit doing the same to the pilot. He was sure Robin never even fathomed picking up a gun, let alone killing someone, he thought. But by the way she looked at Jacob, Frank was certain that she was a mother again. And a mother's love was more powerful than any weapon.

"Everything O.K, Robin?" Frank yelled towards the cockpit.

"My hand is getting a little bit tired, but I'm all right," Robin yelled back. "What's our next move?"

"I don't know," Frank yelled back.

"That's comforting," Robin said sarcastically.

"Do you really think you're going to get past the people guarding the President?" Dr. Taylor asked, with an arrogant scowl.

"You better hope so," Frank barked, grabbing Dr. Taylor by the lapels of his blue suit jacket. "Because the minute I get caught, you're dead."

Frank relaxed his grip and plopped back in his seat. Dr. Taylor was right, he thought. The farmhouse in Virginia, which really was a government facility that the President could escape to if the White House was under attack, was surrounded with the best Secret Service thugs the country had to offer. And the facility was underground, one way in and one way out. How would they explain the bruises? What if the pilot talked? Too many variables beyond his control, he thought.

What to do? Frank kept asking himself. Only one chance, he thought. He grabbed Dr. Taylor and pushed him into the cockpit. "We need to talk," he said to Robin.

"What about?" Robin asked.

"Shut down the radio," Frank said to the pilot, pointing his gun at his head.

The slim pilot's hands trembled as he reached for the controls on the panel. He took off his head-set and handed them to Frank. "How far away are we?" Frank asked.

"Ten minutes," the pilot said, steering the plane to the left.

"If you planned on taking us somewhere else, you're dead. I reviewed your flight plans as you know."

"Hey, I just fly this plane," the man said shrugging his shoulders. "I don't work for the government."

Frank grabbed Robin's arm and pulled her from the cockpit. He closed the door and looked through the glass window inside. Robin immediately gave him a hug, then gazed deep into his eyes. "I never got a chance…"

"Neither did I," Frank interrupted, pecking her on the lips. "I wish it were another place or a different time because I couldn't get you out of my mind the entire time."

"Do you think we're going to make it?" Robin asked, pressing her head against his chest.

"Probably not," Frank said, glancing inside the cockpit. "But I've got a plan."

"Really?"

"Well, it's more of a gamble than a plan. I figure we have a rocky landing."

"A rocky landing?"

"Yeah, that will explain the bruises and cause enough confusion to get inside."

"Then what?"

"We get to the First Lady. I'm pretty sure if she knew that her life was about to be saved by the death of an infant, she'd put a stop to all of this."

"How can you be so sure?"

"It's a long story."

"Not another one," Robin said, raising her eyebrows.

"But, it's a good one. She has spent her entire life working with children. There's no way she would ever let a child die just to save her life. Hey, if we don't make it, I'd like to thank you for making me believe that it could happen again."

"What are you talking about?"

"That I could meet someone like you."

"I know just what you mean," Robin said, pecking him on the lips.

Frank gallivanted through the door and shoved Dr. Taylor aside. "Can you land this thing without the landing gear?"

"Can I do what?" the pilot said, looking at Frank as if he had grown a horn from his head.

"You heard what I said," Frank ordered, pressing the gun to his face.

"We could be killed."

"That depends on how good you are."

"I have a wife and two children...please," the pilot pleaded.

"Then I guess you'll have to be extra careful."

Frank pulled Dr. Taylor from his seat and pushed him through the door. "Robin, make sure our friend here is buckled in."

The plane angled towards the ground as Frank buckled his seat belt. The pilot's face was tight as perspiration dripped from his forehead. The aircraft plunged through the blanket of clouds and the lights of the small runway appeared. The engine screamed as the pilot pulled back on the accelerator. "I'm coming in too fast, I have to release the landing gear," the pilot yelled, frantically.

"No way," Frank said, raising his gun.

The plane started to shake as the pilot fought with the controls. The black pavement of the runway appeared. Frank put his head in between his legs as the plane touched down. The seat belts almost cut off the circulation in his hands as it tightened against his shoulders. The plane shimmied right, then left, lofting maps, coffee cups and pens into the air. In the distance was a farmhouse, which moved closer with each second. The pilot's eyes fought the controls as the plane continued to skid along the runway out of control. The farmhouse was now fifteen feet away. Frank closed his eyes, wishing he could take back his stupid decision. Suddenly, the plane slowed, but the farmhouse still approached. There is going to be an explosion, Frank thought. The pilot was right.

He was going to die without ever seeing his son. The plane drifted to the right, avoiding the farmhouse and stopped in the middle of a cornfield.

The pain in Frank's ribs returned as he unfastened his seat belt. It then throbbed and burned as if someone had lit a fire in his chest. He fought through the agony and rose to his feet. "You O.K.?" Frank said to the pilot.

"I think I broke my wrist," the pilot uttered, holding his hand.

Frank walked to his side. "Good job. Sorry about this," Frank said, pulling his gun from the floor and whacking the pilot on the head. The fewer witnesses, the better, Frank thought.

The pilot's chin dropped to his chest. His body was motionless. Frank estimated he would be out at least twenty minutes. That would be enough time to get inside and either save his son or be killed. He opened the cockpit door, praying that Robin and Jacob were all right. Robin groaned. Her long red hair was stuck against her head with a small pool of blood on her face. Jacob was hyperventilating but appeared to have no injuries. Dr. Taylor was unharmed as well.

Frank rushed to Robin's side and examined her forehead. He peeled away the layers of hair and removed the blood from her face. It was only a minor cut from a flying coffee mug that nicked her head.

"I'm fine, Frank," Robin said, unloosening her seatbelt. "How is Jacob?"

"O.K.," Frank replied, pulling Jacob from his seat. He looked at Dr. Taylor's face, reached back and punched him in the mouth. Dr. Taylor's eyes almost leaped from his face. "What the hell was that for?" Dr. Taylor yelled, dabbing the blood from the corner of his mouth.

"We were just in a plane accident," Frank said punching him again. "You don't look like someone who's just been in an accident. And it just felt good. Now listen, if you say anything out of the ordinary, I'll kill you. The only reason you're alive right now is because I need you. We are your two assistants. Any deviation from that fact, and I will definitely get to my gun way before they can kill me. Do you understand?"

"I guess," Dr. Taylor said, feebly.

Frank stuffed his gun in his leg holster and plopped in the seat beside Robin. "Put your seatbelts back on," Frank said, reattaching his. "Act groggy."

Frank closed his eyes and heard men grunting, obviously trying to pry open the door. Two men, dressed in suits with radios in hand, appeared. One was a bald, African American; the other was white with a crew cut and broad shoulders. They were definitely Secret Service, Frank thought. They walked inside the cabin and tapped Frank on his shoulder. "You O.K., buddy?" the African-American agent asked, unloosening Frank's seatbelt.

Frank groaned, as if he had just awoken, and moved methodically. "Took a pretty good bump on the head, but I think I'll live."

"What happened?" asked the other Secret Service agent.

"Something to do with the landing gear," Frank replied, examining Dr. Taylor's face for any suspicious facial expressions.

"You must be Dr. Loventhol," the African American agent said, pointing at Dr. Taylor.

"I am."

"Are these your two assistants?"

"Yes...Dr. Roberts and Dr. Vastbinder."

"Where are the two CIA operatives that were supposed to escort you?" the other agent asked, walking into the cockpit.

"They had some problems back in New York," Frank said.

"We need to check things out," the African American agent said, skeptically.

They aren't buying it, Frank thought. Now what? The presidential compound was probably underground and surrounded by enough Secret Service agents to comprise an army. Someone had to do something. Robin stood up and walked over to the African-American agent. "Do you realize the time you're wasting? If we don't get this boy's blood to the First Lady in the next thirty minutes, she'll be dead. Our people estimated that the infant's blood doesn't contain enough virus to save her. We need at least twenty minutes to prepare the boy's blood. Now, if you want to explain to the President that his wife died because we wasted all this valuable time, that's up to you."

The African-American agent wrinkled his brown forehead, then sighed and stared at his counterpart. "O.K., let's go," he said reluctantly.

Chapter 46

It had been at least twenty-two hours since Dr. Orpheus Martin had been asleep. His eyes were as dry as the stale donut he tried to choke down. Each blink seemed to scrape the corner of his eyes. His body felt as if he was carrying a truck on his shoulders. He rubbed his face and fought to get comfortable in the wooden chair in front of Agent Dan Johnson's desk. Agent Johnson had left for the moment, which was the first break from questions in over an hour. How many times can someone tell the same story? he thought. And how could one man be so anal? His oak desk looked as if he cleaned it in an autoclave. Quite an impossible feat for a pencil pusher, Orpheus thought. The couch in the corner looked as if it had been in plastic, just like his mother's house. And his line of questions matched his office. Every word Orpheus said was followed by ten questions.

Orpheus took a long swig of his cold coffee, hoping for a jolt of caffeine, and closed his eyes. Slowly, he drifted off into a dream. He was making love to his wife on a tropical island when the slam of the office door almost made him fall from his seat. Agent Dan Johnson appeared, his blue suit buttoned, tie pressed and shoes shined. His hair was short, with a bald patch on top. His eyes were green and honest. He looked like a Mormon, fresh off a bicycle, about to knock on a door. "I brought you some more donuts," Agent Johnson said, handing him a jelly donut on a napkin and sitting in front of his desk.

"Great...another donut," Orpheus said, chucking it on the desk. "You guys must make these things yourselves."

"I know you're tired, but as of now I can't convince a court in this country to allow me to go after the President."

"I'm way past tired," Orpheus barked. "Look, from what you told me, you and Captain Irwin are good friends. Do you think he'd make something like this up?"

"I know he wouldn't," Agent Johnson snapped back. "But, as in medicine, we don't act upon hunches. I need proof."

"What about the blood samples and Nicole Johnson's missing body, or how odd it was for her brother and son to disappear in the same day. Those two boys are here in Washington. I'm sure of it."

"But, there are three different compounds they could be in, if they're here at all. My career would be over if I go busting into one of the President's bomb shelters without an ounce of evidence."

"So, you want to sit here and wait until all the evidence is dead. The infant will die if they use him for the transfusion. He doesn't have enough serum to cure the First Lady. An infant dead! Do you want that on your head?"

Agent Johnson rubbed his face and then leaned back in his chair. He wrinkled his forehead in deep thought, then jumped from his chair. "I've got an idea."

"What, more donuts?"

"I've got some friends who could help us. It's an election year. These people would definitely take the risk, judging how far back they are in the polls."

"How long is this going to take?"

"One phone call, trust me," Agent Johnson said, picking up his receiver. "We could get agents at all three compounds in an hour."

"It better be a quick one."

Orpheus was reluctant to enter Agent Johnson's blue Chevy Blazer, but realized there were no other options. He jumped inside and watched agent Johnson's eyes for the least bit of uncertainty. The most powerful crime family in the world was after him: the U.S. government. And no one was immune to their power. He was in their territory now with only a weak promise of redemption from Agent Johnson.

* * *

Robin Vastbinder wiped the blood from her face and grabbed Jacob's hand. They followed the two Secret Service agents off the runway to the entrance of the farmhouse that reminded Robin of a place fifty miles outside of Boston where she attended summer camp. The air smelled of manure, the grass was thick under her feet. The farmhouse was an A-frame with a wrap-around porch and a swing on the side. But, the wood was worn, the light blue paint chipped. It looked as if no one had lived in the house for years.

The half-lit moon illuminated the cloudless sky, making the stars seem only a few feet away. She wished she could reach out and touch one and go to a safe place where Jacob and her could live. But, as she grabbed Jacob's hand, she knew that the chances of them coming out alive were slim. Frank seemed to swagger behind the two Secret Service men with a confidence that eased some of Robin's fear. His eyes were locked on every gesture of Dr. Taylor as he tagged close to his side. Frank looked so out of place with the white lab coat draped across his shoulders. Hopefully, no one would ask him any complicated questions. They had to be suspicious already, Robin thought.

The two Secret Service agents punched in a code on the panel beside the door and it opened. A large metal door appeared. The two agents placed their hands on the fingerprint recognition panel beside it and this door opened as well. Behind the door was an elevator. Robin filed inside behind Frank and the door closed. The interrogative look in the two agents' eyes made Robin want to vomit. Something was wrong, she was sure of it. The elevator descended slowly, as if it were going to the depths of hell. Hide the fear, Robin kept telling herself. Be strong. She glanced at Jacob's face and realized he was long past the fear; he seemed to be in a trance of uncertainty. But Frank had a strength about him that seemed untouchable. Unfortunately, he was only one man against the world.

Frank coughed twice, clearing his throat and said, "Boy, we're lucky to be alive."

"What happened?" the African American agent asked.

"Damn landing gear," Frank said shaking his head. "How is the pilot?"

"He was sent to a hospital," the other agent said sharply.

The three minutes in the elevator seemed like three hours to Robin. Finally, it stopped. The doors slid open and a huge steel door, twice the size of a bank vault, appeared. It had to be at least a foot thick. The African-American agent talked into the microphone on his collar and then punched in a code. He placed his hand on the panel and the door creaked, like an ocean liner sailing from a dock. A wide hallway appeared with cement floors and five metal doors on each side. Four men walked down the hall, their faces skeptical and empty. They were dressed in blue suits with black ties. "Where is the patient?" Robin asked.

"This way," the African American agent said, pointing.

As the other agents approached, Robin looked at Frank. His eyes moved quickly back and forth as if he were about to make a move. What move? Robin frantically thought. One agent was behind her, the other in front. There was no place to run. As the other agents approached, Robin realized they would never see the First Lady, let alone tomorrow, if they didn't run. Frank looked back and nodded his head in the direction of another corridor that appeared to the left. What was he thinking? Robin thought. What was he going to do? The closer the four agents came, the faster Robin's heart raced. She glanced down at Jacob and fixed on his eyes. They flickered with fear. The agents were now twenty feet away with their hands tucked inside their jackets, about to pull their pistols. Frank grabbed Dr. Taylor, pulled a syringe from his pocket and placed the needle next to his throat. "Robin, pick up Jacob…put him in front of your face," Frank yelled.

"What?" Robin screamed back, repulsed at the thought of using Jacob as a human shield.

"Just do it," Frank ordered. "They won't risk killing the First Lady's only two chances of survival."

"You have nowhere to go," the African American agent barked, with his pistol pointed at Frank. "Our people are all over this place."

"Go ahead, put a bullet between my eyes, but I guarantee you, the last thing I'll do is put a syringe full of air into his neck, and the First Lady will be dead. He's the only one who knows how to save her. Throw down your fucking guns!"

"He's right," Dr. Taylor said, his eyes wide with terror. "Don't shoot, please don't shoot."

"Run, Robin."

"Where?" Robin uttered through the tears that streamed from her eyes.

"Find the First Lady. Save my son," Frank yelled. "If one of you move, he's dead."

Robin slowly backpedaled towards the corridor. She quickened her steps to a jog, then to a full out sprint. The agents froze and then reluctantly threw their guns to the floor. Robin looked back and saw Frank continue the stalemate. She turned the corner, emerged into another hallway and prayed she would see Frank again. Where was the First Lady? The compound had to be as large as a stadium, she thought. She dropped Jacob from her chest, grabbed his hand and continued running down the hall. In the distance the pound of hard-soled shoes against the cement approached. She turned the knob on the door to her right and it was locked. Jacob checked the door on the left and it was locked as well. The clicking approached, this time faster and louder.

One door, last chance, Robin thought, as she turned the knob. It opened. She waved her hand to Jacob and ran inside.

The room was so dark Robin couldn't see her hand in front of her face. Each step was an adventure. She ran her hand against the door, looking for the lock. Outside the door she could hear three voices. Frantically, she searched for the lock as the voices became louder. They had to be right out front, she thought. Reaching down, she pushed in the lock and held Jacob close to her chest.

"All these doors are locked," a deep authoritative voice said beyond the metal door.

"They must've went down corridor B," a raspy female voice replied.

"Let's move."

The loud stomps slowly dissipated into the distance. Robin felt the walls and floor, trying to figure out what was inside the room. She bumped her knee against a table sending a jolt of pain through her leg. She placed her hands on it and felt a chair in front. They were in some type of conference room. Judging from the location, the First Lady had to be at the other end of the compound. She was probably surrounded by Secret Service agents the furthest point from the entrance. "What are we going to do?" Jacob whispered.

"I don't know, honey," Robin said, stroking his head.

"My momma taught me something," Jacob said, reaching in his pocket.

"What?" Robin asked.

"We can get into the tubes above the wall."

"What tubes?"

"The metal tubes," Jacob replied, handing her a pocketknife. "My uncle gave this to me. We could use it to take off the screws so we could get in. They can't find us in there."

Robin felt for the chair and sat down. What was Jacob talking about? The tube? Then it came to her. That's how they must've escaped from the Loventhol clinic, through the air-conditioning ducts. But where was it? She stepped on the table and ran her hands against the ceiling. It was cold cement without a rough edge or blemish. She balanced herself on the edge of the table and felt a metal grate on the far side of the table. "Give me your knife," she whispered.

She grabbed the tiny pocketknife and opened a blade. Slowly, she ran her fingers against the vent and found a screw in each corner. She unloosened all four screws, and then pulled it off. She lofted Jacob inside, then began to pull herself up. Suddenly, the lights in the room came on, but no one came through the doors. They must have surveillance cameras in every room, she thought, quickly pulling herself inside. Hopefully, they didn't see her.

The air inside the crawl space was stale and dry. The metal floor was warm. She had only about six inches of room to move her shoulders as she struggled to maneuver up the shaft. It was dark, except for fractured rays of light that penetrated the tiny grids of another room in the distance. Robin fought to keep up with Jacob as his skinny body whizzed through the shaft like a snake. She snatched his leg to slow him down so she could catch up. She estimated that the First Lady had to be at the far end of the building. She continued to lumber through the cramped metal walls, looking through every vent, until she finally found a room with a hospital bed inside. She strained her eyes and saw a frail woman with flesh hanging from her bones sleeping restlessly on a bed. It was the First Lady. The room had a blue couch and a coffee table with daisies as a centerpiece. An I.V. bag was connected to her arm with blood inside. It had to be the infant's. All the muscles in her body began to relax with defeat. Sean was probably dead.

Chapter 47

The muscles in Frank Roberts' hand cramped with pain as he held the syringe to Dr. Taylor's neck, while watching every move of the five Secret Service agents that surrounded him. He knew it would be only a matter of time before they would take him down. Please God, let Robin get to the First Lady, he kept praying. But, how much time would she need? The chances were small that she could find her in such a large place, but it was the only twinkle of hope he had left.

"You can't win," the African American agent said. "If you give up now, maybe you can make it out of here with only a life sentence in prison."

"I just want my son," Frank yelled though clenched teeth. "Do any of you have children? As long as he's in there, dying, I'm going to be out here dying with him. But the professor here is going with me."

The stalemate wasn't going to last forever, Frank decided. It was time to act. "I'm only going to ask you one more time. Take me to my son."

One of the Secret Service men talked to the microphone inside his jacket, and then nodded his head. "Let's go."

Frank slowly followed them up the hall, waiting for them to make their move. It was definitely a set up. The only question was when. He carefully planted each step all the while glancing over his shoulder, waiting for the attack. At the end of the long hallway was another metal door. The only female Secret Service agent talked into her jacket. A shot rang out from above and a burning pain shot through Frank's hand and blood trickled onto his shirtsleeve. He dropped the syringe and reached for his gun. It was too late. Five men tackled him and pinned him to the ground. He struggled to break free. Unfortunately, the weight of the five men was too much to overcome. It was time to die, he was sure of it. One of the Secret Service men pulled out his gun and pressed it firmly against his head. He closed his eyes and braced himself for the impact of the bullet. There was a silence that seemed a thousand years long. "Don't kill him," one of the Secret Service men said.

"Why?" the other Secret Service agent replied, about to pull the trigger.

"We've got our orders," the female agent replied, calmly. "Bring Dr. Taylor to the presidential suite."

* * *

When were the two Secret Service agents going to leave? Robin thought, staring through the vent above the First Lady's room. They had been in her room for the last five minutes. One of them helped her to the chair as the other brought her a glass of juice. She took a long sip then sighed. "Thank you," she said.

"Do you need us to help you back in bed?" one of the agents asked.

"No, I'm fine, I would just like to be alone right now if that's all right," the First Lady said.

"We'll be right outside the door if you need us."

The two agents leaving the room made the palpitations in Robin's chest slow for a moment, only to return. She waited for a few seconds, then carefully angled the tiny pocketknife through the three-inch grid and unloosened the first screw. The First Lady was still sitting in her chair, staring pensively at the flowers on the coffee table. Quickly, she unfastened the second and the third, all the while praying that the perspiration on her hands wouldn't cause her to drop the knife. Jacob's eyes didn't flinch for even a moment as she pulled the final screw from the vent. It was as if he were in another world. Robin hugged him, trying to calm his fears, then carefully pulled the vent from the wall.

It was about a ten-foot drop from the vent to the floor, Robin estimated. How would the First Lady react? Probably scream and the guards would rush in the room. But, the options were few. The moment was now. In one quick motion, she jumped and fell to the floor. She forgot about the twinge of pain that pulsed through her ankle and ran towards the First Lady. The First Lady's thin eyes, that seemed to dangle from her sunken face, widened. She was about to scream, but Robin pressed her hand firmly over her mouth. "Listen, I'm not here to hurt you, just to tell you that the blood in your bag is from an infant. I know that's hard for you to believe, but the five-year-old boy in the air-conditioning duct will tell you the truth. He's his brother. If you scream, they'll both be dead."

The First Lady's face froze for a moment, and then relaxed.

"Please, don't scream and let me go get the boy," Robin said.

The First Lady nodded her head and Robin carefully pulled her hand away from her face. The thousand pounds of pressure on her chest crept from her heart as she walked back over to the vent. The First Lady had remained silent. She raised her hands and instructed Jacob to jump. He landed in her arms. Robin carried him over to the First Lady and placed him by her side. "If you don't believe me, ask him. Why else would we be here? I'm sure your security wouldn't let a strange woman and a little boy inside one of the most protected places in the world."

"How did you get in here?" the First Lady asked, combing her hand through her gray hair.

"Long story," Robin said, thinking about Frank. "But the real story is that infant and this little boy. Their blood cures cancer and they were about to kill them both to save your life."

"My husband wouldn't allow that," the First Lady snapped.

"Well, he has and the longer we have this conversation, the shorter that infant boy has to live."

The door clicked, then opened. The two Secret Service agents appeared, their guns aimed at Robin's head. "Don't move," one of them said.

"Put down your guns," the First Lady yelled, using the chair to rise to her feet.

"I'm sorry ma'am, but I can't do that," one of the agents said, moving closer to Robin.

"You can and you will," the First Lady barked. "Take me to the infant."

The Secret Service man remained silent with his pistol still aimed at Robin.

"I said, take me to the infant," the First Lady demanded with tears streaming from her eyes.

The agent reluctantly placed the gun back in the holster inside his jacket. "Get her wheelchair," he said to the other agent.

Robin helped the First Lady to her chair, then grabbed Jacob's hand. The Secret Service men opened the door and led them down the hallway. The faces of the two agents that stood in front of the infant's door widened with astonishment. "I can't let you go in there," one of them said with a crack in his voice.

The First Lady stared them down as if her eyes were two cannons about to blow off their heads. Just as they were about to open the door, Robin felt Jacob's hand separate from hers and the barrel of a gun touched her head. She tried to resist, but the two agents behind her pinned her against the wall. Six agents then appeared. Behind one of them, the President of the United States emerged. He walked over to his wife and knelt in front of her. "Please, Sophia, you must go back to your room and finish the treatment," he said, softly, with a crack in his voice.

The First Lady glared in his eyes, then reached up her hand and slapped him in the face. "How could you do this," she said, with tears staining her pale cheeks. "Not this way, Steward, not this way. I could never look you in the face again."

"Please, I can't live without you," the President said, bursting into tears, burying his face into her lap.

"These are children, Steward."

"You'll understand some day," the President said, kissing her on the forehead. "Please take her back to her room. Is Dr. Taylor ready?" the President asked, lowering his head.

"Yes sir," one of the agents said, as if he were a mindless robot.

"How can you let this happen Mrs. Daniels? How can you live another day knowing that two innocent children died to give you life," Robin screamed, fighting to break loose.

The First Lady fought to get up from her wheel chair, but it was obvious that she was too weak. She dropped her head in despair and covered her face as one of the Secret Service agents wheeled her back to her room. Robin's entire body became numb as she watched the First Lady disappear into the distance. It was the same feeling she had when the police arrived at her door and informed her that her son and husband were dead. The hopelessness and shock still whirred in her head and now she had to live through it again. As the agents pulled Jacob away, the second chance of being a mother disappeared like sand being washed back into the ocean. "Please, let me just hold him once more," Robin begged feebly.

The agent ignored her request and dragged him away while his tiny somber eyes looked back at her as if to say goodbye forever. In the distance, Dr. Taylor appeared with an arrogant smirk on his face. He was carrying an ice cooler in his hand, probably filled with the infant's blood, Robin thought.

"Take Jacob to the infirmary," Dr. Taylor said to the Secret Service agent, walking closer to Robin.

"I can't wait till you sit on the electric chair for this," Robin snapped.

"I'm saving lives, Dr. Vastbinder. It's too bad you don't understand that."

"Where's Frank?"

"Probably dead by now," Dr. Taylor said, emotionless. "Another casualty of progress. Progress is always hard. Someone has to die, history has shown us that, now hasn't it? Your life means nothing to the millions I will save one day."

Dr. Taylor smiled and walked away. The two agents, with arms as thick as the steel door at the entrance, pulled Robin from the wall and dragged her down the hallway. It was definitely time to die. Her only solace was the chance to look upon her husband and son's eyes again and feel the warmth of their bodies in her arms that made her feel complete, dispelling the emptiness that tortured her soul over the past year. Hopefully, they would be humane and put a bullet through her brainstem, killing her instantly. Only a second of pain and it would all be over.

Robin tried to struggle at first, but why waste the energy, she thought. Nothing could stop the inevitable. As the Secret Service agent opened the door to end her life, an explosion resonated through the compound almost piercing her eardrums. She fell to the ground, covering her head and the sound of a thousand foot steps marched down the hallway. Bullets whizzed by her head and debris showered on her back. Then, it was quiet. She looked up and the two agents by her side had their hands raised to the ceiling. A group of men in army fatigues, with FBI armbands attached to their uniforms, jogged toward them with machine guns raised in the air. "Drop to the floor and put your hands behind your head," one of them yelled.

The FBI agents handcuffed each Secret Service agent and led them down the hallway. Robin rose to her feet with a surge of energy pulsating through her skin. From behind the soldiers emerged a familiar face. His blue eyes were bright, but had much concern. Robin exploded into tears when she realized it was Frank. His hand was wrapped with a blood soaked handkerchief, but his face was filled with hope. Robin jumped into his arms and hugged him, never wanting to let go. "Where's my son?" Frank asked quickly, pulling her away.

"In that room," Robin replied, pointing.

Frank grabbed one of the Secret Service agents and said, "Find me the keys."

The agent pulled out a key card from his back pocket and somberly dropped it into Frank's hand. Frank ran over to the door with a terror on his face and inserted the card into the panel beside. The door clicked, then opened. Robin followed inside. A crib, with multiple tubes and wires projected from the rails like snakes from medusa's hair, was in the center of the room. Robin became lightheaded when she realized the monitor against the wall showed the infant's heart was in bradycardia. He was dying. Robin ran over to the crib and found a fragile, pale infant with blue fingertips struggling to breathe. His blue eyes were dim with fear as his tiny chest muscles fought for each breath. She reached over and checked the gauge on the oxygen tank by his bed. It was only at two liters. She dialed it up to six and fumbled through the drawers for an I.V. needle. He needed I.V. fluids. Frank's eyes almost jumped from his face when he saw his son for the first time. It was tough for Robin to watch the strong man that she loved look so helpless. "We…need…help," Frank yelled frantically with tears streaming from his face.

Chapter 48

Frank Roberts stared into the multicolored tiles on the floor of Walter Reed military hospital looking for answers. Why did he ever let Nicole Johnson leave? Why didn't he believe her? He could've been washing bottles and humming lullabies instead of sitting in the waiting room praying for one moment with his son. He had replayed that day so many times in his head over the past week that he wished his brain didn't give his mouth a holiday that night. The words left his lips without ever considering the consequences; a chance to never see his future in his son's eyes.

Frank stood up, stretched and looked around the room. The FBI had practically quarantined them from the world. The only people in the room were Robin with Jacob asleep in her lap. Frank began to pace, almost peeling the paint from the tiles, and combed his hand through his hair.

"Robin, I want you to tell me the truth because I can't live on false hopes. I need to know something."

"Infants can take a lot, they're very resilient."

"Then what was that pediatrician talking about?" Frank asked, rubbing his eyes.

"Your son has lost a lot of blood, but he got two units from Jacob."

"What about those respiratory problems he was talking about?"

"Some of his tissue has died from this episode of hypoxia. I've seen a lot of infants in his situation and they seem to regenerate the damage pretty quickly because their metabolism is so fast."

"I can see it in your eyes, Robin," Frank said, sitting by her side. "I know he's not going to make it."

Jacob rolled over, his eyes barely open, and crawled on Frank. He tucked his head on his shoulder and went back to sleep. "He must be exhausted...poor kid," Frank said, rubbing Jacob's back.

"How's your hand?"

"Hurts a bit, but luckily it only needed a few stitches," Frank replied, looking down at the bandage.

"So, what do you think is going to happen?"

"Well, the President will probably be impeached, but as always, no charges will stick. Dr. Taylor and Senator Watson will take the brunt of the shit. Senator Watson will only spend a few years in a federal prison, but Dr. Taylor is going down. He doesn't have the political clout to make it through this. The President will deny knowledge of Sean's blood and so will Senator Watson. Do you think the First Lady will make it?"

"Tough to tell," Robin said, expelling a piece of gum from her mouth and placing it in a tissue. "It's impossible to tell how much viral load she needed for a cure."

"I just feel so helpless, you know? I've been shot at and stabbed bringing down some of the worst scum New York could offer, but this is a thousand times worse."

Robin reached out her hand and caressed his face. Her eyes had deep black circles, but her smile made them disappear. She kissed him softly on the lips and for one second, the fear of the unknown wasn't as bad for Frank. "So where do we go from here?" Robin said softly.

"I can't make you any promises because I know we both got a lot of healing to do. But one thing I do know...we've got two children to take care of."

Frank was about to get up and pace again when he heard a door open. It had to be the doctor, he thought. But the large Afro and wide grin made him realize it was Robin's friend, Dr. Orpheus Martin. Robin jumped from her seat and gave him a hug. "I can never thank you enough, Orpheus," Robin said softly into his ear.

"Don't thank me. It was Frank's boss, Dennis Irwin. He hooked me up with Agent Johnson, who figured out which compound you guys were in."

Each letter of Dennis's name brought a new pain to Frank's heart. But, Dennis had saved his life, while giving up his own. Somehow, he knew Dennis would never let him down. "How's your son?" Orpheus asked.

"It doesn't look good," Frank uttered, dropping his head.

"How bad is it, Robin?" Orpheus asked.

"Well, he's lost a lot of blood," Robin replied.

"I see," Orpheus said, staring at the floor.

"So, where are you going from here?" Robin asked.

"A long vacation, on the government. We're going to some island resort, away from the leech reporters that will probably be hounding me. But the good news is that the wife has bought something from Victoria's Secret, which means the boys will be seeing a lot of the beach and I'll be listening to a lot of Barry White," Orpheus said, cracking a smile. "I've got to go, but once things calm down, we need to get together and make sense of all of this. Frank, your son is in my prayers."

"Thanks, Orpheus," Frank said.

"Take care," Orpheus said, slowly opening the door and leaving the room.

Frank resumed his long, gloomy stare at the ceiling, contemplating the thought of his son's death. He would never see his boy laugh, sing funny songs or grow into the man he could only hope to be. It was about to be all that could've been rather than what is. A thin tear dropped from his face, staining his dusty white dress shirt. Why couldn't it be him in the intensive care unit instead of his son? Why? It was his fault. Just as he laid his head against the wall, the door opened. It was a doctor dressed in green scrubs with wisps of gray sneaking through his black hair. His eyes were uncertain, almost empty. He walked over to Frank and sat in the chair beside him. "Mr. Roberts?" the doctor asked, looking at his son's chart.

"Yes," Frank said, a lump of anxiety creeping up his throat.

"Would you like to see your son?"

"Is he all right?"

"Yes, he is. We'll have to keep him here for a few days, but after that you can take him home."

Jacob immediately awoke. He rubbed his eyes and said, "Will he be able to play baseball?"

"As much as he wants once he gets big enough," the doctor replied, a smile expanding on his face.

"I can't wait to teach him my spit ball," Jacob said excited.

Frank hugged Robin and grabbed her hand. "Let's go see my son."

Frank followed the doctor past the nurses' station, into the pediatric intensive care unit. His heart jumped a thousand times a second as he approached the tiny crib, surrounded by monitors and wires, and looked inside. His son's pudgy little cheeks and thin, blue eyes made him feel as if nothing else mattered. The doctor reached inside and handed him his son. He was so fragile and small that Frank thought he might break him in half if he held him too tight. The warmth of his miniature body could heat an entire town, Frank thought. His rapid little heartbeat seemed to pound against his chest like wings of a butterfly that his own father would catch and put against his face. It was all he ever needed and a thousand times greater than he could've ever imagined.

Frank turned toward Robin and smiled, "I'm going to need your help."

"You got all the help you need," Robin said with tears racing down her cheeks. "So where do we go from here?"

"Probably into some sort of witness protection program."

"Do you think it'll be safe?"

"We'll never be safe as long as these boys have the cure."

About the Author

Dr. Zane Gates is a graduate of the University of Pittsburgh School of medicine and did his residency at Allegheny University hospital in Pittsburgh, Pa. He currently practices Internal medicine in Altoona Pa, where he spends most of his time volunteering at a free medical clinic he founded for the uninsured and helping the children of the housing project he grew up in to dream again. The Cure is his first novel and half of the proceeds will be donated to the Gloria Gates Memorial Foundation for Children

Printed in the United States
118272LV00003B/163-225/A

9 780595 174843